LORD OF MONSTERS

AN OUT OF ABATON NOVEL

BOOK 2

LORD OF MONSTERS

AN OUT OF ABATON NOVEL

BOOK 2

John Claude Bemis

DISNEP • HYPERION

LOS ANGELES   NEW YORK

First Edition, June 2017
10 9 8 7 6 5 4 3 2 1
FAC-020093-17111
Printed in the United States of America

This book is set in 11.5-pt Adobe Caslon Pro/Monotype; Bodoni Classic Pro A,
Bodoni Classic Pro B, and Bodoni Classic Pro E, TT Compotes /Fontspring.
Designed by Maria Elias
Interior illustrations by René Milot

Library of Congress Cataloging-in-Publication Data

Names: Bemis, John Claude, author.
Title: Lord of monsters / John Claude Bemis.
Description: First edition. • Los Angeles ; New York : Disney-Hyperion, 2017.
Series: Out of Abaton ; book 2 • Summary: "Pinocchio and Lazuli
encounter dangerous creatures thought to be long gone from Abaton in this
sequel to The Wooden Prince"—Provided by publisher.
Identifiers: LCCN 2016042690 • ISBN 9781484707418 (hardback) • ISBN 1484707419
(hardcover)
Subjects: CYAC: Fantasy. Characters in literature—Fiction.
Monsters—Fiction. Princesses—Fiction. Magic—Fiction. BISAC:
JUVENILE FICTION / Action & Adventure / General. JUVENILE FICTION /
Fairy Tales & Folklore / General. JUVENILE FICTION / Fantasy & Magic.
Classification: LCC PZ7.B4237 Lor 2017 | DDC Fic]—dc23
LC record available at https://lccn.loc.gov/2016042690ISBN 978-1-4847-0741-8
Reinforced binding
Visit www.DisneyBooks.com

For Amy and Rose
Every day is a glorious adventure!

PART ONE

Presters

1.

The Moonlit Court

The Four High Nobles of Abaton gathered in secret. These lords and ladies would never have done such a thing when Prester John was on the throne. But Prester John was dead. And their new rulers were young and unaware of what was being whispered about them.

"Children. They have their place, of course." Two ribbons of smoke snaked out from the lord of the djinn's wide nostrils. "But on the throne? I think not."

"I find I'm in agreement," said the lady of the undines, the words escaping her green lips in a fountain of bubbles. "It's not just their youth that worries me. The boy is a *human* boy . . . a *Venetian* boy, no less. The humans of the Venetian Empire are perfect savages, are they not?"

The tiny lord of the gnomes nodded. "True. All you are

saying is indeed quite true. But Prester John gave the boy the Ancientmost Pearl before his death. And we can't forget that Princess Lazuli was His Great Lordship's only living child. So by right, the rule of Abaton belongs to them."

"Aren't you troubled by this?" the lady of the undines asked.

"Of course I'm troubled!" the gnome lord said. "Grievously troubled! We don't know if this Pinocchio can even use the Pearl. How do we know whether they'll keep our people safe?"

"We don't," the djinni lord snarled.

"But what is there to do about them?" the gnome lord asked helplessly.

The djinni lord narrowed his eyes until they were slivers of molten orange. He seemed to be considering various possibilities.

Before he could share any of them, the lady of the undines spoke. "I propose we establish a regency council to take over the rule of Abaton. Once the children are older and have proven they can be worthy presters, *maybe* then we can return them to the throne."

"But . . ." The gnome tapped his small earthen fingers together anxiously. "Do we have the authority to replace them with a regency council?"

"Most certainly we do!" the undine replied. "We four lead the elemental houses. Our people—all our people, elementals and lesser races alike—look to us for guidance. They respect us. With Prester John gone, there is nobody our people trust more." She shifted inside the glistening bubble that surrounded her, her long green hair dancing in the watery gloom. "Who would argue if we took possession of the throne?"

Until now Lady Sapphira of the Sylphs had not spoken. She wasn't given to pointless chatter. But at the lady of the undines' question, she felt it necessary to answer.

"I will," she said.

Her expression remained calm. But her words seemed to draw all the air out of the room, as they often did when the lady of the sylphs had something important to say. The other three High Nobles shifted in their seats.

"Lady Sapphira," the djinni lord said with a sneer, "let me speak honestly. Your love for your niece Lazuli blinds you to the best interests of our people."

Lady Sapphira's cool crystalline gaze met his. "Love is precisely what allows me to see what is in the best interest of our people. Better than you, lord. My greatest love is for Abaton and it gives me keen sight. The rule of our land should not be in the hands of a regency council, but in the hands of whoever commands the Ancientmost Pearl."

"And you feel these children—your niece Lazuli and this Venetian boy Pinocchio—are capable of this?" the lady of the undines asked. Her skepticism wasn't lost in the fount of bubbles.

"I cannot speak for Pinocchio's capacity to rule," Lady Sapphira said. "But my niece is the last of Prester John's children. Lazuli is Abatonian royalty. You don't know her as I do, my fellow lords and lady. My niece is no unruly, impulsive child. She might be only fourteen, but she has grace far beyond her years."

Lady Sapphira rose to her feet, hovering ever so slightly. "And she is our prester. She will show you how capable she is on the throne."

Lazuli stood high on the back of the throne and drew her sword. She unleashed a savage cry and leaped.

Her blade met Pinocchio's in a clash of steel on steel that rang through the great domed hall. Lazuli smiled. There was nothing quite so wonderful as a good battle.

3

Pinocchio blocked her blows, but then turned on the offensive, driving her back until Lazuli felt herself bump against a table laid out with a sampling of the cakes and frosted desserts that were to accompany the evening's banquet.

"Yield!" Pinocchio said.

Lazuli lifted an eyebrow. "Don't be ridiculous."

She summoned a gust of wind that carried her gracefully into the air. Lazuli landed on the table and ran to the far end, her silk-slippered feet dodging the platters. Pinocchio made a less graceful bound onto the table. His right foot landed with a perfect splat in a coconut-cardamom pudding. Lazuli shook her head. At least it hadn't been the spiceberry cake.

The cricket Maestro fluttered about on his tiny wings, crying in his tiny voice, "Come now, Your Majesties! Someone will hear you. I beg you, please stop this silliness!"

Pinocchio smirked as he blocked her next swing. "Did you hear something, Lazuli?"

"Maybe," Lazuli said, "our royal musician is working on a new song?"

Clang! Clack! The metallic noise echoed off the high curved ceiling. The throne room was at the very top of the towering palace of the Moonlit Court. Like the rest of the palace, it was more space than substance. Archways encircled the room, opening out to breezy balconies that overlooked jungle and a distant turquoise ocean. The marble ceiling was impossibly delicate—thin as eggshell and just as white—and the bright tropical sunlight seeped straight through, glistening across the polished floors.

The noise was only slightly muffled by fluttering tapestries along the walls.

"Ah, that must be it," Pinocchio said. "Maestro's writing a new sonata. Yes! About our upcoming mission. How Abaton's

4

valiant new rulers, Prester Pinocchio and Prester Lazuli, will lead their army of celestial knights in a daring rescue mission back to the Venetian Empire."

Ping! Clack!

"Or maybe," Maestro chirped, his antennae trembling furiously as he clung to one of the twisting pillars, "he's composing a piece about an insolent pair of presters who acted like perfect barbarians when they should have been getting ready for their banquet!"

"Hmm," Lazuli said. Sweat dripped from her blue hair onto her nose as she drove Pinocchio farther down the table. "Which version do you prefer, Prester Pinocchio?"

"Well, Prester Lazuli . . ." Pinocchio parried her blow. "I'd have to say the first."

"Agreed," Lazuli replied.

"Incorrigible!" Maestro said. "I've come to expect this kind of unruliness from Pinocchio, but *you*, Prester Lazuli! You never used to behave like this!"

"I blame Pinocchio," Lazuli said. "He's a corrupting influence."

"I take that as a compliment," Pinocchio said.

Lazuli gave a nod of appreciation as she hammered her sword against his.

"Go on. Laugh at Maestro. Mock his burden. But you won't be laughing if one of your nobles comes through that door and sees you—" Maestro grew quiet, tilting his tiny head. Then he issued a sharp squeak. "The door! Someone's at the door!"

Lazuli was off the table in an instant. She slipped her sword behind her gown and brought her face into that mask of regal pleasantness that she had learned so well.

Pinocchio stood panting on the table, half-frozen with

indecision. He managed to get the sword clumsily behind his back just as the great red-and-gold doors to the throne room swung open.

A tall man with a mane of silver-streaked hair and a curly mustache entered.

"Father!" Pinocchio smiled.

"Geppetto!" the cricket said, leaping to the man's shoulder. "At last! Implore these two to end this rumpus. Tell them this is no way for proper presters to act, especially before this evening's banquet."

Geppetto deposited himself in one of the chairs at the table and reached for a piece of candied mango before eyeing the frosted footprints beside the plate. With a shrug, he took the candy anyway and popped it in his mouth.

"Our noble guests are down in their chambers, and the servants are setting the tables in the gardens. We're fine. Besides, the throne room is by far the most sensible place for our presters to keep up their skills." Geppetto waved, encouraging Pinocchio and Lazuli to continue.

Maestro's antennae drooped with defeat. "Why did I ever think palace life would civilize you, Geppetto? Have I ever told you that you're a hopeless rapscallion?"

"Yes, daily, I think," Geppetto said, chewing the candied fruit and giving Pinocchio and Lazuli a wink.

"Father, watch!" Pinocchio called from atop the table. "I was just about to disarm Lazuli."

"Were you, now?" Lazuli summoned a gust that not only lifted her onto the table but also blew Pinocchio back into several platters of desserts.

"Lazuli!" Pinocchio regained his balance, kicking off the custard stuck to his foot.

"What?" she said innocently.

"It's not exactly fair when you use your powers."

"Who decided that?" Lazuli replied. "I don't recall the imperial airmen caring what was and wasn't fair. Besides, you're quite welcome to use your own powers."

Pinocchio furrowed his brow. He stretched out a hand toward Lazuli and closed his eyes. Geppetto and Maestro grew quiet, watching. Pinocchio's face turned as red as a pomegranate. His arms started to shake.

Lazuli waited, ready to dodge in case he happened to summon something potentially dangerous.

Nothing appeared.

Pinocchio opened his eyes. He looked at his hand like it had just called him a nasty name.

Geppetto sat back with a sigh. Even Maestro sagged. The cricket might have been perpetually exasperated with Pinocchio's antics, but Lazuli knew Maestro was devoted to him in his own funny way. Those two had been through too much together for him not to be.

"Why won't it work?" Pinocchio said. "I keep trying, but I don't know what I'm supposed to do!"

"The Ancientmost Pearl is a most curious object," Geppetto said patiently. "Its magic will take time to learn, son."

"But our people expect me to command the Pearl! They expect . . ." Pinocchio waved a frustrated hand at the tapestries on the walls. They showed Prester John's first meeting with the four primordial guardians of Abaton. Prester John uniting the warring elemental houses under the banner of the Moonlit Court. Prester John sleeping on the shore of a white-sand beach while dazzling creatures seemed to be emerging from his head, scattering into the seas and jungle.

"I don't even understand what your father's doing there," Pinocchio said, pointing to the last tapestry. "Was he working magic even when he took a nap? He makes it look so . . . effortless!"

"I'm not sure how much of what's on these tapestries has been exaggerated," Lazuli said. Her father's life had been shrouded in such mystery, even to her. And his death, just three months earlier, still left her wishing she'd known him better, wishing he hadn't been so secretive and remote, wishing he could have been more like the adoring father Geppetto was to Pinocchio.

"It doesn't matter!" Pinocchio complained. "The people of Abaton believe them. They know how powerful your father was."

"He had centuries to master the Pearl," Geppetto reminded him. "Don't be so hard on yourself. Be grateful for the gifts we have."

Lazuli knew he was right. Pinocchio had much to be grateful for: he'd brought her and Geppetto, along with Maestro and their friends Cinnabar, Sop, and Mezmer, safely to Abaton. They had this extraordinary life now in the Moonlit Court. But more importantly, he was alive—not a mindless, mechanical servant in the Venetian Empire, but a living human boy. Being an automa was behind him now. None of their people here in Abaton need ever know what he'd once been.

Still, Lazuli hated seeing Pinocchio like this. There really was only one way to keep his mind off his worries about the Pearl. She lunged with her sword.

The corners of Pinocchio's mouth turned up as he parried lightning quick. But in his hurry to secure his grip on the sword, Lazuli's strike sent the weapon clattering to the floor.

"Sorry," Lazuli said.

Pinocchio smirked. "I guess airmen don't warn you when

they're going to attack either." He leaped from the table to retrieve the sword.

Geppetto pulled a watch from his waistcoat pocket. "It's probably best you two get ready for the banquet. The noble lords and ladies will be joining you in the gardens within the hour." He glanced at Pinocchio. "And, son, please make sure your attendants find you a pair of boots without pudding stains."

"Who's going to be looking at my feet?" Pinocchio asked.

"Everyone!" Maestro chirped. "You are the presters. So present yourself properly. No splattered boots, and certainly no swords!"

"I can't wear my . . ." Pinocchio held up his arms before dropping them in defeat. As he followed Lazuli out of the throne room, he grumbled under his breath something about crickets squashing all the joy out of life.

Beyond the throne room's golden doors, a grand marble staircase wound its way through the palace's atrium interior, spiraling to the distant foyer far below. Lazuli and Pinocchio only had one flight of stairs down to the floor, where one direction along the curved gallery led to Pinocchio's chambers, the other to Lazuli's.

They smiled at each other before parting. "See you in a bit," Lazuli said.

Pinocchio gave a nod, a pinch of nervousness in his brow.

She thought about calling over the balcony a few words of assurance, something to help ease his anxieties about the banquet and having to dine with all those stuffy nobles. Maybe the promise of spiceberry cake would do the trick. But when she turned, her gaze caught on movement below.

The palace was unusually quiet. On a normal afternoon, servants and palace attendants would be flooding the central staircase or hurrying busily along galleries and hallways. Not today, however. They were all out in the gardens getting ready for the banquet.

But half a dozen floors below, three figures were huddled together in the shadows of a gallery.

A voice rose in anger: "Of course Lady Sapphira would!"

Lazuli narrowed her eyes, trying to see who was arguing about her aunt.

Another smaller voice said, "Please, Lord Smoldrin. You'll be heard."

She knew Lord Smoldrin. He'd been high lord of the djinn since before Lazuli had been born. Probably since before her mother had even been born. She wondered if the other two were Chief Muckamire of the gnomes and Raya Piscus of the undines, and leaned a little farther over the balcony to try to find out.

She'd long heard of the intense rivalries and jealousies among the Four High Nobles. Aunt Sapphira prided herself on staying above their petty squabbles. But this sounded like more than a mere squabble.

"Your Majesty?"

With a start, Lazuli turned to see one of her attendants behind her in the hall. The sylph maid gave a quick curtsy. "If you're ready?"

"Yes," Lazuli said, pulling away from the balcony and adopting an expression more fitting to a prester. She shouldn't have let her attendant catch her skulking like that. "Yes, I'll be right there."

The attendant made another curtsy and headed toward Lazuli's chambers.

Lazuli looked once more over the balcony. The three High Nobles were gone, leaving an ominous quiet hovering over the halls of the Moonlit Court.

2.

The Uninvited Guest

Pinocchio felt naked without his sword. Not naked exactly. If anything, as he ran down the endless, circling stairs that wound through the palace, he felt overdressed in his long ivory coat, embroidered silk leggings, and red leather boots.

But he didn't feel like himself without a sword on his belt.

However, as he'd been reminded again and again since his arrival, Abaton was a peaceful kingdom. Its people frowned on warfare. They wanted nothing to do with "loutish savagery," as Maestro put it.

Pinocchio didn't feel he was a savage or a lout—whatever a lout was. But he didn't feel much like an Abatonian yet either. Certainly not the *prester* of Abaton.

When Pinocchio came panting to the bottom of the

staircase, Lazuli was already waiting in the foyer. She looked like a real prester in her pearl-emblazoned gown and her crown shining from atop her blue hair. Even with his own golden crown, Pinocchio couldn't help but think he must look like someone merely dressed up as one.

"Are you ready?" she asked. "You look a bit jittery. Is everything—"

But before she could finish, the front doors opened. An owl chimera in a billowy green caftan suit entered, making a quick bow. "Your Majesties! Very good. You're both here."

Dr. Nundrum was the highest-ranking palace official and oversaw the daily affairs of the Moonlit Court. Short and squat with mottled brown feathers, Dr. Nundrum had a perpetually surprised, wide-eyed look, which Pinocchio decided must be the result of being part owl.

Dr. Nundrum adjusted his glasses on his beak, before gesturing to the door. "The guests are all seated. If you'll follow me."

Pinocchio took a steadying breath. Then he exited with Lazuli.

Outside, the sun threw its last radiant shards across the grounds. The gardens were organized in lush, manicured beds of spectacular soaring flowers, ornamental palms, tamarind trees, and topiaries shaped like dancing animals, which actually danced. Funny little naiad faces peered up from the gurgling fountains. The towering palace behind them glowed with otherworldly hues of twilight pinks and purples.

It was an extraordinary sight. Pinocchio could still hardly fathom this was his home.

Three months ago, he'd never have believed he'd be here in Abaton—certainly not as its ruler. It was Wiq who had inspired

Pinocchio to dream of escaping from the Venetian Empire to Abaton. Wiq: his first true friend. Wiq: a slave back in Al Mi'raj's theater in the empire. Wiq: who he'd left behind.

Pinocchio hadn't forgotten the look on Wiq's face as he spoke of Abaton back then, braiding jasmine vines up on the theater's terrace in the starlight, just the two of them alone with their secret plans and emphatic promises.

"It's going to be more wonderful than you can possibly imagine," Wiq had said, his big brown eyes growing bigger. Wiq was a chimera—called a "half beast" in the empire—but his features were more human than most of his kind, except for the soft tawny fur covering his skin and the long, flopping ears. His boxy black nose would twitch when he got excited. It always twitched when he spoke of Abaton.

"But how do you know?" Pinocchio had asked. "You've never been there."

"It has to be!" Wiq had said firmly. "There are no slaves, no conniving alchemists . . ." —Pinocchio had winced at this— ". . . no imperial airmen or soldiers of any kind. Abaton is perfect because there are no humans. Only my chimera people and the elementals and, well . . . more variety of creatures than anyone here in the humanlands could even dream of, all living together as equals under His Immortal Lordship Prester John's just rule. Wait until you see it all!"

Wiq had been right about most of that. Pinocchio had seen creatures here that looked like hybrids of different animals. Creatures that looked like ordinary animals, but spoke. Creatures that didn't look animal at all, but like living snowflakes or walking shrubbery or humanoid gemstones. And they all lived together in such harmony.

If only *Wiq* could see them and all of the other wonders Abaton held. Pinocchio slid a hand to the jasmine bracelet around his wrist. One day . . . One day soon.

Dr. Nundrum led Pinocchio and Lazuli down the winding path into the garden. They reached a central lawn ringed with hedges, where a long banquet table was already surrounded by chattering guests. Tiny pixies served as the illumination, hovering over the scene, their twinkling lights glinting off the gold and glass table settings.

Maestro stood on a small raised platform at the table's center. Seeing his presters approaching, he flexed his antennae and began conducting a miniature orchestra of birds, insects, and baritone frogs. The topiaries nearest to the table swayed to the chirping, croaking chorus.

Pinocchio's heart beat a little faster as the guests rose in unison from their seats.

Wiq might have been surprised to know that everything wasn't perfectly equal for Abaton's citizens. In fact, if Wiq had been here now, he wouldn't have been allowed at the banquet. Even Mezmer and Sop had been told they couldn't come. It was probably for the best that the crass cat Sop remained in the palace, where he wouldn't offend any of these dignified guests. Mezmer, however, should have been there, in Pinocchio's opinion. She was the general of the Celestial Brigade and a descendant of one of Abaton's most revered heroes, the warrior-fox Mezmercurian. But she wasn't a noble or an elemental.

The servants carrying trays and crystal decanters were chimera, but the guests at the table were exclusively elementals: Fiery djinn with their horns and mottled yellow skin. Tiny, earthen brown gnomes who could split apart into multiple smaller versions of themselves. Green, reedy undines—who were never out of water back in the Venetian Empire—but here were walking about, covered in sloshing shrouds that were somewhere between an oblong bubble and a wearable bathtub. And there were sylphs, who were the most similar to humans, except for their bright blue hair and their complete disregard for the laws of gravity.

A beaming sylph came from the table to greet them. "Your Majesties!" She was graceful and lovely and so similar to Lazuli that she could have been her mother.

"Aunt Sapphira," Lazuli said, taking her hands. "The journey from the Mist Cities is so far. Thank you for coming."

"My dearest, I'm here anytime you need me," Lady Sapphira said. She kissed Lazuli's cheek. Then she turned to Pinocchio and curtsied. "Prester Pinocchio, I trust you are adjusting well to life at the Moonlit Court . . . and the heat."

Pinocchio realized he was dripping sweat. How was he expected to wear these royal vestments in a sweltering jungle and not sweat?

"I'm sorry," Pinocchio said, wiping his sleeve across his forehead. "Yes, fine . . . finely. Adjusting finely." Did his speech always have to get so garbled when he was expected to act like a prester?

Dr. Nundrum directed him toward the table. The nobles were bowing, eyes fixed on him as Pinocchio took his seat beside Lazuli's at the head of the table. Geppetto, midway down the table, gave him a wink. A lump caught in Pinocchio's throat. He'd hoped his father would be seated closer, rather than down with the lesser nobles. But the nearest seats were reserved for the four high lords and ladies.

The closest one to Pinocchio was the little gnome lord with his bushy white beard and face like smashed granite. "Prester Pinocchio, the people of Grootslang Hole send their warmest wishes, Your Majesty!"

Pinocchio felt his heart thundering. "Ah, yes, th-thank you, Chief Muckamire. How . . . uh, are things in your hole?"

The gnome lord blinked his tiny black eyes. "Grootslang Hole is no mere *hole*, Your Majesty. It's the ancient city of the earth elementals, a center of knowledge and ingenuity. Grootslang Hole might not be as grand as the Moonlit Court, but no place in Abaton has more libraries or workshops."

"Oh, yes," he mumbled, wondering if it might be best if he just stopped talking. "Sorry. I didn't know."

A small smile formed beneath Chief Muckamire's beard. "You'll just have to visit us soon, Prester." Pinocchio hoped the gnome wasn't too offended by his blunder.

Dr. Nundrum began to direct chimera servants carrying platters with the first course to the tables. Pinocchio watched Lazuli from the corner of his eyes, trying to follow her lead about proper banquet manners. She had unfolded her napkin as she spoke to her aunt.

Pinocchio took his napkin as Raya Piscus, the lady of the undines, leaned over, long seaweed strands of hair swirling around the watery interior of her shroud. Her eyes were like great glowing lamps.

"Life here in Abaton must be quite different from what you were used to in the Venetian Empire, Your Majesty." Bubbles filled her sloshing shroud as she spoke. "I hope you don't feel . . . out of place. Without your own kind."

"I don't think so." Pinocchio had truthfully not felt odd at all that he and his father looked so different from rest of these people. To his mind, these were just Abatonians—lovely and wonderful and endlessly fascinating.

The hulking djinni Lord Smoldrin took a sip from a goblet of flaming liquid. Pinocchio was grateful the servants had only served whatever that was to the djinn, and not to the rest of them. He eyed his own glass. It looked like some sort of frothy juice.

"Have you found interesting things to do, Your Majesty?" Lord Smoldrin had great ramlike horns spiraling from the sides of his head. Pinocchio couldn't help but feel a bit intimidated by him.

"Y-yes, many interesting things." He could tell from the intent way Lord Smoldrin, Chief Muckamire, and Raya Piscus were staring at him that they expected more. "Lazuli has shown me all around the gardens and orchards. And we went down to the harbor yesterday. And of course, the palace is so big. I could probably spend a lifetime exploring all the rooms."

The three nodded to one another, and Pinocchio gave a little exhale of relief.

"Yes." Lord Smoldrin chuckled, issuing a puff of smoke. "Activities that befit your youth. Leisurely pursuits." He tapped a claw to his yellow chin. "I wonder whether you and Prester Lazuli might not prefer to spend more time at such pursuits, and not have to be burdened with all the more complicated aspects of overseeing—"

"Lord Smoldrin," Lady Sapphira said sharply, startling Pinocchio. It seemed to startle the others as well, and Lady Sapphira took a breath, her expression changing from steely storm to regal calm in an instant. So her aunt was where Lazuli had learned to do *that*.

"I'm quite certain," Lady Sapphira said, "that my niece and Prester Pinocchio are interested in more than childish pursuits."

Pinocchio was still trying to understand facial expressions. When he'd been an automa, he'd never had any need to make them, much less read them. If he had to guess, he'd say that the other three elemental nobles looked annoyed by Lady Sapphira's comment. But why would that be?

"My aunt is right," Lazuli said. "While I've made time to show Prester Pinocchio around, we've also begun reviewing petitions from the Southern Townships regarding their plans to add floating irrigation canals into their farmlands. As well as starting repairs to the road linking Caldera Keep with the port at Nolandia."

If Lazuli had been doing that, she hadn't told Pinocchio. But then, he was quite certain there were lots of presterly duties she was handling that he wasn't. They both knew he wouldn't have a clue about any of them.

From the way Lord Smoldrin, Raya Piscus, and Chief Muckamire were frowning at one another, he worried that Lazuli had failed to reassure them about what they were doing as presters.

"And," Pinocchio said, feeling he should do his part to help Lazuli, "we've been working on plans for a rescue mission back to Venice."

Maestro made a discordant squeak, and his animal orchestra fell silent.

Raya Piscus released a fountain of bubbles. Lord Smoldrin spat a flame into his goblet, and Chief Muckamire wobbled in his seat. Even Lady Sapphira looked surprised by this news.

"What is this?" She turned to Lazuli. "You're planning what?"

Lazuli's face went pale.

Maestro hurriedly struck up the orchestra again.

Pinocchio supposed he'd better explain. "A rescue mission to free the slaves. Don't you know? Venice has chimera and elementals enslaved in their empire."

Lord Smoldrin growled, "We are quite aware, Your Majesty.

Raya Piscus's undine spies keep us abreast of the goings-on in the Venetian Empire. But why would Abaton get involved?"

That seemed a strange question. "Because they are your people," Pinocchio replied.

"*Our* people?" Raya Piscus bubbled. "These slaves are not our people. Their ancestors left Abaton for the humanlands centuries ago. The elementals and chimera living in Venice today have only ever known the humanlands."

"And we all know what vile acts the Venetian humans are capable of committing," Lord Smoldrin said. "Twisting our Abatonian magic in order to build machines of war and destruction. Their alchemists are even known to have built mechanical humans to use as servants. What are those abominations called? Automa?"

If Pinocchio had still been an automa, he might have belched up a gasket. As it was, he simply swallowed hard and hoped the conversation headed in a new direction.

Geppetto rose to his feet. The other noble guests down the table looked at him in alarm. Maestro swung his antennae wildly, raising the volume of his orchestra as if he hoped to drown out whatever Geppetto was planning to say. It didn't work.

"I'll remind you, Lord Smoldrin," Geppetto said, glowering at the djinni, "that I was one of those alchemists! And your prester is a Venetian human. Would you accuse us of being vile?"

Pinocchio blinked. This was not the new direction he'd been hoping. He should have known if an argument was going to break out, his father would join in.

The djinni lord gave Geppetto a placating smile. "I do not mean to offend the prester or his alchemist father, Master Geppetto. You left the empire because of its dark ways. And we all know that Prester John trusted you above all other humans."

He waved for Geppetto to sit back down. "All I mean to say is that: when the ground is poisoned, the fruit grows bad. You of all people know Venice is corrupt. Its ways have surely corrupted the Abatonians living under human rule."

"The elementals I knew in Venice were not," Geppetto growled.

"A few, maybe," Raya Piscus said. "But my undine spies often report how many Venetian elementals and chimera have escaped enslavement only to turn to villainy."

Pinocchio knew what Raya Piscus was saying was partially true. Mezmer and Sop had once been bandits in the wilds of the empire. But they weren't bad. They were two of the best people he knew.

Pinocchio was about to say this when his attention caught on something across the garden grounds. A puff of smoke had bloomed in the dusk sky, out past the orchards where the teeming edge of the jungle began. A flying creature emerged from the smoke.

"Prester Pinocchio, Prester Lazuli, I know you mean well," the gnome Chief Muckamire said, bringing Pinocchio's attention back to the table. "But if we rescue these foreign-born Abatonians and allow them to flood our peaceful kingdom, how will we know which are villainous and which aren't? I don't think we can take that sort of risk."

"Agreed," Raya Piscus said. "Our people are anxious enough after the shock of Prester John's death. They don't need their lives disrupted even more." She looked at Lady Sapphira. "This is just what we warned you about. I told you they weren't ready to be presters."

Lazuli turned to her aunt. "What is this?"

Pinocchio didn't wait for an answer. He'd had enough.

"But we are the presters!" he said to Raya Piscus. "And we have decided to give these people the freedom they deserve. It's . . . it's the right thing to do."

"But you have no army, Your Majesty," Lord Smoldrin said. "I understand you've declared this fox Mezmer and her cat companion as knights of the Celestial Brigade." He gave a smoky chortle. "Do you really expect the two of them to take on the military might of Venice?"

"I'll go with them!" Pinocchio said. "Prester Lazuli too. We've faced Venetian airmen before. Right, Lazuli?"

Lazuli looked to Lady Sapphira. Pinocchio didn't need to be an expert in facial expressions to know Lazuli was anxious about what her aunt thought. Lazuli admired her aunt so much. And Lady Sapphira didn't appear pleased.

"Your Majesties!" Chief Muckamire squeaked. "Be reasonable. Surely you aren't planning to go back yourselves?"

"Of course they aren't," Lady Sapphira said, her voice barely audible over the blaring chirps and croaks of Maestro's orchestra.

Lazuli whispered to Pinocchio, "Maybe this isn't the best time to discuss our plans. . . ."

Pinocchio scowled, but found his attention once again drawn to the creature that had appeared so strangely from the smoke.

It wasn't uncommon for Abatonians to fly over the gardens or around the glowing white palace. Most looked docile, cute even—especially the wing-eared kits he'd seen only this morning frolicking above the mango groves.

But this one was glossy black and pounded massive leathery wings. Its body was feline—possibly a midnight-coated lion—although its face appeared human with overlarge eyes of jade green. He'd never seen anything like this in his months in Abaton.

"Are you listening?" Lazuli hissed, over the quarreling voices.

Pinocchio realized he hadn't been. The creature flapped silently in the darkening sky. Rather than continuing on its way, it circled toward the banquet.

"No," he admitted. "But Lazuli—"

"I know the rescue mission is important," she said quickly, struggling to keep her voice low as the rest of the table argued with one another. "But we might have something more serious going on with my aunt and the other High Nobles—"

"Lazuli?" Pinocchio grabbed her arm.

The winged being was definitely coming their way. The guests at the banquet were all so engrossed in the argument, while Dr. Nundrum and the servants were trying to figure out what to do about the next course, and Lazuli was so busy trying to settle the matter that no one had seen it.

". . . right now," Lazuli continued, "we need to focus on assuring the nobles that we—"

"Lazuli?"

"What?" she snapped.

"Are there dangerous creatures in Abaton?"

"Of course not," Lazuli said. "But that's not the point. Our people are worried *we* can't rule—"

"Lazuli!" Pinocchio pointed to the sky.

Frowning with exasperation, Lazuli looked. Her luminous eyes widened as she spied the creature plunging headlong toward the banquet table.

"Doesn't that look dangerous?" Pinocchio asked.

A maw filled with jagged fangs opened wide. The dinner guests finally noticed, first with gasps of surprise, then with screams of terror.

3.

The First Monster

Pinocchio rose from his chair. With a sword in his hand, he was capable of the extraordinary. After all, he had beaten the renowned automa swashbuckler Harlequin. He'd fought imperial airmen and the great mechanical Flying Lions of the Venetian Empire. So at the sight of the creature barreling down on him, his first impulse was to reach for his sword.

Which, of course, he wasn't wearing.

Stupid Maestro and his lecturing that it wasn't proper for the prester to wear a weapon! He had half a mind to tell the cricket. Maestro, however, was busy fleeing in panic like the rest of his orchestra, scattering into the nearest ferns and foliage.

The winged beast streaked over the heads of the screaming guests and servants, extending its lion claws and widening its fang-filled maw.

Terror was alight like a brushfire across the scene, but as Pinocchio met Lazuli's eyes, they didn't show fear. Her eyes seemed to say: *Well, are you ready?*

"What do we do?" Pinocchio gasped.

"For starters," Lazuli said, "duck!"

The creature descended like a missile. Its jagged teeth were inches away as she pulled him flat to the ground.

"I thought there were no monsters in Abaton!" Pinocchio shouted.

The beast, having missed, streaked over the quivering topiary hedges and out of sight.

"There aren't," Lazuli answered.

"Uh, Lazuli?" Pinocchio arched an eyebrow. "Obviously there are."

With a blink of her glowing eyes, Lazuli sprang to her feet, scanning the skies. "We've got to do something!"

"Like what?" His sword, his seven-league boots, his chameleon cloak, anything he had that might have helped him was up in a cabinet in his royal chambers. He looked up at the towering palace of the Moonlit Court looming over him, gauging how long it would take to run up all those stairs. There was no time!

The monster appeared overhead, its black body silhouetted against the purple twilight sky.

"Your Majesties!" Dr. Nundrum squawked, waving his feathery hands in fright and running for a gap in the hedges. "Retreat to the palace!"

Pinocchio was on his feet, but not to retreat. Where was his father?

The scene was complete chaos. The tiny pixies that had been illuminating the table were now scattered, leaving the garden in

24

semidarkness. Many of the guests and servants had leaped into the hedges to hide or were rushing down the paths in pushing, panicked clusters. Lazuli's aunt Sapphira had taken cover under the table, along with Raya Piscus and Lord Smoldrin. But his father and the gnome Chief Muckamire were nowhere to be seen.

The monster roared from above, scanning the mayhem.

"That's a manticore," Lazuli said.

"Yeah?" Pinocchio asked, encouraged. "How do we stop it?"

"I have no idea," she replied. "No one's seen a manticore for centuries!"

There was no time to puzzle out what she meant by that. The manticore was diving toward a group of servants fleeing under a blossom-covered trellis. A gazelle-headed servant tripped before he reached it. Desperate to protect himself, he held up the only thing he had—a silver tray he'd used to deliver dishes to the banquet. The manticore whipped around its tail at him. The end, Pinocchio noticed, was bristled like a cocklebur with long, deadly spikes.

Several spikes fired out, clanking into the tray that the trembling servant held like a shield.

A queasy wave came over Pinocchio at the sight of those spikes and the realization of how vulnerable he truly was. Not only because he had no sword, but also because he was human. Before, when he had been an automa, the alchemied wood of his body had withstood battle-ax blows. But flesh was soft and vulnerable. That monster's spikes could go right through him. Its jaws could tear him to pieces.

A rush of anger thrust that worry aside. What if the gazelle servant had been hit? That monster was endangering his people! Including his father, who was somewhere out there . . .

"Hey!" Pinocchio shouted. "Leave them alone!"

The manticore's glowing jade eyes met Pinocchio's. Its mouth curled into a smile crowded with jagged teeth. The creature looked like it was having fun, as if sending people screaming in terror was the most amusing game in the whole world, only to be topped by devouring presters.

"What are you doing?" Lazuli cried, pulling Pinocchio by the elbow.

"Drawing it away from the others," he said.

"But now it's coming for us!"

The manticore was already beating its wings, building speed as it flew.

"Uh, yes, I see what you mean," Pinocchio mumbled.

He searched for something, anything to use as a weapon. Where were Mezmer and Sop when he needed them? He grabbed the chair nearest to Lord Smoldrin, who was quivering beneath the table. For a hulking djinni who looked like he could eat manticores for breakfast with a side of flaming toast, he sure was cowardly.

Pinocchio shattered the chair against the ground and held up a pair of splintered legs. They weren't swords, but they'd have to do.

The manticore streaked down. Pinocchio reared back with the chair legs, sharp ends forward. But as the monster soared across the top of the table at him, Lazuli pushed Pinocchio aside and thrust out her arms.

A blast of wind ripped through the garden. It caught the monster's wings and sent the creature spinning back into a stand of lemon trees.

"Great shot!" Pinocchio cheered.

"A little wind isn't going to stop that manticore." She fixed

Pinocchio with an adamant look. "But you know what would?"

"What?" Then he understood. "The Pearl?" She knew as well as he did that he hadn't figured out how to use the powers of the Ancientmost Pearl!

Screams and wails carried across the darkening grounds as the monster circled over the fleeing guests. Pinocchio felt that indignant anger rise again. Those were his subjects out there. And he was their prester. The people of Abaton might not have known that Prester John had never bothered to explain how to use the Ancientmost Pearl. They might not have known that Abaton's most crucial magic was now helplessly locked inside this human boy who was their new prester. But they were counting on him to be their protector. They were counting on him to command the Pearl.

Lazuli took him by the arms and shook him. "You have to use it!"

Pinocchio dropped the chair legs. Tentatively he held up his hands. He searched for some recognition, some inkling of a sign, that the Pearl's powers were inside him.

Abaton's magic involved the elemental forces of fire, air, earth, and water. It didn't need to be something complicated, he decided. If he could conjure something similar to what Lazuli had done with the wind.

The manticore was headed for a cluster of fleeing servants.

Hot anger filled Pinocchio's chest. He flung out his arms. He had to stop that thing! He had to—

A tingling sensation moved from his chest down his arms and into his outstretched fingers. He heard a whoosh of wind and the banquet table with all its plates and glasses lifted into the air, flipping end over end out into the flower beds.

He rounded excitedly on Lazuli. "I did that!" he shouted.

"Great!" She pointed into the air. "Next time aim for the manticore."

Lady Sapphira, Lord Smoldrin, and Raya Piscus, having lost their hiding place, were scrambling to their feet and running through the hedges into the garden.

"I can handle the wind!" Lazuli shouted at Pinocchio. "Try something else."

The manticore was heading over a fountain. Water! That was one of the elemental forces. He pointed at the fountain. The water bubbled and frothed, but in the end, only burst the stone sides, sending a torrent out across the grounds, knocking down a few gnomes caught in its flood. Only a splash hit the monster.

Shaking the water from its inky fur, the monster smiled menacingly at Pinocchio before beating its great wings and charging toward him.

Pinocchio focused on another fountain, this time managing to send up a more impressive geyser. The monster banked sideways to avoid the explosion.

Water wouldn't be enough. If he was going to stop this monster, he needed a more powerful elemental force.

Pinocchio stretched out his hands. The warmth that had tingled down his arms rose into a blazing heat. Pinocchio's hands ignited in flames. He hadn't quite expected that! With a yelp of alarm, he flapped and the fire shook off. It landed on the nearby shrubbery, igniting it at once like dry parchment.

His hands were singed black, but they didn't feel burned—didn't hurt at all, in fact.

"Do that again!" Lazuli said. "And this time, throw it. I'll try to use the wind to direct the flame."

A fiery missile. That sounded good. Pinocchio fought to

28

ignite his hands again. He felt them go warmer, warmer, then hot as they began to shimmer. Flames erupted. Pinocchio lobbed the fire at the monster.

Lazuli threw out her hand, sending a streak of wind that caught the ball of flame.

The monster dodged sideways. The flame hit a banana tree, setting its fronds ablaze.

This time, the manticore stopped midflight, staring at them with a mixture of surprise and fright. In the light of the flames, Pinocchio had a good look at its face now—*her* face, he realized, because something about that strangely human inky-purple face was definitely female. A diamond-shaped scar was centered on her forehead almost as if the mark had been burned into her skin with a brand.

The manticore hesitated, suspending her lioness body with heavy flaps. Then she turned her gaze over to where Lazuli's aunt was running down a path.

"No!" Lazuli gasped.

Pinocchio fought to summon another flame. His hands were getting hotter, but it wasn't working fast enough. He wouldn't be able to stop the manticore in time. And Lazuli, in her panic, was running for her aunt rather than summoning wind.

The monster exposed her long fangs in a snarl, diving for Lady Sapphira.

Out of the darkness, a shiny silver figure leaped in front of Sapphira. No, not completely silver. The head was covered in coppery-orange fur, with tall fox ears and a snarling snout. At last, Mezmer!

The manticore swung her tail around, firing several spines, one after the other.

Mezmer took the blow, her armor ringing as the spines hit. Unharmed, the fox knight drew back her spear and launched it with deadly aim straight at the manticore.

All at once, the monster was encompassed by a cloud. Mezmer's spear cut through with a puff and sailed out into the shadows. The cloud faded into wisps. The manticore had vanished.

Pinocchio stared in bewilderment. Where had she gone? Realizing that his hands were igniting with flames, he shook them off, sending sparks into the grass.

From behind him, the cat chimera Sop came running into the garden. He carried a sword in one hand and was hoisting his sagging pants over his belly with the other.

"What did I miss?" Sop panted.

"Only the whole battle, darling!" Mezmer shouted at him. Then turning to Pinocchio, frustration filling her large amber eyes, she barked, "Who's the head of the Celestial Brigade? Me! I'm the presters' protector. I'm the one that's supposed to do the fighting around here. Why didn't you get me?"

Before Pinocchio could explain, Lazuli gave a scream. Looking over, he saw Sapphira touch a hand to her shoulder. The silvery fabric of her gown was growing dark with blood. One of the manticore's spines had found its way past Mezmer.

Lazuli caught her aunt as she collapsed. "Help!" she cried.

Mezmer gathered Sapphira into her arms and barked, "We've got to get her inside."

"To Dr. Nundrum," Lazuli said, clutching her aunt by the hand. "Hurry!"

The panicked guests and servants running around the burning gardens hadn't yet realized that the monster was gone. Their shouts echoed across the grounds.

Sop began clearing a path. "Out of the way! Calm down, you ninnies, and let us through!"

They disappeared into the crowd, fighting their way toward the palace doors.

Pinocchio didn't follow. He had to find his father! He tore through a hedge, peering all around at the crying, swirling figures.

Then from out of the darkness Geppetto appeared, his face creased with worry.

"Father!" Pinocchio hurled himself at him with a great hug. "You're alive. I was afraid . . ."

"Yes, me too, my boy," his father said. He released Pinocchio and looked him up and down anxiously. "Were you hurt?"

"No, were you?"

His father shook his head. "Thanks to Chief Muckamire and his quick thinking."

With relief washing over him, Pinocchio suddenly remembered. "I . . . I did it, Father! I used the Pearl!"

He couldn't even begin to put words to how it had felt. Strange and wonderful and terrifying all at once. The way the fire had bloomed right out of the palms of his hands. And the tingling, like his whole body was charged with electricity when the magic had rushed down his arms.

Amazement lit his father's eyes. "You defeated the monster?"

"Um . . . well, no. Not exactly."

Geppetto peered around at the smoke and flames and then the portions of the gardens that now lay in ruins, including the masonry of a fountain so completely demolished that the water was flooding across the grounds. Thankfully it was putting out fires as it went.

"Did the monster do this or you?" his father murmured.

"Me. Mostly me," Pinocchio said feebly. Lazuli could also be blamed, but he felt it ungrateful to bring this up. "We were giving it a good fight, but then the monster simply . . . disappeared."

Geppetto picked up Pinocchio's hands, inspecting them in the orange light of the flames. "Are they burned?"

"No, they don't hurt. But they still feel strange . . . sort of like—"

Geppetto wiped away the soot and gave a gasp. Beneath the black, Pinocchio's hands were no longer skin. They were hard and run through with lines of grain.

"They're wood!" Geppetto breathed.

Pinocchio felt his heart give a sickening jolt. This couldn't be! This wasn't supposed to happen. He was a boy now, not—

"Your Majesty?" Tiny figures were coming up a path, leaping into one another and merging until they became a single gnome—Chief Muckamire. "Are you all right?"

Geppetto blocked Pinocchio from the gnome, covering Pinocchio's hands and calling over his shoulder, "Prester Pinocchio is fine. All is safe, Chief Muckamire. The creature is gone. But we need to make sure there aren't any others injured and get everyone into the palace."

The gnome lord gave a quick nod and hurried back toward the clusters of trembling guests and servants emerging from the mayhem.

Geppetto turned to Pinocchio, still clutching his wooden hands. "Keep them hidden!" he whispered. "Don't let anyone see. Do you understand, son?"

"Yes," Pinocchio said, tucking his hands into his sleeves and folding his arms beneath his robes for good measure.

"If the others discover . . ." Geppetto shook the thought

aside. He pulled an arm around Pinocchio to lead him into the palace. "We must get you upstairs."

"But, Father, what's happening to me? Why am I turning back into wood?"

Geppetto gave a frown. "I don't know, son. But I can't help but feel it's no coincidence that this has occurred after you summoned the powers of the Ancientmost Pearl."

4.

Dr. Nundrum's Discovery

T he pandemonium that had been echoing throughout the palace was finally dying down. Pacing back and forth outside her aunt's door as she waited for news from Dr. Nundrum, Lazuli wondered if word of the monster's attack had already spread to the harbor—or even beyond. Soon enough, all of Abaton would hear what had happened. She knew she should do something to help calm her people, but now all she could think about was her aunt.

Mezmer and Sop came down the hallway. They looked exhausted. Mezmer's bushy tail was dragging behind her. And Sop's one eye was threatening to close. He slumped to the floor beside the door and adjusted his eye patch.

"The fires are all extinguished, Your Majesty," Mezmer

reported. "Everyone's safely indoors. And thankfully no one was injured except for . . . How is your aunt?"

"I don't know," Lazuli said. "Dr. Nundrum has been in there forever."

At that moment the door opened, and the owl slipped out.

Lazuli grabbed his arm. "How is she?"

Dr. Nundrum removed his glasses and rubbed a feathered hand to the bridge of his beak. "Sleeping, Your Majesty. And she'll be fine. I removed the manticore's spine. Fortunately, it contained no poison. I've put salves on the wound to help it heal and given Lady Sapphira a draft of medicine for the pain. Best wait until morning before you visit her."

Relief almost sent a trickle of tears spilling from her eyes, but Lazuli drew a sharp breath to stop them. She was the prester. "Good. Thank you, Dr. Nundrum."

Her head began to clear, and her concerns shifted from her aunt to what had just occurred.

"Was that really a manticore? Where did it even come from?"

Dr. Nundrum fluttered his feathers. "I have no idea, Your Majesty. Who would have imagined? A monster in Abaton! None have been seen in our kingdom since the days of . . ."

Lazuli waited for him to continue, but Dr. Nundrum seemed to drift down some deep current of thought. His wide owl eyes stayed fixed and unblinking.

"Dr. Nundrum?" she asked after a moment.

He blinked. Then he was alight with manic energy, making several failed attempts at adjusting his glasses before they settled on his beak. "Your Majesty! There's something I need to look up. And you should come with me. To the library." He started to hurry down the hallway. "We should probably gather Prester Pinocchio as well."

"But what is it?" Lazuli asked, following after him.

"I hope I'm wrong. Oh, please be wrong." The owl shook his head. "I'll explain it all in the library. Prester Pinocchio—"

"Sop will get him," Mezmer said, catching up to them.

The cat gave a groan from where he sat on the floor. "Do I have to?"

"A knight of the Celestial Brigade never shirks his duty, dear," Mezmer called back.

"But when there's only two knights in the whole kingdom, I wind up having to do all the duties," Sop complained, staggering to his feet.

When they reached the library, Lazuli and Mezmer cast each other worried glances as Dr. Nundrum first searched one bookshelf and then another, muttering all the while under his breath. Moonlight filtered through the delicate stone of the palace walls, bathing the room in its silvery glow. It would be too dim for reading by.

Lazuli opened a box on the nearest table, releasing a swarm of pixies into the air. She took the lid off a glass lamp and, with a wave of her hand, a breeze gathered the pixies into the lamp's globe. Their warm orange light pooled on the table's surface just as Dr. Nundrum deposited a stack of books with a dusty thump.

"Now, where is it?" he murmured—flipping pages, stopping occasionally before scanning a passage, pushing one book aside for another, searching, searching.

"What's going on?" Geppetto entered the library with Pinocchio and Sop. Maestro fidgeted on Geppetto's shoulder.

Lazuli noticed that Pinocchio was now wearing a pair of

gloves. He wasn't one for fancy additions to his attire. Had he injured himself in the fight?

"Yes, here it is and . . . can that be?" Dr. Nundrum muttered, his hooked beak pressed nearly to the page of a book. "Oh, but . . . no! No, no, no."

"Can you please explain why you've brought us here, Dr. Nundrum?" Lazuli said, her patience wearing thin.

The owl looked up, turning his gaze to each of them in turn. "The monster tonight—"

"About that," Sop interrupted, crossing his arms. "I thought there weren't any monsters left in Abaton. You know, *peaceful kingdom* and all that *we don't need an army because we're perfectly safe* business?"

Maestro hopped from Geppetto's shoulder onto the table beside Dr. Nundrum's book. "There aren't supposed to be any left."

"Well," Sop said, "somebody needs to tell that monster."

"If you'll please allow me to explain," Dr. Nundrum said, his voice quavering. "Did any of you notice the manticore's forehead?"

"Not me," Mezmer said, her ears flicking with agitation. "Especially since we practically missed the entire fight because nobody thought to call the knights of the Celestial Brigade the one time there's an actual threat!"

"I saw her forehead," Pinocchio said. "She had a mark. Sort of like a diamond."

"So what I saw was true," Dr. Nundrum said. "Oh, dear."

"What's it mean?" Lazuli asked.

Dr. Nundrum jabbed a feathery finger to the page before him. "It's the mark of Diamancer. If the manticore had that mark, it means she belonged to Diamancer's army."

Lazuli felt an icy finger of fear run up her spine at the name.

Maestro too looked alarmed as his wings fluttered and his six tiny legs danced frantically. But Pinocchio and Geppetto were exchanging bewildered looks with Mezmer and Sop. Lazuli knew, of course, that they—being from the Venetian Empire—would never have heard about this dark chapter of Abaton's history.

Noticing Pinocchio's confusion, Dr. Nundrum said, "You're aware, Your Majesty, that Abaton was not always peaceful as it is today. Centuries ago, not long after the time when Prester John began trading with the humanlands, we went through a terrible war. One of Prester John's most trusted advisers was Diamancer. But Diamancer had come to believe that Prester John's eternal rule was unfair. He also resented that Abaton's magic was being shared with humans. So he gathered the races of monsters— manticores, wyverns, ghouls, and the like—and led a rebellion."

Dr. Nundrum fluttered a hand at Mezmer. "It was your ancestor the general Mezmercurian who commanded the celestial knights that defeated Diamancer's forces. And since that day, we have known only peace."

"How were they defeated?" Mezmer lifted her snout a little higher and pulled back her shoulders. "Did dear Mezmercurian kill Diamancer in single combat?"

"No," Dr. Nundrum said. "Diamancer would have fought to the end, and made his army of monsters do the same. But when the Celestial Knights cornered Diamancer's forces in the canyons of Magorian Wastes, the monsters surrendered, knowing this was the only way to spare their lives."

"Spare them?" Mezmer said. "They were traitors. Weren't they executed?"

"Certainly not!" Maestro squeaked. "They might have been

traitors, but they were children of Abaton all the same. Prester John could never kill his own children. It would have betrayed his vow as prester-protector and undermined the magic of the Ancientmost Pearl."

"So what happened to Diamancer and his monsters?" Pinocchio asked.

Pixie light glittered against Dr. Nundrum's glasses. "The books of history tell us that they were locked in a secret prison."

Geppetto furrowed his woolly brows. "But how could the manticore who attacked tonight have been one of Diamancer's monsters? It was so long ago."

Dr. Nundrum bobbed his head. "That is precisely why I didn't realize at first who this manticore was! That's why I had to search these books for the explanation. You see, the prisoners are called the Thousand Sleeping Traitors because Prester John cast Diamancer and all the rest into an enchanted sleep until they could repent."

"But that would mean . . ." Lazuli found her words coming out as the barest whisper. ". . . that at least one of these monsters has awakened."

"And found the means to escape," Mezmer added.

Sop swished his tail. "Doesn't look like they've repented, does it?"

"This is most worrisome. Most worrisome indeed!" Maestro looked ready to fly into a fit of panic.

Lazuli was trying to keep calm. She wished desperately that her aunt was awake, that Lady Sapphira was here advising her, telling her what she should do. Everyone was now looking at her expectantly. Even Pinocchio. She had half a mind to remind him that he was the prester too. She wasn't the only one running the kingdom!

She frowned. "I think it's safe to assume that this manticore is the only one so far to have escaped from the prison. Otherwise, the attack would have been much worse. But how long until others wake and find a way out? We need to secure the prison before they do."

"Agreed!" Dr. Nundrum said anxiously.

"So?" Lazuli asked the owl. "Where's the prison located?"

"Oh, yes." Dr. Nundrum was running a feathery finger down the page, reading rapidly. "Well, I can't be sure exactly . . . His Great Lordship, your father, made the prison secret, after all." He continued flipping through books.

Sop gave an impatient tap of his foot. "Can somebody wake up the palace librarian?"

"*I am* the palace librarian. It's just our collection is not as extensive as the one in Grootslang . . . ah, here's something!" Dr. Nundrum squared his glasses as he read. "It's a brief mention of Prester John building an enormous pyramid not long after the Rebellion."

"Does it say where it is?" Geppetto asked.

"The Upended Forest," the owl murmured, giving a quizzical look.

"Upended Forest?" Lazuli said. "I've never heard of it."

"Neither have I," Maestro said. "Is it in one of the jungle realms?"

"No," Dr. Nundrum said, looking from the book around at the others. "Oddly enough, it appears this forest is in a remote portion of the Caldera Desert."

"There aren't any forests in the Caldera," Lazuli said.

"True enough, Your Majesty," Dr. Nundrum said. "But there it is! On the page. Quite perplexing. Maybe this Upended Forest is in fact an oasis. Or was once a forest that the desert has ruined. Whatever the case, it makes sense that such an obscure and clearly quite uninhabited portion of Abaton would be the best location for a secret prison."

"So how do we find it, darling?" Mezmer asked.

"I'll have to investigate further," Dr. Nundrum said. "But once I discover it, we must send Prester Pinocchio right away—"

Mezmer reared up like a mother bear. "Pinocchio go to the prison? We can't send our prester into that kind of danger! Are you mad?"

Dr. Nundrum blinked his gilded eyes. "It's because he's the prester that we must. How else will the prison be opened? It says quite explicitly here"—he touched the page—"that the lock to the prison can only be opened by the prester's hand."

"Then it doesn't have to be Prester Pinocchio," Lazuli said. "I'm the prester too! Ever since I've returned to Abaton as prester, my powers commanding air seem stronger . . . when the manticore attacked, I felt it!"

"That might be true," Dr. Nundrum said. "But Prester Pinocchio commands the Ancientmost Pearl. Only he has the powers to ensure that no more of these monsters escape. There is no one else who can!"

Lazuli saw Pinocchio and Geppetto exchange worried glances.

"Prester Lazuli," Dr. Nundrum said quietly. "I hope that your responsibility to your people will persuade you to stay where you're most needed—here at the Moonlit Court. Your people depend on your presence to assure them all will be safe."

Lazuli tried unsuccessfully to hide her scowl. How was this fair? She didn't want to sit around on the throne while

Pinocchio went off on some dangerous—and most likely exciting—mission.

Pinocchio wrung his gloved hands. "So I have to go to this prison . . . alone?"

"I'll go with you," Geppetto said, giving a squeeze to Pinocchio's shoulder.

"And of course the knights of the Celestial Brigade," Mezmer added.

"All *two* of us." Sop rolled his eye.

"Very well," Lazuli said, masking her disappointment. "Dr. Nundrum, you'll continue to search for more information about the location of the Upended Forest."

"I will search all night if necessary. What's critical is that Prester Pinocchio leave as soon as possible! Abaton depends on him." The owl gave a bow and then hurried off across the library.

"We should get some rest," Lazuli said to Pinocchio and Geppetto. "I'll need to talk to the high nobles first thing in the morning so our people know we have a plan of action."

"Sop and I will keep watch tonight on the upper balconies, in case the manticore returns," Mezmer said, pulling the grumbling cat by the arm toward the door.

"Wait," Pinocchio said. Then turning to Lazuli, he whispered, "We need to talk. Somewhere we won't be overheard."

Lazuli rubbed her eyes, exhausted. "Can't this wait?"

But the look of urgency on Pinocchio's and Geppetto's faces told her that it definitely couldn't.

Up in Pinocchio's chambers, with the cool night air blowing in through the windows, Lazuli stared in disbelief at his outstretched hands. The grains of wood ran from his fingertips down to his wrist, merging back into smooth, soft flesh.

She had to open and close her mouth several times before she could get any words out. "How did this happen?" she gasped.

"When I used the Ancientmost Pearl," Pinocchio whispered.

Geppetto frowned, dark circles under his eyes.

Maestro flittered with agitation. "But they'll turn back, right? They have to! In the empire, the Pearl changed Pinocchio from wood to flesh and blood. It'll do it again. Won't it?"

"Only if he doesn't use the Pearl," Geppetto said.

"But if more monsters begin escaping from the prison, he'll have to," Mezmer said, digging her fingers into the coppery fur on her face. "Darlings, I think we're in big trouble."

"There has to be a way," Lazuli said.

Sop was wringing his tail in his paws. "Any ideas, Your Majesty?"

Lazuli frowned. "If we only knew what caused the manticore to awaken."

"And how to get her back to sleep," Mezmer added.

"But we don't," Geppetto growled. "And we have no time to figure this out before we have to leave to locate the prison."

Pinocchio squeezed the wooden hands into clacking fists. "I . . . I don't even know if I *can* open the prison. Dr. Nundrum said it could only be opened with the prester's hands. What if they won't work, because mine are . . . like this?"

Lazuli could see the solution plainly enough. But how would she explain it to her aunt and Dr. Nundrum and the high nobles?

"I'll come," she said.

"You'll *what*?" Maestro chirped.

"I'm coming with you. I'll have to," Lazuli said. "You heard Dr. Nundrum. If the prison can only be opened by the prester's hand, well . . . I'm the prester too. We'll just have to hope it works for me."

43

No one argued. Pinocchio even smiled, a look of relief washing across his face.

Lazuli smiled back. She was glad for the excuse. She didn't want to miss out on the fun, after all—if you could call facing a prison full of potentially awake and ferocious monsters fun.

5.

Departure

In the morning, everything around the Moonlit Court seemed in a hurry. Servants were frantically trying to clean up the decimated gardens. Palace officials were rushing letters from Dr. Nundrum up to the palace aerie, where they'd be sent to historians all around the kingdom, anyone who might have clues about the location of this ancient prison where Diamancer and his monsters had been hidden. Even the wind coming off the ocean blew in wild, panicky gusts.

The palace grooms were fighting the gales as they brought the various mounts out from the stables. The elemental nobles, eager to get back to their respective cities, were pouring out from the palace with their belongings, ready to depart.

The djinn boarded a luxurious carriage as big as a cabin lifted by a flock of flaming birds. The undines did their best to keep a safe distance from the djinn's birds as they passed, heading for the harbor, where they'd shed their sloshing shrouds and swim back to their underwater realm of Piscaray.

The gnomes sat in long lines down the multitude of saddles strapped to the backs of massive millipede-like creatures called slithersteeds. Chief Muckamire called his farewells to Dr. Nundrum, Pinocchio, and Geppetto before departing. The sylphs were waiting for their lady while the grooms brought out their half-eagle, half-lion griffin mounts, who were snapping their golden beaks and flexed tawny muscular wings in the morning sun.

Lady Sapphira, her arm bandaged, was still speaking to her niece at the top of the steps.

"What do you mean *you* have to join them?" she asked.

"Aunt Sapphira," Lazuli said, keeping her voice low to not be overheard by the servants and nobles collecting on the palace steps. "You know Prester Pinocchio isn't familiar with our kingdom. He'll need my help."

Her aunt's eyes narrowed suspiciously, and she gave a hint of a smile. "You have always longed for more adventure than the Moonlit Court could provide. It's what has set you apart from all your father's other children. But your people need you here, on the throne, assuring them that Abaton is in safe hands."

Lazuli opened her mouth to argue, but her aunt cut her off. "Please listen to me, my dear niece. It's not simply your people you must reassure. I hesitated to share this with you, lest it cause you undue concern. But given this grave turn for our kingdom, you must know that the other three high nobles were advocating to have you and Prester Pinocchio replaced by a regency council."

"What?" Lazuli gasped. "They don't feel Pinocchio and I can rule?"

"I hope for now I have persuaded them otherwise," Sapphira whispered. "But do not underestimate the power and ambition of the elemental houses. If they decide to work against you, they could convince the people of Abaton that their presters are too young and inexperienced. You must show them otherwise!"

Lazuli felt torn. Part of her longed to unburden herself from having to rule. Let the high nobles have it—especially if her aunt was part of this regency council. But she also realized all their hopes for rescuing the slaves of Venice would fall away. And besides, the council would expect to be given the Ancientmost Pearl.

"Lazuli," Aunt Sapphira said, taking her by the hands. "You know how dear you are to me. With no children of my own, I have come to see you as the daughter I never had, especially after my sister's death. You are clever and bold. I feel if you will allow me to guide you that you will make a truly great prester."

Lazuli felt her cheeks grow warm at the compliment. She couldn't help but think if things had been different, her aunt, however, really would have made the best choice for prester.

"I can't imagine how I could rule without your guidance, Aunt," Lazuli said.

"Then you must assure the high nobles and your people that you can keep them safe, that you can rule decisively. Send Prester Pinocchio to end the threat of this monster. He will have his knights to protect him."

"But if I joined, wouldn't that show our people that Pinocchio and I can keep them safe?"

"Leaving the thone unsecured? No! You must focus on what is in the best interest of your people. Your presence in the Moonlit Court will instill confidence that you are in command."

Lazuli understood what Lady Sapphira was saying, but her

aunt didn't know what was going on with Pinocchio, the truth they were hiding from the kingdom.

Lazuli looked her aunt in the eye. "Aunt Sapphira, you saw what happened when Pinocchio used the Pearl last night."

She pursed her lips. "Prester Pinocchio protected us. Maybe he did more damage to the gardens than to that manticore. Still, he's capable of handling this undertaking without you."

"I'm not sure he can," Lazuli said, wrestling with how much to reveal. "You see . . . Pinocchio can draw powers from the Pearl, but I feel he needs to be cautious in doing so."

"Why?"

"There might be consequences. Not good consequences."

Her aunt tilted her head. "For him or for Abaton?"

Lazuli considered this question. Part of her wanted to simply tell everything, so Sapphira could understand the full scope of their dilemma. Maybe her aunt would even know something they didn't about the Pearl, some explanation for why he was changing back and, better still, a way to stop it from happening.

But this felt like a betrayal of Pinocchio. Besides, Lazuli couldn't help but fear that if Lady Sapphira knew what Pinocchio really had been—what he was becoming once again—she and all the people of Abaton would be horrified. They might demand that Pinocchio give up the throne, that he give up the Pearl. And giving up the Pearl . . . No, she couldn't tell.

Lazuli shook her head, not answering the question. "I don't mean for you to doubt his abilities. Pinocchio will make a great prester. I am certain. But until he understands how the Pearl is to be mastered, I have to help him."

Her aunt opened her mouth, but Lazuli plunged forward. "You said yourself, I need to focus on the best interests of my people. And now more than ever—with the manticore's attack, with the threat of more monsters escaping—I must go with him. I have to be certain that he will be successful. For all our people."

"But we don't even know where the manticore came from," Aunt Sapphira said. "How long will it take to locate this hidden prison?"

"All the more reason for me to help," Lazuli said. "I will show my people and the high nobles that we can do what no regency council ever would. I can work with Pinocchio to stop monsters from returning to Abaton."

Aunt Sapphira held her gaze for a long moment. She then gave a sigh before gesturing to one of her attendants nearby. "Bring me the parcel stored at the top of my trunk."

The sylph hurried to the griffins. He returned a moment later with something thin wrapped in a square of velvet.

Her aunt opened it and handed Lazuli a small gilded mirror of black glass. "With this, you'll be able to speak with me, no matter where you are. Will you promise to seek my counsel on any matter you need? I am here for you."

Relief flooded through Lazuli. Her aunt was allowing her to go! But then she turned this thought over in her mind. She didn't need anyone's permission. Still, she was glad Sapphira wasn't upset with her, glad that this could be settled before they parted ways.

"Yes, of course, Aunt."

"Good girl," she said, patting Lazuli's cheek affectionately. "Be safe. Remember that you are the prester and not some foolhardy knight. If there is danger, let Mezmer and Sop deal with it. Your people need you to return safely to the throne."

Lazuli nodded briskly, a small bubble of guilt rising. This was not a promise she intended to keep. If there was danger, Lazuli would never stand aside to let others handle it.

Sapphira gave her a hug before following the other sylphs onto the backs of the griffins. Once they were seated, the griffins charged in formation down the lawn, building speed with their powerful lion hindquarters. They threw out their wide wings and sailed above the jungle and into the dawn sky.

Lazuli watched until they were mere specks. A little hollow feeling formed in her chest at her aunt's departure. She cupped the mirror in her hands, tempted to test it, to hear her aunt's reassuring voice just once more. The weight of all there was to do pressed heavily on her.

"What's that?"

Lazuli turned to find Pinocchio coming up the stairs.

"Oh," Lazuli said, showing him the mirror before wrapping it back in the velvet. "In case we need to reach my aunt."

Mezmer burst from the palace doors. "He's found it, darlings! Dr. Nundrum found the location of the Upended Forest. We depart as soon as you're ready."

Pinocchio grew alight with nervous energy. "I need to get my sword. And my seven-league boots. Don't you think I should bring them?"

"Bring it all," Mezmer said, a dreamy smile slipping up the sides of her snout. "Finally a glorious mission fit for a knight of the Celestial Brigade. Hurry, my darling presters. Hurry!"

Lazuli followed them back into the palace. "Wait," she said as Mezmer veered off toward the library. "How are we getting there?"

The fox flung out her arms. "With royal flair, of course! Better than any griffin or flying carpet. You won't believe how he's cleaned the old gal up."

"Who's cleaned up what?" Lazuli asked.

"Ah, yes." Mezmer lifted a furry finger. "There is just one

little catch." Her eyes darted apologetically to Pinocchio. "You're not going to like this, darling."

"No," Pinocchio said. "Please tell me Cinnabar's not coming."

"Sorry, dear, but it's his special project."

Down from the Moonlit Court, hugging the great green lagoon that served as Abaton's harbor, was the town of Crescent Port. Compared to the grand elemental cities, it was small. But the capital's neighboring town was bustling with activity—chimera traders exchanging goods in great open markets, spice vendors filling barrels with delicious powders and herbs bound for the best kitchens in Abaton, so many shops and apothecaries and teahouses crowded together that they seemed about to spill over into the narrow streets.

But today the whole town was down at the docks, where, hovering over the glassy waters of the lagoon, there was a flying ship. Pinocchio stood beside Lazuli and the others staring up at it in amazement.

The former Venetian war galley no longer looked like the near wreck it had been when they'd arrived in Abaton. Venice's crests and colors had been stripped, and the ship's prow had been replaced with the painted figurehead of a snarling sea monster, eyes rolled back and swirls of decorative froth extending from its teeth across the sides of the ship. Pinocchio assumed this impressively terrifying vision was meant to be the Deep One, the guardian of Abaton. After all, this ship had flown from the Deep One's mouth after it had swallowed them. The sails were dropped, but Pinocchio could see that even they were new, as was every rope, rigging, and tackle.

"Cinnabar's certainly been busy," Lazuli said.

Pinocchio had wondered what the ill-tempered djinni had

been doing since arriving in Abaton. He supposed this was a better project than what he'd imagined Cinnabar had been up to. Namely, plotting to have Pinocchio overthrown.

"The ship looks great," Pinocchio grumbled. "But why does he have to come with us?"

"We'll need all the help we can get dealing with this prison," Lazuli said. "Cinnabar proved he handles himself well in the face of danger."

"You're kidding, right?" Pinocchio said. "He shot you with a crossbow."

"An accident," Lazuli reminded him.

It had been an accident, but that was because Cinnabar had been trying to shoot *Geppetto* in a misguided scheme to return the Pearl to Prester John. Who needed enemies like the manticore when you had an ally like Cinnabar around?

The last of the palace servants were climbing down the rope ladder dangling from the ship to the docks.

"Everything seems to be in order, Your Majesties," Dr. Nundrum said, checking off a list. "Stocked and supplied. Everything's taken care of." The owl tucked his pen behind an ear tuft and rolled up the parchment, his hands slightly shaking.

"Are you all right?" Lazuli asked.

"It's just . . . well, with you both away, I'll be managing the affairs of the palace until your return . . . and if there's another attack . . ." His eyes widened with concern. "Please hurry, Your Majesties!"

"We will, Dr. Nundrum," Lazuli said calmly.

He fluttered his feathers anxiously. "Waste not a moment in locating the Upended Forest—"

"Thank you, Dr. Nundrum," Lazuli said. "We understand the urgency of the situation."

"Of course," the owl said. "Yes, of course you do." He gave a bow. "Your Majesties."

Pinocchio caught Lazuli's glance. He hoped the poor owl was going to be able to manage his duties, and not simply hide under his bed until they came back.

"Anytime you're ready, Your Majesties." Cinnabar's yellow-and-black mottled face peered down from the ship. Unlike the other djinn and elemental nobles of Abaton, who wore robes of garish colors decorated with ridiculously complex stitch-work designs, Cinnabar dressed much as he had as a slave in the Venetian Empire: somber, simple, and a uniform soot black.

The djinni attempted a smile, but as usual it looked more like he'd just eaten something revolting.

There was no denying the fact that Cinnabar loathed Pinocchio. Maybe it was that Pinocchio had been an automa, and since Cinnabar had been a slave to one of the empire's alchemists, he despised all alchemical creations. Or maybe Cinnabar was just naturally hateful. Back in Venice, the djinni had made no attempt to hide his feelings, but now that Pinocchio was the prester, he had no choice but to mask his dislike, however poorly.

Sop scampered up the ladder first, eager to see the ship. Lazuli followed, hardly needing to hold on to the slats as she practically hovered up in typical sylph fashion. Pinocchio climbed after her. But as he came over the railing, he tripped and would have fallen on his face. Cinnabar caught him by the hand.

The djinni was about to let go, as if holding Pinocchio's hand might leave a stink. But then his eyes became slits. He gave Pinocchio's glove a squeeze, pressing against the wood.

Pinocchio tore his hand from Cinnabar's grasp.

The djinni gave a smarmy bow. "I merely meant to assist you, *Your Majesty.*"

Pinocchio backed away, scowling, and went over to where Lazuli was admiring the ship.

Sop came charging up from belowdecks, whiskers wild. "Do we get to pick our own bunks? I call the one up front."

Mezmer climbed over the railing. "Darling, this is a royal vessel. The presters get first pick." She reached back to help Geppetto aboard.

Maestro was chirping from Geppetto's shoulder, "I swore I'd never again leave the Moonlit Court."

"No one forced you to come," Geppetto said stepping onto the decks and smoothing his mustache.

"Yes." The cricket sighed. "But how would you manage without me and my vast understanding of Abatonian culture?"

Pinocchio shook his head. For someone so small, Maestro had an awfully big sense of self-importance.

Sop clapped Cinnabar on the shoulder. "You've had way too much time on your hands, old chum. I'm not complaining. This is amazing! But why haven't you been enjoying palace life with the rest of us?"

Cinnabar pushed his sleek hair over his horns. "I thought my time best spent repairing the ship for our return to Venice. Besides, I haven't exactly been warmly welcomed by my brethren here."

"Those high-horned snobby djinn aren't toasting you with fancy parties?" Sop asked. "I'm shocked."

Cinnabar curled a lip.

"I'm sorry the elemental nobles haven't treated you more kindly, Cinnabar," Lazuli said with a frown. "They don't seem to appreciate what you and the rest of our enslaved people have endured under the Venetian Empire. Once we figure out this issue with the prison, I promise Prester Pinocchio and I will work on changing the nobles' minds."

Cinnabar made a bow, cutting a skeptical eye that Pinocchio didn't miss.

Mezmer pulled up the ladder and clapped her hands in satisfaction. "Well, Cinnabar, I hope she flies as well as she looks."

Sop bounded up to the ship's wheel. "I get to steer first."

"No, you don't," Cinnabar snarled, chasing after him. "After all my work, I won't have you damage anything with your reckless flying."

The crowd gathered along the lower streets of the capital city, watching their presters' departure with excitement. As the sails unfurled and the ship set off, Pinocchio stood with Lazuli at the railing, waving to the well-wishers. The motley faces of the Abatonian citizenry peered up from the rapidly shrinking Crescent Port.

Soon they were passing the Moonlit Court, the towering white palace tapering up into the sky like an ivory horn. The ship gave a gentle, side-to-side rock as it ascended above the jungle cliffs and caught the higher currents streaming off the ocean.

While Cinnabar steered and Sop manned the lines, Mezmer spread an aged brown map on the deck, discussing their route with Geppetto and Maestro.

But Pinocchio continued to watch the djinni. "I really don't like Cinnabar coming along," he whispered to Lazuli.

"You're being silly," she said.

"Am I? I think he realized my hand is wood. When he helped me on deck."

"He'd find out sooner or later," she said. "Besides, he already knows your secret."

"Which I'm sure he'd love to share with all our subjects," Pinocchio said.

Lazuli rolled her eyes. "No, he wouldn't. He's on our side.

You're going to need to trust him if we're to work together to stop this threat. Stop worrying about grumpy Cinnabar and start worrying about our mission."

He *was* worried about their mission. Plenty. But as he looked away from scowling Cinnabar and to the great vista of dark green jungle peaks spread out before their ship, he realized he was excited too. He couldn't help it.

The notion of going to a prison full of sleeping monsters should have completely terrified him. But this was exactly the sort of thing he was good at. He was terrible at court. Lazuli might not have loved it either, but at least she could gracefully manage etiquette and political maneuvering. But, for Pinocchio, strapping on a sword and facing the dark unknown . . . that was what made him feel alive. Truly and thrillingly alive.

He felt a shiver run through him.

He only hoped he'd return to the Moonlit Court alive. And not as a mindless, wooden automa.

Pinocchio and Lazuli spent the first afternoon aboard the ship practicing their swordplay up on deck as the misty range of volcanic jungle rippled beneath them. Geppetto and Maestro were set up down in the galley poring over the books borrowed from the palace library, desperate to discover more about the prison. Cinnabar was hunched at the helm, snapping commands for Sop to recheck lines and double-check riggings.

"Come on," Sop begged. "I sailed us out of the Deep One, didn't I? Just give me a turn."

"After all I've done to get her in shape," Cinnabar said. "Not a chance. And if I see you using any part as a scratching post . . ."

Sop rolled his eye.

That evening, Cinnabar anchored the ship to a craggy peak

for the night. After a supper around the galley's long table, Pinocchio set off for bed.

He had no idea how long he was asleep, but when he woke, something was scratching against the wall. For half a sleepy moment, he thought it was Sop. He opened his eyes.

Thin moonlight gathered on the circular porthole window. Pinocchio tilted his head, listening, but the sound had stopped. Maybe it had just been in a dream. He still wasn't used to dreaming. Automa never did. Such a funny part of being alive and having to sleep with these strange stories playing in your head.

A shadow crossed the porthole. Pinocchio shot up. A thump sounded outside before the scratch-scratch-scratching returned. It was coming from the other side of the hull.

Something was out there in the dark. And it wanted to get in.

6.

Skulkers and Storms

Pinocchio tore back the sheets and leaped from his bed. He pressed his face to the porthole's glass. All he could see was the faint silvery mist hugging the jungle below. What was out there?

He grabbed his sword and slipped into the narrow hallway. "Father!" he hissed.

Geppetto opened his door, the pixie lamp in his hands illuminating his wide eyes. "I heard it."

Maestro poked his antennae out from the collar of Geppetto's nightshirt. "M-m-monsters!" the cricket stammered.

"Maybe not," Geppetto whispered. "Stay calm."

They crept down the hallway. As they passed Cinnabar's room, the djinni peered out. "Why are you stomping around?" he grumbled, still half-asleep.

"Something's outside," Pinocchio said.

Cinnabar's eyes blazed with alarm, and he spun around, emerging an instant later with a crossbow. "I'll wake Prester Lazuli," he said, sliding a bolt into the crossbow and cranking back the string. "Where are Sop and Mezmer?"

"Up on deck, keeping watch," Geppetto said. "Meet us up there. And be quiet."

The djinni nodded, slipping down the hallway toward Lazuli's room.

The ship had been stocked with an assortment of ancient weapons that Dr. Nundrum had gotten the palace servants to round up from wall displays around the Moonlit Court. Geppetto took a slender sword from the rack in the galley as he followed Pinocchio toward the gangway stairs.

Pinocchio opened the hatch onto the upper deck and emerged into the moonlight. He moved in a crouch, sword at the ready, peering around for signs of danger. The sky was empty except for the speckled sea of stars. But fog rose from the jungle below, stealing up the sides of the ship in serpentine ribbons.

Pinocchio spied Sop, sprawled on the deck beside the mast. He ran to him and grabbed his shoulder, whispering, "Sop! Are you hurt?"

The cat opened his eye. He sat up, scratching his whiskers. "Sorry. Must have dozed off."

Geppetto grumbled, "You're supposed to be keeping watch. We heard something."

The cat sprang to his feet, much more lightly than seemed possible given how round he was. "Where's Mez?"

The fox was already coming down from the quarterdeck with her spear just as Cinnabar and Lazuli emerged from the gangway. Pinocchio was glad to see Lazuli had her sword.

"I don't see anything out here," Cinnabar said, frowning at Pinocchio. "Are you sure Your Majesty wasn't dreaming?"

"I heard it too," Geppetto said. "It was coming from the bottom of the hull. A scratching sound. Like claws on wood."

Mezmer ran to one side of the ship, Sop the other, each peering over. Cinnabar raised his crossbow, aiming it around at the dark. Pinocchio huddled closer to his father and Lazuli, standing back-to-back in the center of the deck.

Mezmer moved along the railing, staring down. "I don't see anything," she whispered.

"Maestro," Sop said. "Fly down there and check it out."

"And get eaten?" the cricket chirped. "Absolutely not!"

"I'll go," Lazuli said. "I can hold on to the sides."

Pinocchio had seen Lazuli walk down vertical faces before. One of her many sylph talents.

"Your Majesty, darling," Mezmer said. "As general of the Celestial Brigade, I am charged with protecting you. I have to insist that you—"

A door slammed. They all looked at one another. Then Sop sprang toward the gangway. He grabbed the hatch. "It's locked!"

The others ran to help. Sop and Mezmer threw their shoulders against the wood, but it didn't budge. Faint sounds of overturning furniture came from belowdecks.

"Someone's down there!" Cinnabar hissed.

"Or something," Sop said.

"Break it down!" Mezmer ordered, slamming the blunt end of her spear against the hatch.

Sop hacked with his sword until the wood splintered. Then with a kick, he had the hatch open. Mezmer charged down first, quickly followed by the others. Pinocchio didn't relish the idea of combat in these cramped quarters. But the galley was empty, as were the hallways and cabins. It was only when they reached Pinocchio's room that Mezmer raised a hand in warning.

"The door's locked," she whispered. "It's in there."

Sop was about to kick it open, when Lazuli pushed him aside. "Stand back," she said. Then, sheathing her sword, she raised her hands, palms out. A blast of wind funneled down the hallway. Pinocchio staggered against the wall, as did everyone but Lazuli.

The door flew off its hinges with a thunderous crack of wood and landed on Pinocchio's bed. Mezmer raced in, followed by the others.

Crowded together in the tight space, they found the room empty. But the porthole was open. Pinocchio pushed his head and shoulders through.

A shadow with wide wings disappeared into the jungle mists below.

Pinocchio felt arms grab him by the waist, pulling him back inside. Mezmer scowled at him as she put him down. "Let me do my job please, dear!"

"She's gone," Pinocchio said.

Mezmer checked anyway, poking her head out the porthole. "Why didn't she attack us?" the fox said, sounding almost disappointed.

"I don't think she was here to attack us," Lazuli said. "Look."

She waved a hand to the mess of Pinocchio's room. His belongings were pulled out from his trunk, scattered across the floor, along with his sheets and pillows.

"The manticore was looking for something," Geppetto said, kneeling to touch the torn hole in the mattress.

"But what would she want in my room?" Pinocchio asked.

"What else?" Lazuli said, crossing her arms. "The Ancientmost Pearl."

After Cinnabar cast off the following morning, Lazuli found Pinocchio up at the bow, keeping watch with Mezmer. The fox had a tight grip on her spear, eyes straining as she scanned the jungle.

"You're worried the manticore will return?" Lazuli asked.

"I doubt she'll give up that easily," Mezmer said, tapping a finger to the railing. "We have to be prepared. But I do find it strange, how this monster came for the Pearl last night. She was quiet, stealthy. Why didn't she try to take it by force?"

Lazuli had no answer, except that maybe they were lucky. And might not be next time.

"Do you think the manticore wants the Pearl in order to release the other prisoners?" Pinocchio asked.

"She obviously found a way to escape," Mezmer said. "I don't think that's why she's after the Pearl."

"Maybe she needs the Pearl to wake the others," Pinocchio said. "Maybe to wake her leader. What was his name?"

"Diamancer," Lazuli said. Saying the name sent a shiver of fear up her spine. Images from the ancient books of history she'd read bubbled up from her memory. Visions of the hordes of terrifying monsters clashing with the knights of old.

"It will be one thing to figure out how the manticore woke," she said. "But it won't do us much good unless we know how to get her back to sleep in the prison. Before she figures out how to waken them all."

Mezmer gripped her spear in a choke hold. "My ancestor Mezmercurian led the greatest army Abaton's ever known against Diamancer. Where are *our* glorious knights?"

"I think we've got a more pressing problem," Pinocchio said, pointing off the stern.

Lazuli spun around. A black mass of storm cloud was looming dead ahead.

"All hands on deck!" Cinnabar shrieked. "Man the lines. Let out the sails!"

"Don't set your loincloth ablaze," Sop said, running from one rigging to another. "I've got it."

Lazuli could scarcely believe how fast the swirling storm rose up. The sky darkened, and the temperature dropped. Ominous-looking purple-black clouds crackled with skeletons of lightning. Cinnabar tried to bank the ship around the storm, but the swelling mass just seemed to envelop them.

"Should we drop sail and wait it out?" Geppetto cried over the rising wind.

"After all I've done to get this ship fixed up?" Cinnabar snapped. "I'll not have it burned to ashes by lightning. We've got to outrun it!" He turned to Lazuli. "Your Majesty, a little help?"

Lazuli blinked, realizing an instant later what he meant. She held up her palms, summoning with all her might. The riggings creaked as the additional wind filled the sails. The ship accelerated so fast Lazuli had to adjust her stance.

But when she glanced over her shoulder at the storm, she found it coming ever closer. The front of the squall line was ripping leaves and fronds from the treetops, seeming to devour the jungle in its rushing path.

Lightning cracked, and thunder shook the boards beneath her feet. Heavy drops of rain began to hit the deck, landing like lead shot.

Mezmer shouted, "Cinnabar, you've got to get belowdecks before your elemental heat is doused!"

The djinni looked loath to leave his post. But water and djinn didn't mix. Sop nudged him away from the wheel, adjusting his eye patch and putting on a determined face.

"I can handle it."

Casting a look of utmost pleading at Sop, Cinnabar dashed for the gangway just as the squall hit the ship.

Against the driving rain, Lazuli continued to direct the wind into the sails. She heard Pinocchio shout, "I can help you, Lazuli!"

But Geppetto grabbed him by the arm, growling, "No! Your hands. We can't risk any more!" He pulled Pinocchio reluctantly below as rain lashed in sheets across the deck.

The ship rocked violently side to side. Sop yowled, holding fast to the wheel. Lazuli, light as she was, might have been swept away in the rising gale, except Mezmer grabbed her around the waist, holding her down.

Lazuli gave up trying to add extra wind to the sails. They had plenty now. She focused her efforts instead on containing the gusts battering them from all sides. The mainsail's boom swung wildly, stretching the canvas until it was about to shred.

She wished she could simply use her powers to drive the storm back. There were sylphs, especially among the farmers along the Arable Flats, who learned to command the weather. But this skill had never been seen as something for a proper princess to learn. There were many things her father had neglected to do to prepare her for being prester. She supposed he never imagined his daughter's responsibilities would include keeping a flying Venetian warship from being smashed to bits in a storm.

The ship pitched dangerously to one side, and Lazuli fought to keep it upright. Disquieting groans were coming from deep in the belly of the vessel, reverberating through the mast and shrieking down the overextended lines.

"She won't hold!" Sop yelled. "We've got to—"

With a crack like a cannon blast, the boom snapped. The upper portion shot from the base into the billowing black. Sail and rigging ripped away, flying off in the storm. The ship was thrown into a dizzying spin, whirling around faster and faster.

Lazuli found herself clinging to Mezmer, both of them screaming. Then a mountain peak appeared from the gloom. Lazuli wanted to close her eyes, but terror forced them open. And with each spin of the ship, the jagged fist of rock drew closer in her swirling field of vision until finally, with a colossal smash, they collided.

Lazuli's head smacked against the deck and all went black.

"Your Majesty?"

Lazuli just wanted her maid to let her sleep a little longer. But the light filtering through her eyelids told her it must be late. Why hadn't they woken her earlier? And why was her bed so infernally hard?

Then she realized she wasn't in her chambers back in the Moonlit Court. The storm! The mountain peak!

She sat up, nearly banging heads with Sop, who was crouched over her.

"Are you all right, Your Majesty?" he asked.

The back of Lazuli's head was throbbing. She sat up, rubbing it, but didn't feel anything worse than a painful lump.

The storm had blown over, leaving blue skies and steaming jungle in its wake.

Mezmer gave a groan from where she was sprawled next to Lazuli. "Are we dead?" the fox asked.

"We will be when Cinnabar sees what's happened to his ship," Sop answered.

Lazuli got to her feet and stared around at the damage. The mast and sails were gone. Tattered lines lay tangled across the decks. The side of the ship that had struck the mountain was a ruin of broken boards and railing, although the ship had now drifted away from the craggy peak, hovering lazily.

"At least we're still floating," Lazuli said. The alchemied timbers would hover even if the ship had come completely apart. They'd witnessed that after the Deep One had devoured the rest of the imperial fleet on their journey from Venice.

The hatch to the gangway creaked open, and Pinocchio, Geppetto, and Cinnabar spilled out onto the deck. They stared openmouthed around at the decimation.

"My . . . ship," Cinnabar gasped. "No! No!" His cries turned to wails as he rounded on Sop. "What did you do to her, you idiotic fleabag!"

"Now, now," Sop said, holding his paws up protectively. "Let's keep a level head about this. It's not so bad."

"Level head? Not so bad?" the djinni shrieked. "I'll level your head! Look at this. How are we going to fly? We're stuck, adrift over endless jungle!"

"Can't Lazuli just push us with a wind?" Pinocchio asked.

"Push what?" Cinnabar growled. "We've got no sails. No mast even if we wanted to rig up a temporary sail. Sylph wind won't get us anywhere."

"So what do we do?" Pinocchio asked.

Mezmer was already coming up from belowdecks with the map. She unrolled it on the deck. Maestro landed on a corner and scuttled on his six legs, inspecting the drawing.

"I think we're somewhere around here," the fox said, tapping the map. "In the southernmost reaches of the Farrago Jungle."

"Barely inhabited," the cricket said. "A few chimera villages scattered about, but they won't be able to help us. Not with us way up here."

"How far are we from Grootslang Hole?" Lazuli asked.

Mezmer traced a finger. "It's the closest city, but how would we get there? We're too high to descend on ropes. Even if we could, with all this jungle, it might take weeks to walk anywhere inhabited."

"You should have equipped your ship with a flying carpet," Sop suggested to Cinnabar.

"I should have pushed you over the side in the storm," the djinni growled.

Geppetto waved his hands. "We just need to send word for help."

Pinocchio brightened. "Lazuli, the mirror from your aunt. You can contact her."

Lazuli bit her lip. What would her aunt think to learn that things had gone wrong so soon into their mission? She cringed at the thought.

"The Mist Cities are too far," Lazuli said. "We'll be rescued faster if we contact Chief Muckamire at Grootslang. Maestro, you'll have to fly there."

The cricket jerked and flattened his wings. "Fly? Me? But I . . . Oh, I knew I never should have left the Moonlit Court. I swore to myself—"

"Stop griping and get flying," Sop said. "You're in Abaton. What bird is going to eat the royal musician to the presters?"

"Fine," Maestro grumbled. "But if I sprain a wing and can't play music again, you'll all be sorry."

7.

A Champion Arrives

The hazy red sun flared like an ember before extinguishing beyond the mountains. The still air was thick as syrup and dripping with heat. Pinocchio leaned on the railing wondering how long it would take for Maestro to reach the gnomes. He watched as dancing lights rose from the treetops of the jungle below. They swirled around in the dusky sky, chasing one another and emitting tinkling chimes.

Lazuli came up beside Pinocchio, just as one of the lights flitted past the ship. It looked less like a living creature and more like a soap bubble.

"They're pretty," he said. The bubble dipped below the railing, chiming lightly. "What are they?"

"Aleyas," Lazuli said. "Playful little things."

"Can you help out your presters?" Pinocchio called to the

aleya. "How about bringing us a nice spiceberry cake from the Moonlit Court's kitchens?"

The aleya paused a moment before streaking back to the others.

"I think you scared her," Lazuli said.

Pinocchio gave a sigh.

"How are your hands?" Lazuli turned, leaning back against the rail.

Pinocchio checked to see if Cinnabar was around before he slipped off his gloves. The grains of wood were as pronounced as ever. He rapped his knuckles on the railing. *Clunk-clunk.*

"They haven't changed," he said, tugging the gloves back on.

"Strange," Lazuli said with a frown. "I thought they'd turn back faster."

"Me too." Pinocchio found his fingers fidgeting with the jasmine bracelet around his wrist. "What if they don't? What if . . . ?" He gave a frustrated scowl. "I don't even know what to do. Dr. Nundrum expects me to use the Pearl to secure the prison, to keep these monsters from escaping, but I barely know how to summon flame, much less something really complicated."

"I'll be there to help you," Lazuli said. "We'll figure it out. We always do. You doubt yourself too much."

He didn't think his doubts unwarranted. After all, discovering what powers to use would be hard enough, but adding to that was the fear that he might also turn back into an automa. They were facing a serious dilemma.

"Darlings," Mezmer called from the stern. "Best get below-decks and try to sleep. We're keeping a better watch tonight. Right, Sop?"

The cat held up two teapots. "Will be wide-awake. All night." He drank straight from the steaming spout.

69

Lazuli nodded back toward the gangway. Pinocchio followed her. When they were almost to the hatch, the aleya soared up in front of him, bobbing up and down.

"Oh, you again," Pinocchio said.

The aleya sped down to bump against his hand. She felt like a sack of jelly. He drew back his gloved hand. "What are you doing?"

She made an urgent chime and bumped his other hand. Maybe she wanted him to hold her? That seemed odd.

"I think she wants to give you something," Lazuli said.

Pinocchio noticed now that something was dangling beneath the aleya. He stuck his hand out, palm up. The aleya dropped a cluster of yellow fruit.

"Spiceberries," Lazuli said, giving a laugh. "Your favorite! She must have found them in the jungle."

"Thanks," Pinocchio said, popping one into his mouth and relishing the sweet, fiery taste.

The aleya made an excited tinkling before shooting back into the sky.

"You certainly have a way of making friends in the funniest places," Lazuli said.

Pinocchio hadn't always had friends. When he'd been an automa serving in the floating palace of the doge of Venice, Pinocchio had never thought or even been capable of making friends with the other mechanical servants. But then Prester John had hidden the Ancientmost Pearl inside him, and a whole new world opened before Pinocchio.

Wiq had been his first true friend. It hadn't been easy at first. Wiq had hated Pinocchio for being an automa. It seemed all Abatonians—whether here in their homeland or enslaved in the humanlands—shared this loathing for alchemy and its inventions.

But Wiq had been able to look beyond what Pinocchio was.

In his cabin, with night falling outside, Pinocchio cringed at the thought of what Wiq must think of their friendship now. He could almost imagine Wiq, up on the theater's terrace looking out night after night across Siena's cityscape and wondering what had become of Pinocchio and his promise.

Pinocchio turned the bracelet around his wrist. The flowers and leaves had long dried and fallen off. The braided vine was beginning to fray.

"I haven't forgotten," Pinocchio whispered. "I swear I haven't."

He squeezed his eyes shut, trying to fight back the images that formed: Wiq, lonely and friendless in the depths of Al Mi'raj's dungeon. Al Mi'raj's master, the lord mayor of Siena, selling Wiq from the theater to an alchemist's workshop, where he'd work day after dreary day building war machines for the empire until, like Wiq's parents, he was worked quite literally to death.

Pinocchio tucked the bracelet protectively beneath his sleeve.

The ship had grown silent, except for the occasional cackling laugh from Sop up on deck. Pinocchio rose from his bunk. He needed to see his father. He always had a way of cheering Pinocchio up. He'd last seen Geppetto in the ship's galley, poring over Dr. Nundrum's books, trying to find some overlooked clue about the enchantment keeping the monsters in their prison. Maybe he was still there.

But when Pinocchio reached the galley, it was empty. His

father must have already gone to bed. Pinocchio was about to head back when his gaze caught on the open book on the table. He'd flipped through it earlier. Many of the pages were lavishly illustrated with colorful pigments and gold foil. Some contained strange symbols—a mouth, an eye, a feather, a flame. Most, however, showed pastoral scenes from around Abaton—elephant-headed chimera dancing on mountaintops or herds of one-horned horses galloping across rippling dunes.

But the illustration on the page his father had left open was not so tranquil.

The scene showed a battle. On one side was the towering Moonlit Court with rows of armored knights behind their leader, a fox chimera Pinocchio knew to be Mezmer's ancestor, the legendary general Mezmercurian. On the opposite side, an army of monsters was charging toward them. They were a gruesome lot. Several seemed to be dragons. Others looked like flaming demons or skeletal ghouls. Lots of them were almost like chimera—hybrids of animal and human, although these monsters were much more beastly, often four-legged with massive claws and gnashing fangs, as the manticore had had. In fact, Pinocchio saw several manticores among the horde.

Pinocchio's attention was drawn to a lone figure toward the front of the army who didn't look nearly as monstrous as the others. He could have been a human or even a sylph, except that his skin was crimson red.

"Diamancer," a voice said behind him.

Pinocchio turned. Cinnabar stood in the doorway.

"How do you know?" Pinocchio asked.

The djinni gave a shrug. "When I wasn't fixing up this ship, I visited the palace libraries to fill my time. There's quite a lot to learn, if I'm to understand my new home."

Pinocchio turned back to the image of Diamancer. "He looks so ordinary," he said. "Compared to the other monsters. He hardly looks a threat at all."

Cinnabar chuckled mirthlessly. "Isn't it surprising how ordinary the most powerful and dangerous look? You'd never suspect what they really are . . . unless you happened to know." He seemed to emphasize his last five words.

Mezmer's boot heels clunked on the deck up above.

Pinocchio frowned at Cinnabar. "Are you talking about Diamancer? Or are you talking about me?"

The djinni smiled, eyes narrowed. "It's true, Your Majesty. You don't seem dangerous at all to your subjects. If only they knew you as I know you."

"I'm not dangerous!" Pinocchio said. "And I'm your prester. I don't think you should be talking to me this way."

Cinnabar bowed. "Of course, Your Majesty."

Pinocchio felt his heart thundering against his ribs. He wondered again if the djinni had realized his hands were wood when he helped him aboard. "And, Cinnabar, you know you have to keep my secret. You promised before we arrived in Abaton that you would."

"Yes, Sop's colorful threats still paint a vivid picture in my mind's eye." He turned to go.

"Cinnabar," Pinocchio said.

The djinni paused, impatience roiling on his face.

"I . . . I know you don't like me," Pinocchio said. "But I'm not your enemy." How could he explain this? Pinocchio decided to pull back his sleeve, exposing the jasmine bracelet. "Do you know why I wear this?"

"Do tell me, Your Majesty."

"Because I too left a friend behind in the Venetian Empire.

I promised to rescue him. And I will! Along with your friend Zingaro and the others who deserve the goodness of Abaton."

Cinnabar's face was impassive, but something shifted in his eyes.

"So," Pinocchio said, "I just thought you should know that . . . that you and I want the same thing."

Cinnabar's mouth twisted. "That might be, Your Majesty. But will you be *able* to save Zingaro and your friend and the others? I can't help but wonder if the Ancientmost Pearl could be in better hands . . . so to speak."

He slipped back into the darkened hallway.

Pinocchio lay in bed, unable to sleep as Cinnabar's words churned about in his head. Despite the jungle heat that filled the cabins, he felt cold. Given Cinnabar's choice of expressions about Pinocchio's hands, he had to know what was happening under his gloves. But what would the djinni do about it?

He wondered if the truth behind Cinnabar's hatred of him was that Pinocchio wasn't what he appeared to be. That he was pretending to be human, when in reality he was an automa.

Was he really an automa masquerading as a living boy? Pinocchio rubbed his wooden hands together, hating their hardness, hating the awkward way the gears made his fingers move, wishing they were nimble and soft again.

Whether Cinnabar could be trusted to keep his secret worried him, but what kept Pinocchio tussling in his sheets and unable to fall asleep was the fear that maybe Cinnabar was right.

Laughing voices on the deck above woke Pinocchio. Pink morning light was coming in the porthole window. He sat up. So he had managed a bit of sleep. It certainly hadn't been a restful night.

A sharp *thunk* sounded. He heard Mezmer cry out, a merry note in her voice. And then someone else replied, a voice he didn't recognize.

Pulling on his tunic and boots, Pinocchio opened his door to find his father emerging into the hallway. "What is going on up there?" Geppetto grumbled.

They were joined in the galley by Lazuli pulling a robe over her nightgown. Pinocchio pushed open the hatch just as the stranger was saying, "That, my friends, was not dumb luck."

Stepping out on deck, Pinocchio tried to find who was speaking. He saw Mezmer and Sop grinning wildly as they rummaged through the broken boards. Cinnabar was there too, looking grumpy as usual. Otherwise they appeared alone on the deck.

Then Pinocchio heard Lazuli gasp. Something swooped past the ship, a blur of feathers and fur. Was that a griffin?

On the creature's back rode a sylph, dressed in a riding suit of blinding white. He drew back a long curling bow. With a laugh, the sylph said, "I assure you this one will not be a lucky shot either. Go ahead, General Mezmer. Toss it."

Mezmer held up a chunk of wood no bigger than a tea saucer before pitching it off the starboard side. The sylph archer took aim.

Pinocchio thought the target too small and moving too fast to be hit. But with a *thunk*, the arrow sank into the chunk of wood before arrow and target spiraled down into the treetops below.

Mezmer applauded. "A perfect shot, dear! Never seen one better."

"Uh, Mezmer," Pinocchio said. "Who is this?"

The griffin landed on the quarterdeck. The sylph leaped lightly off its back, making a bow.

"Rion of the Mist Cities, Your Majesty. Here to enlist, if my presters will allow me."

As Rion rose, Pinocchio saw now that although he was tall, he was still a youth, not much older than Lazuli.

"Enlist?" Lazuli asked. "Enlist in what?"

Rion waved a hand at Mezmer. "Why, the knights of the Celestial Brigade, Your Majesty. I set off on my griffin as soon as I heard what happened at the Moonlit Court."

"And you found us . . . here?" Pinocchio asked.

Rion gave a loud bark of a laugh. "No, Your Majesty. I was headed for the Moonlit Court when I ran into this venerable cricket who alerted me to your need."

Maestro fluttered onto Geppetto's shoulder.

"Did you know he composed the first cantata to include soprano mosquito?" Rion made a gesture as if tipping a hat. "Surely you're a genius, Maestro."

"Some think so." The cricket sighed.

Sop folded his arms with a smirk. "Oh, yeah. Who else?"

"General Mezmer shared the ill news of the storm," Rion said. "And of your quest to locate the infamous prison where Diamancer and his traitors are escaping. So my arrival could not be better timed. I am here to serve, Your Majesties. Your champion has arrived."

Mezmer was grinning broadly, beside herself with excitement. Pinocchio felt it too. He was definitely going to get Rion to show him how to shoot like that.

Lazuli was eyeing Rion suspiciously. "Do you know my aunt?"

"Why, of course," Rion said. "Who in Abaton doesn't know Her Graceful Commander of the Winds, the High Lady of the Sylph House, the Noble Elemental of—"

"Did she send you?" Lazuli asked flatly.

Rion froze. Ever so slowly a guilty look melted over him. "Your Majesty, Lady Sapphira was concerned about you joining Prester Pinocchio on this dangerous journey. I . . . I hope that you won't refuse my services."

"Refuse!" Mezmer barked. "Darlings, who said anything about turning away a willing knight? Prester Lazuli, surely you wouldn't—"

"Of course I wouldn't," Lazuli said. But Pinocchio noticed a hint of annoyance pulling at the corners of her otherwise poised expression.

Rion smiled in relief. "Very good! Most grateful. Now . . ." He clapped his hands together and peered around at the ruined deck. "Let's just see about some ropes." He gestured to Cinnabar. "Good sir, the rigging by your foot. Can you bring it here?"

Cinnabar picked up a tangle of rope that had snapped when the sails came loose in the storm. "What for?"

"Why, to tow your ship to the gnomes for repairs." Rion flashed a winning smile. "The quest must go on!"

Rion's griffin—who turned out to be named Quila— beat the air with powerful strokes of her wings. The lines stretching from the bow to her harness creaked under the strain. Quila was a stout, muscular creature, however, and her hooded amber eyes betrayed no complaint as she pulled the ship.

Rion lounged in the saddle, half-turned so he could address the audience gathered at the ship's bow. Pinocchio leaned forward on the railing with Mezmer, listening raptly as Rion spoke. Arms folded, Lazuli had put on that aloof royal demeanor she often wore when she was around her subjects. Pinocchio wondered if he'd be more presterly if he tried it once in a while. But for now, he was too fascinated with Rion's lesson.

"You see, it's not about making the right aim. It's not about letting go when your arm is steady. It's about *allowing* the arrow to reach the target. It wants to hit that target! You must *feel* when the arrow is ready, then release it and let it follow its desire."

Sop gave a doubtful snort from where he lounged on the deck. Pinocchio cut his eyes at the cat. But Rion continued as if he hadn't heard.

"Yes, learn to communicate with the arrow." Rion patted the feathers protruding from his quiver. "And I guarantee, you'll soon be shooting nearly as well as I do." He flashed another smile.

"Where did you learn?" Pinocchio asked. "I thought there weren't any trained warriors in Abaton."

"Archery is a popular sport in the Mist Cities, Your Majesty," Rion said. "I do not claim to be a warrior. Simply a lad with good aim and a sense of duty to his homeland . . . and to his presters, of course."

Pinocchio looked over at Lazuli with a grin. But her expression hadn't wavered. Wasn't she even a little impressed with Rion?

The bubblelike aleya who had given Pinocchio the spiceberry had been tagging along since the ship set off, bobbing beside Rion like an overly friendly puppy. She made a musical chime. Rion chuckled. "Thank you," he said to the aleya.

"You understand her?" Pinocchio asked.

"Only a bit of Aleyan," Rion said. "I pride myself in picking up what phrases I can from the lesser races of Abaton."

Pinocchio sighed. He could speak to aleyas. He was an expert archer. What else was this Rion good at?

As Mezmer began asking Rion about archery in the Mist Cities, Lazuli turned to Pinocchio and said quietly, "You do realize all that letting the arrow follow its desires is nonsense?"

Pinocchio scowled. "What are you talking about?"

Lazuli rolled her eyes. "He's a sylph. He's just controlling the wind to guide the arrow."

"He's still really good."

"I'm not saying he's not," Lazuli replied.

"But you don't like him."

"I'm not saying that either," Lazuli said. "It's just . . . he's a bit of a show-off—don't you think?"

Pinocchio's scowl deepened. He didn't see what was so bad about Rion teaching them a thing or two about archery, especially when he was so good. In fact, he hoped Rion could give him some lessons, maybe when they reached Grootslang Hole.

Lazuli looked back at Rion. "It's strange, but he seems familiar. . . ."

"You've met him before? Seems like you'd remember someone you thought was a big show-off."

Lazuli gave him a smirk. "Forget I called him that."

"Look at Mezmer." Pinocchio waved a hand toward her. "See how happy she is. She's found exactly the kind of knight she dreamed of for the Celestial Brigade. If only we had more like Rion."

Lazuli gave a little nod of reluctant agreement.

Pinocchio couldn't help but think that Rion was going to be dead useful when they faced the manticore again. Maybe—was it too much to hope?—he might even help with their rescue mission back to Venice. Assuming they got this monster problem contained first . . .

Sop, yawning with exhaustion from all-night guard duty, said, "Come on, Mez. Let's get some snore-time."

Mezmer sighed, reaching out to help Sop to his feet.

"Yes, go and rest assured, General," Rion called. "Quila and I will guard the presters against any dangers."

The griffin gave a shrill note of agreement. The call was not nearly as majestic as Pinocchio had imagined, especially given how tough the griffin looked. Quila sounded more like a squeezed chicken.

Rion pursed his lips with seriousness at Pinocchio and Lazuli. "I want to apologize, Your Majesties, for not bringing other recruits from the Mist Cities. Many are afraid to travel, given the current situation. My grandfather is contacting the heads of several chimera clans he has dealings with, and hopes they'll—"

"Is your grandfather Zephyr?" Lazuli asked.

"Why, yes, Your Majesty," Rion said.

"You came with him to the Moonlit Court."

Rion gave a chuckle of embarrassment. "I was hoping you wouldn't remember that, Your Majesty. It was many years ago, and we were just children."

Lazuli laughed, her regal demeanor falling away. "Oh, yes. I recall I followed you around everywhere, begging you to play with me in the gardens."

"I fear I wasn't too polite to you then," Rion said. "But I swear, Your Majesty, it was only because I was painfully shy as a child."

Pinocchio had a hard time believing Rion had ever been shy.

"Wasn't there an old gnome at the dinner who fell out of his chair?" Rion asked.

"Oh, right! I think the chair broke. And do you remember the cake Cook made?" Lazuli asked, beginning to chuckle.

"The one that exploded!" Rion barked, joining Lazuli in laughter.

"Why did it explode?" Pinocchio asked eagerly.

But the two were laughing too much to answer. He wished one of them could stop for half a moment to let him in on the joke.

As Lazuli finally took several shuddering breaths and wiped her eyes, Pinocchio tried again. "So why did the cake explode?"

"Oh, I—I don't know," she said. "She mixed up the ingredients. Something she accidentally put i-in it, I suppose."

"Pixie eggs, don't you reckon?" Rion asked.

Lazuli's eyes grew wide, then once more, they burst into fits of renewed hilarity.

Pinocchio crossed his arms. "I don't get it," he said flatly.

"P-p-pixies don't lay e-eggs," Lazuli gasped between laughs. "It's . . . it's this old . . . ex-ex-expression." She doubled over. "It's . . . just what we sylphs . . . say when something surprises us."

Rion gulped a deep breath and said quickly before he started laughing again, "I'm sorry, Your Majesty, I guess you have to be a sylph to get the joke."

"I'm not a sylph," Pinocchio said. Maybe he should take this as his cue to leave these new friends to their old jokes.

Lazuli caught his eye. He could see that she recognized his irritation and was trying to stifle her mirth, but that only made Pinocchio more annoyed. He hated to feel like he was spoiling Lazuli's good time.

"I'm going to go check on my father's research," he said, turning on his heel.

81

"Don't be cross, Your Majesty," Rion said, straightening in his saddle. "We'll stop talking about the cake."

"I'm not cross," Pinocchio said rather crossly, despite his best efforts. "Talk about your pixie eggs all you want. I'm sure it's much funnier when you don't have to explain the joke to me."

"Pinocchio," Lazuli said softly, reaching out for his arm.

But he evaded her grasp, and made his way to the gangway with as much casualness as he could muster.

Pinocchio found his father sitting at the galley table with Maestro on his shoulder. Geppetto looked up from his books. "What's all the laughter about?"

"Nothing," Pinocchio said, flopping into a seat. "Father, I need to ask you something. Do you think I'm funny?"

"Funny?" Geppetto raised an eyebrow. "What do you mean by *funny*?"

"Do I make you laugh?" Pinocchio searched his father's tired face. "Do I make . . . others laugh?"

Maestro flittered. "Being funny is far too overrated, in my opinion. I, for one, take great pride in avoiding the temptation of humor whenever possible."

"You have a lot to be proud of, Maestro," Geppetto said drily.

"I do," the cricket agreed. "I really do."

Geppetto scooted his chair closer until he and Pinocchio were knee to knee. He gave a gentle smile. "Why are you asking? You have a wonderful sense of humor, son."

"You're just saying that because you're my father."

Geppetto chuckled. "You're right—a father always sees his child in the best light."

"In the best light?" Pinocchio wasn't sure what that meant.

"I always see the best in you," his father explained.

"You don't think I can do wrong?"

"I'm not saying that."

"But what if I'm doing something wrong, and I don't mean to?"

Geppetto twisted the tip of his mustache. "I don't think I'm following you, son."

Pinocchio glanced down the hallway, making sure no one was listening. He lowered his voice. "Yesterday . . . during the storm, you stopped me from helping Lazuli control the wind."

"Because I didn't want the Pearl changing you anymore," his father said.

"But I'm the one who has the Pearl, Father. If we're to secure the prison and stop these monsters from escaping, I'll have to use it."

"No, son," Geppetto said. "You won't." He clapped a hand to the book on the table. "Why do you think I'm reading all these? I'm looking for another solution. A way for this problem to be solved without you having to use the Pearl!"

Maestro bounced from Geppetto's shoulder to the table, turning to face him. "But, Geppetto, you said yourself—you only see Pinocchio in the best light. It's blinding you. You don't want him to use the Pearl because you're afraid of the costs. But what will the costs be for Abaton if he doesn't use the Pearl?"

"He has to learn how to master the Pearl without it changing him back!" Geppetto growled.

"How?" Maestro asked.

"I don't know." Geppetto made a fist. "I've searched every page of these books Dr. Nundrum gave us and found nothing. The answer must be somewhere in Abaton's records, in some other book. I'll . . . I'll find out."

Pinocchio shook his head dismally. "Cinnabar's right. He said the Ancientmost Pearl's in the wrong hands."

His father shook his head irritably. "Don't listen to him, Pinocchio—"

"But what if bad things happen to Abaton because I refuse to use the Pearl? The people trust me to be their prester!"

"And if their prester becomes an automa, they'll cast us out of Abaton!"

Pinocchio swallowed hard. "Is that why you . . . is that what you're afraid of, Father?"

Geppetto pulled back, hurt. Then his careworn face drew into a knot of utmost tenderness. He cupped his hands over Pinocchio's. "My boy. My dearest son. No. I'm not afraid of losing Abaton. What terrifies me is that if you turn back into an automa, I'll lose you."

8.

Grootslang Hole

Despite what Chief Muckamire had said, Grootslang Hole turned out to be a hole. Or maybe more of a pit. Pinocchio wasn't disappointed, however. It was a pretty extraordinary pit.

The ancient city of the gnomes was tiered like a gigantic amphitheater, rings of palaces and guildhalls, taverns and smelting furnaces going down step by concentric step until the lowest streets must only have gotten direct sunlight for about a minute each day.

By the time Rion had docked the ship along the uppermost wall, Chief Muckamire was scurrying to meet them. "Your Majesties! My goodness. Your ship! Have the monsters attacked you as well?"

"No," Mezmer said. "A freak storm wrecked our ship."

"And reckless piloting." Cinnabar cut his eyes at Sop.

Lazuli looked sharply at Chief Muckamire. "Did you say *as well*? Has the manticore attacked again?"

"Haven't you heard, Your Majesty?" the gnome replied, fumbling his fingers together. "Not just the manticore. A dozen monsters—maybe more! Word just arrived this morning."

Pinocchio felt a ripple of fear run through him. "Where? Back at the Moonlit Court?"

"No, a village at the far edge of the Caldera Desert. Just a remote mining town, really, called Sunder. From what I gathered from Dr. Nundrum's letter, the monsters appeared in the middle of the night. Fortunately, most of the village's inhabitants are nocturnal chimera who scour the desert sands for luminous astergems. So nearly everyone was out of the village at the time. But their homes are in ruins."

"If Sunder is in the Caldera, it could be near the prison," Lazuli said. "Did anyone see which way they went? Are they attacking elsewhere?"

"The few that witnessed the attack said it was as if the monsters appeared from the sky in puffs of smoke," Chief Muckamire said. "And disappeared that way after they laid waste to the town."

"That's what the manticore did at the banquet," Pinocchio said. "She disappeared into smoke."

Chief Muckamire cast an anxious glance at their ship. "Wherever they're headed next, we must find a way to get you to the prison immediately—"

"Shouldn't we find these escaped monsters first?" asked Lazuli.

"Your Majesty," Chief Muckamire said. "Which is more urgent? A dozen escaped monsters or having the entire thousand of Diamancer's army released upon Abaton? I've already spoken to the other high nobles, and we all agree—your aunt included—what's most critical is that Prester Pinocchio stop the others from escaping the prison. The Noble Houses will do all we can to protect our people from the dozen who have gotten out. We've already sent letters out to township mayors, urging them to create safe shelters and defenses."

Mezmer put her hands to her hips. "It's times like this you wish Abaton still had an army."

Chief Muckamire furrowed his brow.

"How quickly can your gnomes repair the ship?" Geppetto asked.

Already a troop of tiny gnomes was gathering beneath the ship with Cinnabar, talking to one another and inspecting the damage.

Chief Muckamire scratched his beard. "We have many fine carpenters in Grootslang who can begin right away. But I can't imagine they'll finish in less than a week."

"A week!" Mezmer barked. "We can't wait that long."

"Isn't there another way for us to travel?" Pinocchio asked. "Flying carpets?" He glanced at Rion and Quila. "Griffins?"

Chief Muckamire gave an embarrassed shrug. "Our people aren't much for flight. We have slithersteeds and rhinocerovers we could offer."

"Not fast enough," Mezmer said. "Don't get too comfortable with all the gnomish hospitality. I'll find a quicker way to get us to the prison." She pointed to Rion. "Can I trust you to keep a good watch over the presters, dear?"

The sylph gave an eager smile. "Certainly, General. But where are you going?"

"To do a little investigating. Come along, Sop."

The cat slumped his shoulders, following. "Can we investigate a good place to eat first?"

Chief Muckamire motioned for the presters to follow him, leading them from the uppermost walls down onto a broad boulevard crowded with gnomes and the occasional chimera merchant. They parted for their presters, bowing or curtsying, all eyes following them.

Pinocchio couldn't help but think their expressions seemed to be searching for assurance that he would save them from this threat. He folded his gloved hands beneath his cloak guiltily and tried not to meet their gaze.

"Chief Muckamire," Lazuli said as she walked beside the gnome. "Dr. Nundrum was able to tell us the location of the prison, but nothing about what we'd find there. If Prester Pinocchio and I are going to stop more of these monsters from escaping, we need to know how they're waking."

"Indeed," the gnome lord said. "And how to get them back to sleep."

"Do you know?"

"Me?" Chief Muckamire blinked his tiny black eyes. "No, I can't say that I do, but of course there are our libraries. The finest in all of Abaton. I could have my most learned historians begin searching at once. If the answer is not here among Regolith's memories, I'd be quite surprised."

"Regolith?" Geppetto asked. "Who is Regolith?"

Maestro made an impatient flutter from Geppetto's shoulder.

Chief Muckamire said, "Why, Master Geppetto, surely you know . . ." But then the gnome shook his head. "Forgive me. I forget that much about Abaton must still be unfamiliar to you." He waved a small hand to the tiered city surrounding them. "The city of Grootslang Hole was built on the spot where the primordial giant Regolith descended beneath Abaton in the earliest days."

"Have you ever seen Regolith?" Geppetto asked.

"Oh, no!" the gnome said with an emphatic wag of his beard. "We'd never dare interrupt his slumber. But like the Deep One who guards our shores, each of the primordials protects Abaton in a different way. Prester John gave Regolith Abaton's deepest memories to guard."

Pinocchio wanted to ask what the other two guarded, but already Chief Muckamire was continuing. "Our libraries are filled with books written by gnomish seer-scribes recording Regolith's vast memories. So if the answer to your question has been documented, Prester Lazuli, it will be here."

"We appreciate any help you might provide, Chief Muckamire," Lazuli said.

The gnome lord gave her an anxious glance. "Of course, I'm sure you can appreciate that the task might be quite difficult. As I said, Regolith's memories are vast, and truthfully our libraries only reflect a fraction of what the primordial himself knows. But we will do our best. And as quickly as gnomishly possible, Your Majesty."

"I'll be happy to help," Geppetto said, "if that's quite all right."

Pinocchio suspected his father was hoping to find more than just the answer to why the monsters were waking.

"Certainly, Master Geppetto. We'd welcome it," the gnome said. "We can begin as soon as I show our presters to their chambers."

Pinocchio frowned. Mezmer and Sop were off exploring the city. His father would disappear with the gnomes in the libraries for who knew how long.

"What are we going to do?" Pinocchio asked Lazuli.

Her eyes were narrowed in thought. "I'll need to contact my aunt to discuss what she and the other high nobles are doing to defend against continued attacks."

Pinocchio sighed. "What I am supposed to do, then?"

"I don't know," she said distractedly. "Discuss archery with Rion."

Rion drew up straighter. "Have you ever thrown a sylph lasso, Your Majesty? I placed first in last summer's Galetide Games." He gave a wink. "I'll show you my secret technique."

Pinocchio gave an appreciative nod, but couldn't help but think everyone had something important to do but him.

"Even if every gnome in Grootslang Hole were searching the libraries, it could take weeks. Months, even." Aunt Sapphira shook her head from the small mirror in Lazuli's hand. The glowing glass bathed the otherwise windowless chambers around Lazuli in blue light.

"I know, Aunt," Lazuli said. "But we need to discover how to get them back to sleep once we reach the prison."

Sapphira pursed her lips, as if she were trying to be patient with her niece despite the urgency of the situation. "Let me remind you that you are the prester. Your subjects expect you to present confidence. If Chief Muckamire sees you as weak, it might not be long before others begin to doubt their presters' abilities."

"We simply asked for help," Lazuli said. "Was I wrong—?"

"Prester Pinocchio has the Pearl," Sapphira said from the mirror. "You assured me you'd be able to guide him in using it to stop this threat. I understand your concerns, but there are times for action. Your people need you to act swiftly, my niece and prester. Reach the prison before more of Diamancer's forces escape."

Lazuli took a deep breath, hoping her face looked more confident than her shaky hands felt.

Sapphira gave a nod. "You are in good hands with Rion. He's the finest archer in the Mist Cities. A real knight."

Lazuli felt a knot of annoyance at her aunt's jab at Mezmer and Sop.

"Be assured," her aunt continued, "I am taking care of the coordination with Dr. Nundrum and the other high nobles to protect against future attacks. As we speak, we're moving those in the most vulnerable townships into the safety of the elemental cities. Your focus needs to be on the prison."

"Yes, Aunt," Lazuli said. "Thank you."

The mirror dimmed to black. Lazuli sat holding it a moment longer. She dreaded the thought of going into the prison without a way to stop these monsters that didn't require Pinocchio using the Pearl. But what was she to do?

She rubbed her throbbing temples and stood up. She stepped out from her room into the antechamber. Rion sprang to his feet from one of the small, stone chairs set against the walls. She'd forgotten he'd be standing guard out there. Couldn't she have a moment's peace to think?

He jabbed a thumb at the chair. "You've got to hand it to the gnomes. They make the most amazingly uncomfortable furniture."

Chief Muckamire's palace was underground, driven deep into the earth about halfway down the ringed city. Unlike the airy, light-filled Moonlit Court, the gnomes preferred darkness and claustrophobically small spaces. And they clearly preferred every furnishing to be made of stone, most emblazoned with jewels to a stupendous degree.

Lazuli was tired of thinking and tired of being on her feet. She went to the chair and slumped down. "Oh, you're right. That's terrible." She gave a small laugh. It felt good to laugh after the head-throbbing conversation with her aunt.

"Where's Prester Pinocchio?" she asked.

Rion sat next to her. "He went back upstairs to his chambers to practice tying lassos. He's got a promising throw. I suppose you got in touch with Lady Sapphira?"

"Yes." She rubbed her temples.

"Your aunt is quite extraordinary," Rion said. "Clever. Determined. All the people of Abaton respect her." He looked over at Lazuli. "You're quite like her, Your Majesty."

"Thank you, Rion," Lazuli said.

He smiled. "And quite like your father too, I'd say."

Her head only seemed to ache worse at the mention of His Great Lordship Prester John. "My father made ruling Abaton seem so effortless," Lazuli murmured. "I wish he were here. I wish he could tell me what to do."

Rion sat up straighter. "You're doing splendidly. Really, you are. Besides, you can't be expected to rule as he did. And you will lead us through this crisis. Not as he would have done. But in your own way."

Lazuli wished that were true. But she was grateful for Rion's assurances.

"May I ask something, Your Majesty?" Rion said. "About your father?"

"I suppose," she said.

Rion seemed to consider his words before he spoke. "Why

did he give the rule of Abaton to both you and Prester Pinocchio? Are you betrothed?"

Lazuli burst out in laughter. She tried to cover her mouth, hoping it would cover the color flushing into her face. "Pinocchio and I married? No, we rule together, but . . . as friends. My father thought it best that we share the responsibility."

Lazuli couldn't help but think that somehow she took on more of the responsibility, but that was how things were—how they had to be.

Rion gave an awkward smile, blinking away his embarrassment. "I'm sorry."

"No, it's quite all right," Lazuli said.

"But . . ." Rion furrowed his brow. "If I understand correctly, he gave the possession of the Ancientmost Pearl to Prester Pinocchio. Not to you."

Lazuli grew quiet. The throbbing in her head seemed to have stopped, only to be replaced by a tension that ran through her entire body.

"I don't mean to question His Great Lordship," Rion said. "But would it not have made more sense for you to have been given the Ancientmost Pearl?"

Things would have been so much easier if Pinocchio had been an ordinary boy. But if he had been an ordinary boy, they might never have become friends, might never have kept the Pearl from falling into the hands of the doge, might never have reached Abaton. Still, Rion's words stung with a needle of truth.

She began to sit up. "I don't think we should be discussing—"

Rion got to his feet. "Forgive me, Your Majesty. I have overstepped my bounds. I would never speak ill of Prester Pinocchio. Our hope for saving Abaton lies in his command of the Ancientmost Pearl. I only meant to say that, like your aunt, you're enormously respected by your people. If you but had the Pearl, I'm sure you—"

"That's quite enough, Rion!" she said sharply.

Pinocchio stepped in from the hallway. "What's quite enough?" He had a long coil of rope in his hands.

Rion cast his eyes to the floor.

"Nothing," Lazuli said, turning toward her chamber.

"Wait!" Pinocchio said. "Where are you going?"

"Nowhere."

Pinocchio's eyes flashed excitedly from Lazuli to Rion. "Then follow me."

Rion stepped to attention. "Where to, Your Majesty?"

"You'll see." Pinocchio handed Rion the rope and hurried down the hallway. Rion drew up his shoulders and marched after him.

Lazuli fell in behind. Her heart was still racing, and she wondered if she should apologize to Rion. It was her own fault. She was his prester, and she'd forgotten to act like a proper prester in front of him. All their laughing and chumming around about pixie eggs and bad gnomish furniture. She could almost hear her aunt tsking in her ear.

But what really bothered Lazuli wasn't that Rion had spoken too personally with his prester. It was that he had spoken honestly. And his words scared her. How much longer could they keep Pinocchio's secret if even one of their own knights was beginning to doubt him?

"Where are we going exactly, Your Majesty?" Rion asked Pinocchio as they stepped out the front doors of the palace.

Despite being midway down the tiered enclosure of a city, the boulevard was blindingly bright after the shadowy interior of the palace. On several of the curved streets opposite the palace, Lazuli noticed tents being erected. She wondered if they were to house evacuees who were coming to Grootslang Hole seeking protection.

Pinocchio pointed to the great shaft running through the interior of the city. "Down to the lowest street."

Rion furrowed his brow uncertainly. "General Mezmer asked me to watch over you and Prester Lazuli."

"And you will," Pinocchio said.

Rion looked to Lazuli questioningly, as if her orders could trump Pinocchio's. It only tightened the knot of worry in her stomach.

"Why are we going down there?" she asked Pinocchio.

"To find the hole," he said.

Rion lifted an eyebrow. "But we're in Grootslang Hole, Your Majesty."

"Not that Hole," Pinocchio said. "*The* hole. The place where Chief Muckamire said Regolith decended beneath the earth."

Rion lifted both eyebrows. "Why are we going there?"

"To find Regolith, of course."

Lazuli's mouth fell open. She made a sputter before composing her face. But she couldn't help staring at Pinocchio with wide eyes.

"Don't you see?" Pinocchio said. "Chief Muckamire said Regolith guards Abaton's deepest memories. Maybe there is a way to find out from Regolith directly how to stop these escaping prisoners."

"But . . ." Lazuli made a few halting noises. "Regolith has been sleeping since the earliest days of Abaton."

"We'll just have to wake him, won't we?"

"How, exactly?"

Pinocchio shrugged. "I commanded the Deep One, remember?"

"Yes, but—"

"Hopefully I'll be able to command Regolith to wake," Pinocchio said.

Rion stared from Pinocchio over to Lazuli, a silent plea on his face for her to please overrule Pinocchio's idea.

"Look, who knows if my father and the gnomes will find the answer in their library," Pinocchio said. "We have to do this."

"All right," she said decisively. "Lead the way, Rion."

"But, Your Majesty—" At her glare, Rion gave a sigh and began to descend the steps into the street. "All right. Let's pay a visit to Regolith."

9.

The Eye of Regolith

Pinocchio wasn't entirely certain how this plan was going to work. Could Regolith even talk? The Deep One hadn't. It had only eaten them. But if the primordial had answers to how they could stop these monsters without him having to draw on the magic of the Pearl, it would all be worth it. Well, not worth being eaten. Hopefully being prester protected him from that possibility.

Wide stone stairs connected the ringed levels of the city. Rion led them down—past bustling markets and noisy gnome blacksmith shops, past grand mansions inlaid with garish riches, past modest houses carved simply into the stone.

Hoping the noise of the city covered his words, Pinocchio said quietly to Lazuli, "So were you arguing with Rion back in the palace?"

"Not arguing, exactly," she said.

"What was it about, then?"

"I don't want to discuss it," she said with a frown.

"Why not?"

She gave him an exasperated furrow of her brow. "Look, Pinocchio. We are the presters. We need to present ourselves . . . properly to our subjects. We need to project confidence so they will respect us."

"Did you not project confidence to Rion?" he asked, trying to follow what she was saying.

"I'm not talking about me. I'm talking about you."

"What?" He blinked. "I thought we were talking about Rion."

"Pinocchio, you need to act more like a proper prester around Rion and the rest of your subjects. You treat everyone like your friend."

"Rion *is* my friend," Pinocchio said. "He's great. He taught me this thing with the lasso—"

"He's not your friend," Lazuli said. "He's one of your knights."

"Sop's one of my knights."

She made a grumble. "Sop is different."

Pinocchio wasn't sure why she was so upset with him. He knew he was the prester, but couldn't a prester be . . . well, normal in front of his people? "You're always trying to play this part, Lazuli. The perfect prester. Wearing that perfect expression whenever you're in front of your people."

"I'm not playing a part."

"But why can't you just show them you as yourself?" he asked.

She stopped. Pinocchio walked a few steps more before he realized it. He turned back to Lazuli. She was glaring at him, but whether she was angry or hurt was hard to tell.

"I can't," she whispered fiercely. "And neither can you. Don't you realize you can't show your people your true self either?"

His heart gave a lurch. She was right. Of course he couldn't. His people could never know what he'd been, what he was becoming.

Rion had realized his presters weren't following him any longer. "Your Majesties?" he called.

Lazuli raised a finger for him to wait. She looked back at Pinocchio. "We need to be careful. That's all I'm trying to say. Just because someone is a friend doesn't mean that they can't become an enemy. Do you understand?"

He nodded, although he wasn't entirely sure he understood. But as he clenched his gloved hands together, he supposed if Rion or any of his people discovered what was happening beneath those gloves, they might not be so friendly any longer.

They followed the steps down. The noise and crowds thinned until at last they were in the quiet dimness of the city's lowest street.

Rion looked around. "Gloomy down here."

Pinocchio had to agree. The place was lonesome and cast with deep shadows. Something icy hung in the air. The inner side of the small circular street was bordered by an ancient stone wall, caked in lichen and dust. But on the outer side of the street, where the buildings had been on the upper streets, there were no doors, no signs of habitation—only alcoves set one after the other into the rock. Candles and other offerings had been placed in each.

As Pinocchio walked, he saw that each alcove had one of four images carved into the worn stone: a toothy mouth, a feather, and something that might have been an egg or a seed, but the vast majority were carvings of a half-closed eye.

"What are these?" he asked.

Lazuli pointed to a carving of the mouth with a bowl of water before it. "This one's a shrine to the Deep One," she said.

Pinocchio looked at the next alcoves, comprehension coming over him. "These are for the primordials?"

But of course they were. The four ancient elemental beings were highly revered in Abaton. Since there were candles in front of the carvings of the seed, Pinocchio supposed the seed must have something to do with the Primordial of Fire. Strings of small flags fluttered in the breeze before the images of the feather. Was the Primordial of Air some sort of bird?

Lazuli pointed to nuggets of unpolished silver and gold lying before the numerous half-closed eyes. "These are for Regolith. The gnomes revere the Primordial of Earth highest, which is why there are more shrines for him. But all the primordials protect Abaton, so all are honored."

"Most cities in Abaton have shrines like these, Your Majesty," Rion said. "There's even one, if memory serves, in the far corner of the gardens at the Moonlit Court. Haven't you seen it?"

Pinocchio shook his head. He turned to the stone wall that formed the inner circle of the street. The wall was a little taller than he was, too high to see over it from where he stood. "So down there—?"

His heart thumped madly in his chest. Pinocchio approached the wall and pulled himself to the top. Below lay an enormous black pit.

Lazuli and Rion leaped on gusts of wind to land on either side of him. They looked down. Pinocchio noticed that Rion pulled back ever so slightly.

There were no stairs, no ladder, just rough rock leading down into the earth. Lazuli and Rion would have no trouble as sylphs.

They could simply walk down the walls. But Pinocchio had guessed he might need another way into the hole.

"Rion, your rope," he said, quelling the anxiousness in his voice.

"Yes, Your Majesty," Rion said, taking it from his shoulder. "I can secure it up here and help lower you down—"

"Aren't you coming?" Pinocchio asked.

Before Rion could answer, Lazuli said, "No. This place is only for Abaton's presters to enter."

"Are you sure, Your Majesty?" Rion asked. "General Mezmer instructed me to watch over you." Even as he said it, his eyes pinched anxiously, as if his deepest hope was for her to refuse his offer wholeheartedly.

"I'm sure," Lazuli said. "We won't need your protection down there."

Pinocchio swallowed hard. Sure, this had been his idea, but he had to trust that Lazuli would've told him if it was a huge mistake. What were they going to find down there? What was Regolith anyway? Chief Muckamire had simply said he was a giant. But a giant *what*?

Rion threw the coil of rope into the darkness, holding on to the end. He dropped lightly back to the street, securing the rope around his elbow, and took a firm double grip. "I've got you, Prester Pinocchio. Whenever you're ready."

Pinocchio grasped the rope with his gloved hands and walked slowly over the edge, leaning out to plant his feet against the stone sides. Lazuli began walking down next to him.

"Lazuli," Pinocchio whispered. "At the first sign of danger—"

"I know," she said. "We climb back up the wall."

They went down. Little by little, Pinocchio eased himself along on the rope. Lazuli's eyes cast a thin blue light. Pinocchio looked over his shoulder to see what was below, but the illumination from Lazuli's eyes didn't reach the bottom.

"I'll go ahead," Lazuli said. "To see how far down it goes."

Pinocchio concentrated on the rope, eyes up, since looking down sent his head spinning slightly. Soon he found the knotted end of the rope in his palm.

"I'm out of rope," he said, partially to Lazuli, partially to Rion.

"Not too much farther," Lazuli called up. "Too far to drop, however. The walls are uneven. You might be able to hold them. Think you can scale down?"

Pinocchio didn't like the idea of letting go of the rope, but he shored up his courage and felt around with his fingers until found a sturdy lip of rock. He secured his feet on another outcropping and let go of the rope, starting a tentative descent.

He took a breath to steady his nerves. One step at a time. Nice and slow.

"How much farther?" he called.

"A ways," Lazuli answered.

"I thought you said—"

Pinocchio's foot slipped off its perch. He smacked against the rock face, holding on only with his gloved fingers. The alchemied wood of his hands was strong. They could hold him. Heart racing, he kicked to find a foothold.

But before he could, his wooden fingers began to slide in the gloves' soft interior. He was slipping.

"I'm going to—"

And down he fell.

Pinocchio lay on his back, stunned, his breath knocked from his lungs. Above, the solitary hole of light seemed no bigger than a coin.

The silhouette of Lazuli's head eclipsed it. "Are you all right?"

He touched the ground beside him. It was sand, deep and soft almost like snow.

"Yeah," Pinocchio grunted.

He got to his feet, feeling stiff and struggling to take a full breath. His eyes adjusted to the dimness, and he found it was like being at the bottom of a well, except filled with sand, heaped into a gentle dome toward the middle, with no passage, no door, and definitely no Regolith.

He furrowed his brow. "There's nothing down here."

Lazuli was casting her luminous gaze around at all the walls like a dim searchlight. "There's got to be something."

Pinocchio pulled off his gloves and stuffed them into his belt. He could make out the end of the rope dangling maybe thirty feet above. This was pointless. Wherever Regolith was—buried deep under the earth, covered, forgotten, unreachable—they weren't going to find him. And how was he supposed to get out?

Pinocchio felt around the walls searching for a handhold, but down here, the wall was much smoother, more weathered. He found a grip, but his toes couldn't find purchase and kept coming loose. Grunting, he tried to pull himself up by his arms. His wooden hands might have been strong enough, but the muscles in his arms weren't. He'd never get up that way.

"I'm calling for Rion," Pinocchio said.

Rion had said Quila didn't like enclosed spaces, which was why the griffin had remained up on the ship rather than coming into the city. But she was going to have to now. Someone had to get him out.

"No, wait," Lazuli said, feeling around on the walls as if hoping to find a hidden passage. "Regolith has to be here. Call to him."

"Are you serious?"

Lazuli stared at him. She looked serious.

Pinocchio cupped a hand to his mouth. "Hello! Regolith? Are you home? Your presters need you." He sighed. "I told you—"

A sound like a hissing snake rose behind him. Pinocchio spun around. Lazuli leaped over next to him, looking at the floor with alarm. The sand was shifting, spilling away from the dome in the middle of the floor until bare rock was exposed.

Pinocchio and Lazuli flattened against the wall, staring wide-eyed.

A crack formed. It ran perfectly straight across the circular floor. Then the two halves of the bare rock floor slid apart, drawing back almost to their feet.

Beneath the sliding plates of rock was a circle of glossy black stone, surrounded by a ring of white. The rock closed over it again, sealing for only an instant, then opening once more.

Pinocchio realized what he was seeing and it nearly stopped his heart.

An eye. An enormous eye. It had blinked.

The look of alarm dropped away from Lazuli's face. She gave Pinocchio an enthusiastic nod. They'd found Regolith.

"You're . . ." Pinocchio gasped for breath. "Regolith? You guard Abaton's memories?"

The eye blinked. When it had opened again, the black pupil was replaced with an image of swirling green. Something was coming into focus—leaves, a forest . . . no, a jungle as seen from the sky! It was dizzying. Pinocchio felt like he might fall. He staggered back against the wall.

The eye was showing him a scene of a man standing in a dense jungle wilderness, peering into a great hole plowed into the earth.

The man wore snowy robes with a golden crown atop his long silver-white hair. Despite the color of his hair, his face was youthful—strangely so, because it didn't seem someone so young would have such a look of serene wisdom about him. How could he look both young and old at—?

Then Pinocchio understood. He'd seen this man before, but not like this. When Pinocchio had seen Prester John, he'd been ancient, bald and heavily wrinkled. He'd been dying in the depths of the Deep One.

"Father!" Lazuli gasped. "Is that you?"

But Prester John didn't seem to hear her, didn't seem to know she and Pinocchio were even there.

Lazuli winced as she realized her mistake. Her father was dead after all. "This has to be something that happened long ago," she whispered.

In the memory, Prester John opened a hand, holding an orb swirling with light and color. Pinocchio recognized the Ancientmost Pearl, even though he'd never seen it with his own eyes.

Prester John spoke in a clear, commanding voice, facing the cavernous hole. "And to you, Regolith, I ask that you remain beneath Abaton. Tread no more upon its surface."

In his other hand, he held a stone jar, which he tipped over the hole. Silvery sand poured out, an impossible amount given the size of the vessel.

"Sleep, Regolith. Sleep and guard the memories of Abaton."

The great rock lids blinked. When they opened, the image on Regolith's eye was gone.

Pinocchio stared at the black pupil ringed with white, hearing his own heavy breaths coming from his lips. He had just commanded the primordial Regolith!

"You did it!" Lazuli said. "You asked what it guarded, and Regolith showed us, with the memories it's guarding."

Pinocchio felt a thrill of power, warm and tingly, dancing in his chest. But then the prickly feeling seemed to also be moving down his arms.

With a start, he pulled up his sleeve. Wood had formed, along his wrists now and down almost to his elbows.

Panic erupted in Lazuli's eyes. "I . . . I didn't think talking to Regolith would do this!"

Pinocchio scowled. "I don't think it's that. It must be because I woke Regolith. It's obeying me because of the power of the Ancientmost Pearl."

"Then we have to stop!" Lazuli said.

Pinocchio was tempted to agree before he changed any more. But he had already awakened Regolith and now was his chance to find out why this was happening.

He looked at his arms, the horror of seeing more wood making him almost sick to his stomach. If Regolith was revolted or angered by what he saw, the eye gave no indication.

"Why . . ." Pinocchio swallowed hard. There seemed no reason to keep his secret from the ancient being. "Why is the Pearl turning me back into an automa?"

Lazuli gripped his arm, looking hesitantly from Pinocchio to Regolith's enormous eye.

The eye didn't blink, didn't move.

Pinocchio tried again. "Why is the Pearl turning me into wood?"

Nothing happened.

"So he's ignoring me now?" Pinocchio asked.

"I think," Lazuli said slowly, puzzling this out, "if Regolith can only answer by showing memories . . . well, there aren't any memories of Abaton that can answer your question?"

Pinocchio sighed. He tried to think of another way to put it, but found nothing. And he noticed that the wood little by little was continuing to creep up his elbow.

"We should stop," Lazuli said urgently.

Pinocchio shook his head. They had their mission. They needed to know more if they were to stop the monsters from escaping the prison.

Quickly, before Lazuli could stop him, he said, "The prisoners . . . the monsters who rebelled against Prester John . . . we need to know how they're escaping."

The eye blinked. This time the pupil became a leaden gray. As the image came into focus, Pinocchio saw a barren, rocky plain. Prester John, robed now in black but otherwise no different from the other memory, stood before an army of kneeling creatures. Monsters! These were the monsters.

They were much more terrifying than what Pinocchio had seen in the painting in his father's book. Great hulking beasts with blackened claws and fangs that could rip arms out of sockets. Skeletal things that looked rotten and yet somehow alive, with festering yellow eyes blinking from mangled faces. A manticore—there she was, just as Pinocchio remembered her from the attack at the banquet—lay defeated on the ground among the others.

But at the front of the horde, a man with crimson skin sat on his knees, looking down at his bound hands.

"Diamancer," Prester John said. "Let me ask again, do you repent for your crimes?"

The crimson man looked up. Pinocchio drew back in horror and heard Lazuli gasp. Diamancer had no eyes. The skin ran smooth and unblemished where his lids should have been.

Diamancer smiled, a cruel and hateful smile, before whispering, "I do not."

Prester John turned. Behind him stood a fox chimera wearing a full suit of shining armor. He held a tall lance and a battered shield. General Mezmercurian was larger than Mezmer, broader of shoulder, and with scars and patches of missing fur on his snout.

Other soldiers were lined up behind their general. Regiments of sylphs, gnomes, djinn, undines, chimera, and other creatures. Most were soldiers in the prester's army. But the ones in the front, with their gleaming armor and brave faces, were clearly the elite knights of the Celestial Brigade. Mezmer would have given anything to command knights like these.

Prester John faced the monsters once more. He raised his voice. "Do any of you ask for your prester's forgiveness?"

Some of the monsters growled. A few squeaked, although Pinocchio couldn't tell if it was in fear or defiance. None answered.

"So be it," Prester John said, an unmistakable note of sadness in his voice. "Then until the day when you repent for your crimes, you will no longer be free to endanger Abaton."

He took several steps back and raised a hand. From out of the ground, tendrils of leafless vines erupted. They whipped around, snaking together and enclosing the huge army in wooden walls that rose into the steely overcast sky. The wood swelled, fusing together until the walls sealed into the shape of a great pyramid. Prester John waved a hand, and the prison lifted into the sky.

The eye blinked. For an instant, Pinocchio thought the memory was over. He began to shout at Regolith that he hadn't answered his question. But when the eye opened once more, a new scene appeared.

Pinocchio felt the tingling in his arms, creeping ever higher.

Lazuli cast him a worried glance. But Pinocchio gritted his teeth and watched what was unfolding in the great eye.

Prester John was surrounded by darkness. Beside him stood Mezmercurian holding a lamp swirling with pixies that cast a bubble of light. The general no longer wore armor, simply a suit of forest green. He carried no weapons.

"You have served Abaton well, General," Prester John said. "You have done so much already for our people—"

"Then allow me to do a little more, Your Majesty," Mezmercurian rasped.

Prester John nodded somberly. "Very well." He handed a stone jar to the fox. "I make you the warden of the Sleeping Thousand."

As Mezmercurian lifted his lamp, Pinocchio saw what lay on the floor. Spreading out into the darkness in every direction were Diamancer's monsters—eyes closed and partially covered in drifts of what looked like snow or even ancient layers of dust.

Prester John said, "And so the Sleeping Thousand will remain until the day of their repentance or until Abaton falls. Be careful when you check on your charges. Do not uncover them or they will awaken."

Pinocchio frowned. Uncover them from what?

Regolith blinked.

A new scene formed. This time Mezmercurian lay in a bed. He was clearly aged. His coppery fur was frosted with white. His once bright eyes were ever so clouded. The room was modest, the furnishing spare. The rumble of distant ocean came from the open window.

Prester John approached the fox's bedside.

Pinocchio tried to focus on the scene, but the tingling of his arms was rising nearly to his shoulders.

"Pinocchio?" Lazuli said, worry thick in her voice.

He desperately wanted to stop, but Pinocchio reminded himself that it was now more than just this lone manticore who had escaped. The village of Sunder had been destroyed by dozens of monsters. Who knew how many others were being attacked! He had to do this. They had to understand what was going on in the prison.

"I've called for you, My Immortal Lordship, because it is time." Mezmercurian's voice was thin as tissue, dry and fading. "Another must be chosen to take over as the warden."

Prester John looked down on him, his expression stony. But in his eyes, Pinocchio caught the faintest flicker of sadness.

"Pinocchio!" Lazuli said again.

Pinocchio ignored her, trying to find out as much as they could from the memory.

"The Sands of Sleep," Mezmercurian said, lifting a paw toward the table by his bed.

"Yes," Prester John whispered. He picked up the stone jar.

"I will give the wardenship to another," Prester John said. "But what you have done will never be forgotten. Not by me. Not by Abaton. You do your ancestors a great credit."

"Thank you." Mezmercurian shifted, trying to sit up, but Prester John placed a hand on his shoulder.

The tingling rose into Pinocchio's own shoulders. He trembled; the fear that the wood had reached that far seemed to make his body revolt. He had to stop before—

Pinocchio looked once more at the stone jar. It was the same one that Prester John had used when he'd poured the sands over Regolith. The sleeping monsters weren't covered with snow or dust. They were covered with sand. The same sands that had kept Regolith asleep.

"The prison has long remained hidden in the Upended Forest, Your Majesty," Mezmercurian said. "But it is growing inhabited."

Prester John nodded. "Yes, it might be time to—"

Pinocchio shouted, "Enough! Enough, Regolith. Go back to sleep!"

The great rock lid slammed shut. Quickly, Lazuli pushed sand back over the lid, kicking it, brushing it until it was scattered once more over Regolith. Pinocchio dropped to his knees, clutching his hard wooden shoulders and shaking. The tingling subsided.

Lazuli put a hand on his shoulder. Her voice quivered. "Pinocchio? Are you all right?"

He nodded, even though he wasn't. And she knew he wasn't.

"The Sands of Sleep," Pinocchio breathed.

Lazuli nodded. "Yes. If the monsters were uncovered from the Sands, they would awaken."

Pinocchio slid his fingers into the soft sand piled beneath him. Why had it not caused him to fall asleep? Maybe the Pearl was protecting him. But it had not affected Lazuli either, which was perplexing.

"And we can use the Sands to put them back to sleep," Pinocchio said, the realization jolting him upright.

He untied his cape and spread it on the ground. He piled sand into the center before drawing up the corners into a makeshift sack that he tied off with ribbon at the collar.

"How were they uncovered?" Pinocchio asked.

"I'm not sure," Lazuli said. "From what the memory revealed, the prison is governed by a warden that my father selected. Maybe the current warden uncovered them accidentally."

"But who's the warden?"

"That, we'll have to find out," Lazuli said. "Maybe it's

recorded in the gnomes' library. But for now at least, we know how to handle these monsters without you having to draw on the Pearl."

She nodded at the sack in Pinocchio's wooden hand.

Pinocchio looked up the shaft. The coin of sky was graying with dusk.

He approached the wall and grabbed one of the narrow clefts of rock. He'd have no trouble now climbing out. His transformed arms had automa strength.

But as he followed Lazuli up, climbing hand over hand out from the shadows, Pinocchio knew he would have given anything to not have that sort of strength.

10.

The Kirins

"I . . . well, I can scarcely believe it, Your Majesties," Chief Muckamire said in a stunned squeak, from the edge of his chair. "It's . . . You . . . Regolith? You actually woke Regolith!"

The others in the gnome lord's cavernous parlor seemed to be in similar states of disbelief now that Lazuli had finished. She'd told the story in what had felt like one long, breathless sentence—leaving out only the parts that the gnome and Rion couldn't know, about what was happening to Pinocchio.

The glow from the fireplace danced off Mezmer's and Sop's shocked faces. Geppetto leaned forward in his stone seat, nearly statue-still, with Maestro clinging to his shoulder. The only trace of movement came when his father's eyes flickered to Pinocchio's hands with equal parts suspicion and dread.

Only Rion, standing against the far wall behind Mezmer and

Sop, didn't look shocked. But then he'd learned what had happened on their race back to the palace. And besides, he was now clearly put out, since Mezmer had chastised him for allowing the presters to awaken Regolith without their general's involvement.

"Chief Muckamire," she said. "We learned that my father gave the responsibility of watching over the prison to a warden. Do you know who it might be?"

"Your Majesty," Chief Muckamire answered, "I was only remotely acquainted with the fact that there was a prison at all. I've always assumed the details were a secret only known to your father. No, I have no idea who the current warden is. If there even is still a warden! Who knows what decisions your father made regarding the prison in the centuries since the memories you witnessed occurred?"

Mezmer took a step toward them. "If General Mezmercurian was the warden, it could be that after the Celestial Brigade was disbanded, Prester John took over the responsibility of acting as warden."

"In which case," Geppetto said, pulling on his mustache, "the prison has been unattended since His Great Lordship's death. This might explain why the prisoners are wakening."

Pinocchio said, "But in the memory, Prester John said he would give the wardenship to another."

"We'll need to find out for sure," Lazuli said. She faced Chief Muckamire. "Can you search the libraries?"

"Most certainly, Your Majesty," the gnome said.

"And I'll contact my aunt to see if she has any knowledge," Lazuli said. "Dr. Nundrum also might know."

"Whatever the answer, we now have the Sands of Sleep, which is no small success," Mezmer said with a flick of her ears. "We leave in the morning, darlings."

"*Tomorrow* morning?" Lazuli must have misheard her. "But what about the ship? It can't be ready yet."

"No, it's not. However . . ." Mezmer rubbed a furry knuckle across her already spotless armor, looking pleased. "Sop and I are happy to report that we have arranged for another means of travel."

"You have?" Lazuli asked.

Sop groaned and put a paw over his face.

"What? They're perfect, darling," Mezmer said to the cat. "Don't complain."

"What's perfect?" Pinocchio burst out impatiently.

"Wini," Mezmer replied. "And her sisters, Fini and . . . what was the other?"

"Rainbow Dew Drop," Sop grumbled.

"No, it wasn't." Mezmer said. "It was something like Pini." Her fox face brightened. "They're kirins."

"What are kirins?" Pincchio asked.

"They're often called unicorns back in the humanlands," Maestro chirped authoritatively.

"But don't call them that," Mezmer added. "Wini made it quite clear they don't appreciate that term."

"She also made it quite clear that she loved munching buttercups when she wasn't reciting poetry to the solstice winds." Sop shook his head. "We can't take these unicorns . . . kirins, whatever, to a prison full of monsters! This is dangerous work!"

"I admit," Mezmer said, drooping slightly, "they're not exactly what I dreamed for the knights of the Celestial Brigade. But they're quite keen to be of service to their presters. Besides, we couldn't find anyone else who could fly and was capable of carrying all of us."

"They fly?" Pinocchio asked.

Mezmer gave an enthusiastic nod. "Quite swiftly."

"But three kirins," Lazuli wondered. "How can they carry us all?"

"Ah, well . . ." Mezmer said hesitantly. "All of us won't be going."

"What?" Pinocchio said. "Who's not going?"

Geppetto's face was lined with concern. "We were just discussing before your return—"

"There's no discussion!" Chief Muckamire barked. "I told you, Master Geppetto. We can't. I won't allow my gnomes. What you're suggesting is . . ." He lowered his voice as if the word was cursed. "Alchemy."

"Quite right," Geppetto said, splaying his hands. "Yes, alchemy. But if we're to keep the people of Abaton safe from the next attack, we can't just shelter them in the cities. We've got no army. How would you defend Grootslang Hole? How would we protect the Moonlit Court?"

Lazuli shook her head. "I don't understand. What's this about?"

Chief Muckamire puffed up his beard. "Master Geppetto is suggesting that we build weapons of war using Venetian alchemy."

"Cinnabar's former master in Venice designed defenses for the Fortezza Ducale," Geppetto said in a near growl. "He knows how to build alchemical weaponry."

Chief Muckamire narrowed his eyes as if Cinnabar just dropped several notches in his measure.

"We can start with the flying ship," Geppetto said. "Equip it like a real warship."

"*We?*" Pinocchio asked. "You mean you'd stay here."

Geppetto's eyes flickered to his son. He frowned. "Yes, I would need to assist Cinnabar."

"With alchemy!" Chief Muckamire said. "What would my people think if I allowed it—much less if I assisted? His Great Lordship Prester John would never have allowed it!"

Lazuli sat up straighter in her seat. "Chief Muckamire," she said, mustering as much presterly confidence as she could pack into her expression. "There were many things my father didn't allow. But let me remind you that he gave the Ancientmost Pearl to Pinocchio. He allowed the son of a Venetian alchemist to become our prester."

She drew a breath. "The people of Abaton were his children, and he loved them as deeply, as Master Geppetto loves Pinocchio. My father tried to give his children a peaceful world, a glorious one. But now my father is gone. And Abaton has been dealt a threat he could never have foreseen."

Lazuli nodded to Pinocchio. "Abaton has changed. We must all change if we are to keep it safe."

Chief Muckamire said nothing. He sat pensively in his stone seat, hands folded across his lap. "Change can be unsettling," he said at last.

Lazuli nodded.

"His Great Lordship asked little of his high nobles," Chief Muckamire said. "We represented our elemental houses. We were brought to court on occasion for ceremonies and banquets. But we were never asked to help share the burden of ruling."

Lazuli hesitated, feeling her aunt would be furious with her for saying it. "I'm asking you to help, my lord. Our people need us."

Chief Muckamire nodded. "Then we must protect them."

He glanced at Geppetto, worry still carved into his craggy face. "Very well, Master Geppetto. Will you teach my gnomes some alchemy?"

"It's not fair," Pinocchio said. His arms were folded atop the table in the windowless cavern of his chambers. He pressed his face against his arms, but at the feel of the hard wood, he reared back up. "I thought when we came to Abaton, I'd be human forever. I thought I'd never . . ."

Geppetto put his hand gently on Pinocchio's head, smoothing his hair. "I know, son."

Pinocchio didn't like the way his father sounded. Resigned. Hopeless. "Is there nothing we can do? Didn't you find anything at all in the libraries?"

Geppetto sighed, gesturing to a pile of books scattered across the table. "Some passages that provided promising insights, but no real answers."

Maestro skittered across the binding of one of the books. "Read him the part about the palace!"

Geppetto sank into the chair next to Pinocchio. He opened a dusty slate-bound tome and flipped to a page marked with a tattered ribbon. "The text is not easy to follow. The gnomish scribes wrote it based on visions they claimed Regolith sent them. But this one passage we found speaks of the earliest days of Abaton and how the magic was wild and raw and untamed. How even Prester John didn't seem sure how he was manipulating it."

Pinocchio understood the feeling. "Go on," he murmured.

"When Prester John first came ashore in Abaton—"

"Where did he come from?" Pinocchio interrupted. "How did he arrive?"

Geppetto shook his head. "The scribe doesn't say. At least not in this book. But when he first arrived, the island was split into four kingdoms, each ruled by an elemental house. They were at war with one another. Keep in mind, in these early days, there were no chimera or griffins or kirins. Besides the elementals, only birds and ordinary beasts inhabited the island."

Pinocchio blinked in surprise.

"But there were the primordials," Maestro chirped.

"Yes, there were the primordials—however, Prester John had not yet learned to command them. The primordials spoke to him. In a dream." His father pinched a corner of his mustache as he searched the page. "According to this passage, the primordials told him to unite the warring elementals, to dream of an Abaton at peace, in harmony. After he woke, he spent many days trying to figure out how to unite the elementals. Then one night, sleeping on the sands beside the lagoon—"

"Where Crescent Port lies now," Maestro added.

"Prester John dreamed of a towering white palace. In the morning, he discovered that the Moonlit Court had risen overnight in the nearby jungle."

"He dreamed the palace into existence?" Pinocchio gasped. Then he remembered something. "I saw a tapestry with something like that. In the throne room. But it showed creatures seeming to come out of Prester John's head."

"I'm getting to that," his father said, tapping a finger to the page. "With a palace, Prester John was happy, but he grew lonely. He wanted companionship, and so again he dreamed. Soon the birds and creatures began to speak. He discovered other beings that had not been there before—extraordinary creatures, chimera and all the other races of Abaton."

"So am I understanding this right? Prester John *made* the creatures of Abaton?" Pinocchio asked.

"Oh, yes," Maestro said, hopping from one side of the book to the other. "We crickets have many songs celebrating His Great Lordship for bestowing upon us our prodigious virtuosity for music."

The cricket seemed ready to launch into a demonstration, but Pinocchio cut him off. "Were there monsters then?"

His father raised his woolly eyebrows. "It seems odd, doesn't it, that he would dream of such terrifying creatures. Prester John, in fact, notes how the first manticores and wyverns and other monstrous races frightened him. They seemed born of his nightmares. He later decided they were a sort of test given by Abaton itself, a test of a kingly father's need to love all his children, no matter how frightening they might have looked."

Pinocchio thought about this a moment before saying, "But what happened with the elementals?"

His father nodded. "Each of the elementals sent envoys to the Moonlit Court to find out who had built such an extraordinary place. They were greatly impressed. But when Prester John asked them to end their disagreements and unite under him, they laughed and were going to leave. So he introduced them to the chimera and talking animals and other creatures he'd made. Again they were impressed, but refused. At last he showed them the monstrous races. At the sight of the creatures, the envoys all fled from the palace back to their people."

Pinocchio cupped a hand to his face as his father continued.

"Prester John was saddened. He thought he'd failed to honor what the primordials had asked of him. He went to bed for many days, disheartened. During that time, storms began to savage Abaton. Earthquakes and volcanoes. The island was nearly ruined. The elementals arrived at the Moonlit Court and woke

Prester John. They begged him to save them. But even when Prester John woke, he couldn't stop the destruction.

"He went to each of the primordials, asking how he could save Abaton. They told him he was responsible for the wild magic, that it was born of his thoughts. But Prester John didn't know how to stop what was happening. The Deep One, at last, gave him a means of containing the powers. A vessel, if you will."

"The Ancientmost Pearl," Pinocchio said.

His father smiled. "Exactly."

"But I thought the magic came from the Ancientmost Pearl," Pinocchio said.

"So did I!" exclaimed Geppetto, holding the book. "Until I read this. The Ancientmost Pearl became a *container* for the magic, a means of bending the powers more expressly toward his will—not unlike the way a prism bends and manipulates light. And with the Pearl, Prester John was at last able to stop the storms and ruin. He built Abaton anew. And the elementals, seeing his power, united under him."

He set down the book.

Pinocchio squinted. "Is this all true?"

His father gave an uncertain smile. "There is truth in every story. But I can't say how much actually happened and how much was just the interpretation of the gnome scribe who wrote it down."

"But . . ." Pinocchio was struggling to understand what it all meant. "What does this have to do with me turning into wood?"

His father clasped a hand over Pinocchio's. "The Pearl was never inside Prester John as it is inside you. When you became human, who knows what transformation the Pearl made?"

He leaned forward, pressing a hand tenderly to Pinocchio's

chest. "I feel your heart beating, when there was no heart before—where, as an automa, you had a springwork fantom until Prester John replaced it with the Pearl. Is the Pearl still inside you? I can't say . . ."

"But the magic is, right?" Pinocchio said.

"Yes," Geppetto said, nodding heartily. "But if the Pearl as a container has transformed, then has the magic begun to go wild again, as it did for Prester John in those earliest days? This might be our best clue to why you are transforming back."

Pinocchio knew he had some control over the powers. He'd woken Regolith. He'd summoned fire and water and wind against the manticore. But clearly there were things the Pearl was doing that he had no idea how to stop—namely turning him back to wood.

Pinocchio asked, "If Prester John wasn't able to stop the wild magic until he got the Pearl, how am I supposed to?"

Geppetto frowned, shaking his head. "All I know is that until we fully comprehend what's taken place with the Pearl, you must not draw on its powers anymore. Not unless it's life or death. Promise me you won't! Not until Maestro and I can figure out more."

Pinocchio nodded. He had the Sands of Sleep. He had Mezmer and Rion and Lazuli to help him. Sop might come through in a pinch. Hopefully, together, they would be able to handle whatever lay in the prison.

A knock sounded at the door. "Yes?" Geppetto called.

Chief Muckamire entered. "Your Majesty. Master Geppetto." He made a bow. "Forgive my intrusion. Is this a bad time?"

"No, please come in," Geppetto said. "What can we do for you?"

The gnome gave a hesitant smile. "I wanted to say . . . well, despite my earlier reluctance, I'm glad that we'll be able to put your . . . skills to use. In the defense of Abaton."

Geppetto looked a little tentative, but said, "I'm glad you feel that way."

"I'll admit, when you first arrived, I was uncertain whether your loyalties were truly with our people."

"Chief Muckamire," Geppetto said with a frown. "My concern is for protecting—"

The gnome waved his hands. "Yes, I know. Why else would you agree to stay behind while you send Pinocchio off . . . well, we all well know the danger."

Pinocchio swallowed hard. Chief Muckamire didn't know the half of it.

The gnome shifted. "So I can appreciate that you might both be feeling anxious about . . . leaving each other."

He came forward, a small silver box clutched in his hands.

"I wanted to offer something that I hope will ease your worries," Chief Muckamire said. "Meant to give this to you at the banquet, Your Majesty, but with all the commotion and whatnot . . . well, here it is." He thrust the box into Pinocchio's hands. "Open it, my prester."

Pinocchio lifted the lid. The box was filled with dirt.

"Oh, it's dirt. Uh, thank you. Is this . . . some sort of protection?"

Chief Muckamire gave a jolly laugh and shook his beard. "Not the dirt, Your Majesty. And not protection exactly." He gestured to the box. "Riggle."

Pinocchio wasn't sure if this was some strange command, but before he could wonder further, a worm, about the size of a baby's finger, squirmed out from the dirt. Pinocchio had been in Abaton long enough to know a worm like this was surely no ordinary worm and, more likely than not, could speak.

"Are you Riggle?" he asked, already preparing to feel foolish if he was wrong.

"He's a superfluous worm!" Maestro said, tipping his antennae forward curiously. "I've never met one."

The worm bent his nubby head in what Pinocchio imagined must be the worm equivalent of a bow. "A pleasure to serve you, my prester," Riggle said in the tiniest voice imaginable.

"Riggle will allow you to keep in touch with your father and us here in Grootslang," Chief Muckamire said.

"Um . . . how?" Pinocchio asked. He didn't look like he'd be able to crawl back to Grootslang Hole any faster than they'd be traveling.

"We gnomes, as you know," Chief Muckamire said, "can split into a dozen or more smaller versions of ourselves, but we have to stay in the same general proximity to one another. While superfluous worms like Riggle can never fuse back together, they can be separated from their other forms by incalculable distances. Most helpful for communicating from afar. Allow me to demonstrate. It requires a special blade."

Chief Muckamire drew a knife of polished jade from his belt and held out his hand for Riggle to squirm from the box into his palm. Then with a quick slice, the gnome severed Riggle in half. Pinocchio winced. He really hoped that didn't hurt too much.

One half of Riggle slithered back into the box while the other half remained in Chief Muckamire's palm. "So you'll take this Riggle. Master Geppetto will have his. And if you need to speak to your father, you may simply speak to your Riggle." He handed the box to Pinocchio.

"And you'll pass the message along?" Pinocchio asked his Riggle.

"Yes, Your Majesty," both Riggles said simultaneously.

Would the wonders of Abaton ever stop surprising him?

The following morning, Pinocchio dug through his trunk deciding on the barest necessities for the journey. He wanted to feel brave. He wanted to project confidence. So he dressed in a white tunic and leggings. He put on his gloves and the seven-league boots. He strapped his sword to his belt and tucked the box with Riggle in a satchel with the Sands of Sleep. He took a deep breath and nodded to himself. He was ready.

Out on the palace steps where they were to depart, Chief Muckamire was overseeing a group of servants strapping bags of supplies onto Quila's saddle. The griffin endured it with noble patience. Pinocchio wondered why it was that some Abatonian creatures like griffins and the gnomes' slithersteeds were treated more like beasts of burden than others. Maybe they weren't as intelligent. Quila didn't seem to speak, after all. He'd have to ask Lazuli.

But Lazuli was busy, talking with Rion. He heard Rion say, "But, Your Majesty, this is too dangerous for you. I promised Lady Sapphira I would keep you safe. Stay here in Grootslang, and let me assist Prester Pinocchio."

"I'll remind you I faced extraordinary dangers when I was in the Venetian Empire," Lazuli said. "Pinocchio as well. We're both quite capable—"

"But he has the Ancientmost Pearl to protect him," Rion said. "You don't."

"I told you I'm going," Lazuli said. "Enough about it, please, Rion."

Pinocchio was just frowning at this exchange when Sop sidled up next to him. "What's with the outfit?"

"This?" Pinocchio glanced down casually at what he was wearing. "What about it?"

Sop's eye flicked to Rion and his cloud-white clothes before narrowing at Pinocchio.

"Can't a prester dress how he wants?" Pinocchio snapped.

"Of course, Your Majesty." Sop gave a knowing purr.

"There you are," Lazuli called, spotting Pinocchio and coming over. "You've got the Sands?"

Pinocchio patted the satchel at his side.

She gave an approving nod. Then she narrowed her eyes, looking him up and down. "Why are you dressed like a sylph, anyway?"

Pinocchio glanced at Rion. Was it too late to change? "I'm not—" he began.

But the sound of hoofbeats on the steps drew Lazuli's attention.

"Here we are, darlings," Mezmer cried, climbing down from the back of one of the three kirins.

The creatures pranced in circles before them, throwing high their pearly horns and shaking their flowing silken manes. They weren't quite as horselike as Pinocchio had imagined they'd be. Their overlarge eyes were much more human. And the silvery fur along their backs became multicolored scales at their haunches.

"May I introduce Wini, Fini, and Pini," Mezmer said, throwing out a hand.

The kirins bowed their heads to their presters. "An honor to escort you, Your Majesties," one said. The other two giggled.

Pinocchio was beginning to see what Sop meant.

Mezmer had gathered several shields from their ship and proceeded to strap them on either side of the kirins. "A little extra protection," she said, winking at the sisters. "Shall we go?" Mezmer was trembling with excitement.

Pinocchio felt a tremble as well, but not quite for the same reason. He looked over to Geppetto. Since he'd rescued his father in the Deep One and arriving in Abaton, they hadn't been parted. In many ways, he was glad his father wasn't coming. Danger surely lay ahead in the prison, and his father would be safer here in Grootslang Hole.

The image of Diamancer bloomed in his mind. Diamancer with his eyeless face. Diamancer smiling at Prester John as he refused to repent for his crimes against Abaton.

If Diamancer escaped, would anywhere in Abaton be safe—for his father, for any of them?

Pinocchio extended a tentative hand to his father.

Geppetto didn't take it. Instead he pulled his son into a great hug. Pinocchio squeezed back. But over his father's shoulder, he caught the others watching. Reluctantly, he wriggled free. He could tell his father wasn't ready to let go, and a little lump of guilt seemed to catch in his throat.

"Yes," Geppetto said, patting him on the back. "Yes, better get onto . . . which one are you?"

"Wini," the kirin said, kneeling so Pinocchio could climb on. "Don't worry about holding on to my mane, Your Majesty. I'll keep you upright."

Wini had a pleasant, woodsy smell about her.

"Thank you," he murmured, his throat still feeling tight.

Sop and Mezmer climbed on the other two kirins. Lazuli got onto the saddle behind Rion. Pinocchio felt the slightest pang at being left out, seeing them ride together. But of course, as sylphs, they both weighed nearly nothing, so they must be easy for the griffin to carry along with the supplies.

Quila took off first, making a few clumsy bounds down the palace steps to gather speed before throwing out her enormous wings.

"Ready, Your Majesty?" Wini asked.

Pinocchio looked once to his father before nodding. The kirin sprang so suddenly that he thought for sure he'd fall off her back. But then Wini jerked to a stop, hovering in the air. Pinocchio pitched forward. He had to stop himself from grabbing her mane. This might not be the most relaxing ride.

"Good-bye, Your Majesties!" Chief Muckamire called from below.

His father waved to him.

Gnomes from the palace and along the tiered streets shielded their eyes against the rising sun to watch the presters. Pinocchio noticed that Cinnabar hadn't come to see them off. No surprise. Then he realized he hadn't said good-bye to Maestro. But it was too late.

The kirins shot into the sky, kicking their hooves against empty air. They followed Quila up from the city of Grootslang Hole and out over the jungle. In the distance, the sea of green gave way to golden flatlands. And beyond that—somewhere out there—was the prison Prester John had hidden. But what they'd find inside, none could say.

PART TWO

The
Prison

11.

The Wanderer

Grasslands stretched to the horizon—a cloudless blue sky above, golden sun-dappled flatness below. They passed over scatterings of villages. Some were mere clusters of tidy mud huts, others were larger towns on the banks of picturesque rivers, all places so charming Lazuli longed to go down and explore them. There was still so much to Abaton she had never seen.

"Someone decided to tag along," Memzer called from Fini's back.

Lazuli turned in the saddle and spied the little aleya bobbing along behind their party.

"Get back home!" Mezmer barked at her.

The aleya made a musical tinkle, attempting to hide behind the tail of Pinocchio's kirin.

"She says she wants to help her presters," Rion translated.

"Tell her she can't," Mezmer said. "This is knights' business."

The aleya answered with urgent chiming.

Rion chuckled and called over to Mezmer, "She says, then make her a knight. I don't think she'll be persuaded to leave, General."

Mezmer scowled. "Make her a knight? Ridiculous! She can't even carry a sword. I have high standards for the Celestial Brigade."

"Clearly," Sop said.

"She's not in the way," Pinocchio called. "Just let her come if she wants."

Mezmer shook her head but made no argument. The aleya flitted up next to Pinocchio, giving him an appreciative chime.

Lazuli was just thinking how perfectly typical this was of Pinocchio, when Rion looked over his shoulder at her. He said nothing, but she knew what he was thinking. He'd been so insistent that she not join their mission, claiming that her aunt would be furious if anything happened to her under his watch.

Lazuli shifted back slightly in the saddle, putting more distance between her and Rion. She was glad to have a loyal knight eager to keep his prester safe. But did he have to be so annoying about it?

The grasslands began to wither into the crimson-colored sands and rock that marked the Caldera Desert. The villages grew fewer, just clusters of tents gathered around the occasional oasis. They saw few travelers as well. Once, later in the morning, a line of colossal tortoises appeared, strung together in a merchant caravan led by jackal-headed chimera drivers, most likely bound for the distant markets of the djinn city of Caldera Keep.

By the afternoon, all signs of life disappeared entirely. Great, windswept dunes of vermilion red and sunset orange began to fill the landscape below, some as tall as mountains. It was as desolate a place as Lazuli could imagine. Surely the most remote location in all of Abaton.

Mezmer brought her kirin up beside Quila. Hot wind plastered back the fur from her face. "We're looking for a river," she called to Rion and Lazuli. "According to Dr. Nundrum, there's only one and it'll lead us to this Upended Forest. Although how there could be a river, much less a forest, out here, I haven't a clue."

"We'll find it," Rion said confidently.

"Have you flown this way before?" Lazuli asked.

"No, Your Majesty, but Quila has keen eyes."

"So does Sop," Mezmer said, pulling back into formation. "At least the one."

They flew for what seemed hours with only endless empty dunes in every direction. Even high in the sky, the air was like an oven. Lazuli was beginning to wonder if Dr. Nundrum might have been mistaken or if the map he was using was so old the river had since dried up.

"What's that?" Sop cried, pointing to the right.

At first, Lazuli thought it might be a stunted tree atop a distant, heat-shimmering dune—maybe part of the Upended Forest! But as they flew closer, they discovered it was a solitary traveler taking slow, measured steps.

"Where did he come from?" she wondered aloud.

"And where's he going?" Mezmer added.

"Nowhere fast," Sop said, which was true, as the traveler had hardly taken three steps since they'd started watching him. "Should we ask if he knows anything about a river?"

Mezmer gave a pat to her kirin. "Take us down, Fini."

They landed in the sand in front of the traveler and dismounted.

"Greetings, wayfarer," Lazuli called to him. "Are you lost?"

The traveler stopped and pulled back the dust-rimed hood of his cloak. He was a chimera of some reptilian variety and so massive and intimidating with all the spines and frills around his face that the aleya gave a squeak and hid behind Pinocchio's back.

He had the oddest eyes Lazuli had ever seen. They protruded out from the sides of his face like miniature volcanoes with beady black orbs at the ends. The chimera rotated the strange telescopic eyes in a circle before fixing one on Lazuli and one on Pinocchio.

"Not. Any. More. Your. Majesties." He spoke almost as slowly as he moved.

"You recognize us as the presters?" Pinocchio asked, clearly surprised.

The corners of his scaly lips inched into a smile, and he brought a clawed finger up with protracted effort until it pointed at Pinocchio. "You. Are. Human," he said simply.

Lazuli had gotten so used to Pinocchio being human she had almost forgotten that he must look a bit strange to their people.

"What is your name, sir?" she asked.

"Kataton."

"Kataton, we're searching for a river that runs through the Caldera."

The lizard said slowly, "The. Crimson. River."

"Yes," Mezmer hurriedly replied. "Can you point us in the right direction?"

"Better. That. I. Show. You."

Rion made an impatient sigh. "Can't you just—"

Pinocchio cut him off. "Wini, can you carry two of us?"

The kirin batted her long eyelashes. "I'm strong enough to carry more."

"Good," Pinocchio replied. "You can ride with me, Kataton. Lead us to the river, please."

Kataton made a stiff bow before lumbering toward Wini. Lazuli and the others were all saddled back up while Kataton was still coming over. Sop twiddled his thumbs. "Are you always this slow?"

"Not. Always." Kataton chuckled as he hoisted one leg over Wini's back. "I. Can. Be. Quite. Fast. When." He settled on behind Pinocchio. "Necessary."

Sop gave him a dubious one-eyed glare.

Once they were airborne, Kataton lifted a claw and pointed. "That. Way."

It wasn't long before they reached the Crimson River. Lazuli realized why it had been hard to spot. The thin ribbon of ruddy water lay nearly hidden between the enormous dunes rising on either side.

Lazuli heard Pinocchio ask Kataton, "What were you doing out here all alone, anyway? Do you live nearby?"

"My. Village. Was. Destroyed," Kataton said. "We. All. Left."

"Are you from Sunder?" Lazuli asked.

"Yes. Your. Majesty."

"Where are the others?"

"Gone. On. Without. Me."

As slow as Kataton was, Lazuli wondered sadly if the other villagers had simply abandoned him in their haste to reach the safety of Caldera Keep or some other city.

"Did you see the attack?" Pinocchio asked. "Or were you out in the desert gathering gems?"

"I. Saw," Kataton said. "I. Am. A. Cook. I. Was. Baking.

Beetlebread. For. The. Harvesters'. Breakfast. When. They. Came." His eyes protruded a bit farther. "A. Dozen. Terrifying. Monsters."

"How did you escape?" Lazuli asked. In her mind, she was imagining Kataton lumbering slowly along as the attack rained down on him.

"I. Led. The. Children. And. The. Elders. Into. My. Cellar." Kataton nodded. "As. Quickly. As. I. Could."

Sop gave a cough.

"Your. Majesties," Kataton asked. "Are. You. Searching. For. These. Monsters?"

"We are," Lazuli said. "We've learned that they might be escaping from an ancient prison hidden in the Upended Forest. But where it is—"

"Farther. Down. The. Crimson. River," Kataton said.

Lazuli gave a jolt of surprise. "You've heard of this forest?"

"Yes. Your. Majesty." Kataton swiveled his tiny eyes. "Go. That. Way." He pointed to where the river trickled off to the right.

Rion banked Quila, and the kirins trailed behind as they followed the river into the late-afternoon sun. The river at last widened, forming a lake nestled in a valley of red dunes.

"Down. Here," Kataton said.

They landed beside the shore, but there were no trees of any sort growing by the lake.

"This can't be the Upended Forest," Sop said, leaping off Pini and throwing a hand out irritably.

"Maybe it's upended because all the trees were blown over long ago," Mezmer offered.

"No," Kataton said, easing off Wini's back. "It. Is. Beneath. Us."

Sop traced a circle around his ear. "I knew this limp-lipped lizard was crazy. Now he's gotten us lost."

"Look," Rion said. He pointed to the center of the lake.

Lazuli had been so busy searching the shoreline she hadn't noticed until now that there was a hole in the middle of the lake. Water cascaded down, disappearing through an opening like a great drain.

"I had my suspicions all along the forest had to be underground," Rion said confidently. "Why else would it be *upended*? We just need to go down those falls to reach it."

"That. Is. Right," Kataton said.

Lazuli could see the confusion on Pinocchio's face. She wasn't quite sure either what they were dealing with, but Mezmer began to take charge.

"Can we fly down, then?" the fox asked Rion.

Quila made a disgruntled squawk.

"She won't go in there," Rion said. "Griffins hate enclosed spaces." He pointed to Wini. "Kirin, you and your sisters will have to take us down into the forest."

Mezmer stepped past Rion with an irksome scowl. "I can handle this, my good knight." She turned to Wini. "Are you nervous in enclosed spaces, dear?"

"Not at all, General," she said, throwing her horned head to one side to let her mane flow luxuriously. "Would you like me to check out what's below before we carry you down?"

"That would be excellent, darling," Mezmer said.

Wini sprang into the air and disappeared down the hole in the middle of the lake.

Mezmer shook Kataton's hand. "Thank you for your assistance, dear. Safe travels to you."

"I. Can. Stay," he said. "To. Help. My. Presters."

"This is hazardous business, what we have to do," Mezmer said.

"I. Am. Not. Afraid."

"I appreciate your bravery but—"

"Mezmer." Pinocchio motioned for her to come over. Lazuli followed, along with Sop and Rion. When they were out of earshot, Pinocchio whispered, "I think we should bring him."

"What? Why?" Rion scowled. "He'll just slow us up."

Pinocchio flashed him a look of annoyance before turning back to Mezmer and Lazuli. "Kataton said he could move quicker when necessary. And considering what we might be facing in the prison, another knight would be useful."

"He's not a knight," Mezmer said.

"But he could be," Pinocchio said. "Besides, I like him. He's . . . calm."

Sop rolled his eye. "If he were any more calm, he'd be dead."

Pinocchio frowned.

"We could be endangering his life to bring him," Lazuli said.

Pinocchio opened his mouth to argue, but she kept on. "*However*, if he understands the dangers and is willing to help, then Pinocchio's right, we can always use another knight. Besides, we might be underestimating Kataton. Give him a chance to prove himself."

The corners of Pinocchio's mouth inched into a smile. Lazuli hoped she wasn't making a big mistake. But Pinocchio felt strongly about Kataton, and she'd learned his instincts about people were usually right.

Mezmer scratched her chin, ignoring Rion's disgruntled puffing. "Very well, darlings. We'll see if he still wants to go once he realizes what's down there."

"I'll talk to him." While Pinocchio hurried over to explain

their mission to Kataton, Wini returned from the lake, shaking wetness from her fur and scales.

"The forest is down there, General, behind the falls. But it's overgrown. We can carry everyone down, but my sisters and I won't be able to accompany you, dense as it is."

Sop laughed. "You're just scared, aren't you? Come on, you've got that horn. Do you know how many monsters you could impale with that thing?"

Wini looked appalled at the suggestion.

"Thank you, Wini," Mezmer said. "Probably best that we leave guards topside anyway."

The kirin pranced back to her sisters.

Lazuli looked up at the sky. "The sun will set soon. Should we wait until the morning?"

"It'll be dark either way down there," Mezmer said. "Besides, we've lost enough time already with this mission."

"Agreed," Rion said.

Lazuli wondered whether she should contact her aunt with the mirror, to let her know they were about to go to the prison. Afterward, she decided. She was already growing nervous and knew her aunt would be able to tell. Best not to worry her.

"Kataton's coming," Pinocchio announced.

Mezmer untied the shields from the kirins and handed them out. "Do we have an extra weapon for him?"

Kataton slowly took out a hand ax from the back of his belt. At Mezmer's look of surprise, he said, "For. Chopping. Beetlebread."

"If you ever offer to bake any of that beetlebread for us," Mezmer said, "be sure to remind me I prefer having teeth." She gave a twirl of her spear. "Wini, anytime you're ready."

12.

The Upended Forest

The kirins shot into the sky. With Kataton hanging on behind him, Pinocchio couldn't stop from grabbing Wini's mane this time. She pitched alarmingly forward as she dove over the circular waterfalls at the center of the lake.

Pinocchio had half a moment of regret, thinking he might have contacted his father through Riggle, just to let him know their plan. But already the blinding light of the desert had given way to near darkness, and Pinocchio was focusing on holding on and getting his eyes to adjust.

Wini flew deep into the cool shadowy falls. Leaves poked through the sheen of water. Pinocchio expected to see a pool in the cavern below, but the water just kept falling into darkness. Where was the forest floor?

Rather than continuing down, Wini leaped through the

watery curtain. On the other side, they emerged in the branches of a dense forest.

"You're letting us off up in the trees?" Pinocchio asked, wiping the water from his face. "Why aren't we going down?"

"Safer that I let you off here, Your Majesty," Wini replied.

Kataton climbed off the kirin's back onto a stout branch. He offered Pinocchio a hand. Pinocchio steadied himself on the heavy bough, peering past his toes to see how far the ground was below. He reeled with shock, realizing why Wini hadn't taken them down.

The branches and twisting trunks tapered to smaller limbs tipped with broad leaves that expanded into a thick canopy. It looked like the tops of the trees were beneath them. How could that be? He glanced up quickly. The tree trunks were rooted into the ceiling of the cave.

The others, catching hold of branches and climbing from the kirins, gasped in astonishment at the upside-down forest.

"If the trees grow from up there," Sop asked, pointing a retractable claw up, "then what's below?"

No one could see. But judging from the way the roar of the falling water disappeared without a splash, the bottom of the cavern—if there even was a bottom—was incomprehensibly far down.

Wini poked her head one last time through the falls. "I'll be waiting, General. Just give a call when you're ready to come out."

"Thank you, dear," Mezmer said. "All right. Let's—" She gasped, doing a double take at Pinocchio. "What are you doing here?"

Pinocchio wasn't sure what Mezmer meant. Could she really have forgotten he was there? But then he felt something tickle his neck.

"That anxious ol' goat Geppetto insisted I keep an eye on Pinocchio."

"Maestro!" Pinocchio couldn't believe it. The cricket leaped from his neck onto his forearm. "Where have you been all this time?"

"Down in your satchel," Maestro grumbled. "And that worm's incessant humming was driving me insane. Doesn't he know how to carry a tune?"

Pinocchio hadn't heard Riggle once since they'd left, but then Riggle was awfully small.

"I . . . I don't need you to keep an eye on me." Pinocchio glanced at the others, feeling his face grow hot, especially at Rion's amused grin.

"I told your father that, but you know how he worries." Maestro flicked his antennae. "Not like you ever listen to my advice anyway. And don't scowl at me like that! I'm not happy to be here either."

Pinocchio knew perfectly well his father had sent Maestro to make sure he didn't use the Pearl, but he couldn't explain that in front of Rion and Kataton. So now he wound up looking like a coddled little child.

Lazuli came to his rescue. "We should get going. Prester Pinocchio, why don't you lead us?"

Pinocchio drew his sword and irritably hacked away some foliage, to get a better view for how to maneuver across this forest. As Wini had said, the forest was dense, with branches from one tree tangled together with the next. Honestly, he had no idea where to go. But now that he was leading, he felt he should do so with a bit of confidence.

"Keep an eye out for the prison," he said over his shoulder.

"The pyramid in Regolith's memory was pretty big. Would be impossible to miss, I think."

Balancing on the branches, Pinocchio had to crouch and duck and clamber, always with one hand holding something, especially as he crossed from one tree to the next.

The others followed, making as little noise as they could, eyes scanning constantly for signs of danger. The aleya threw a faint light from her bubblelike body that helped them see. The sensation of being in this strange, inverted forest was dizzying. As Pinocchio climbed from one branch to another, he had to remind himself that he wasn't the one who was upside down.

"Have you been down here before, Kataton?" Pinocchio whispered.

"Never. Your. Majesty," he replied, moving slowly, but really no slower than the rest given how precarious the journey across the bouncy branches and sloping trunks was.

"What is this?" Mezmer asked. She touched the tip of her spear to a dirty strand draped between two branches.

Pinocchio thought it was a vine, but as Mezmer pulled back her spear, the strand clung to the blade. "It's sticky," she said, giving a sharp pull to free her spear.

Rion poked another strand with his bow. "Like a web."

"I don't like this," Maestro piped anxiously from Pinocchio's shoulder.

"Then you shouldn't have come," Pinocchio mumbled.

"Try not to touch it," Mezmer said. "Keep going, Pinocchio, dear. But weapons ready, everyone."

This became increasingly difficult as Pinocchio found more of the dark webs blocking their path. He sliced through them easily with his sword, but he kept getting his hands and legs caught. It slowed their progress, and Pinocchio was just thinking maybe they should find a different route when something burst through the trees.

A flurry of wings and screeching hit Pinocchio. Startled, he reared back and lost his footing. Before he could stop himself, he was falling, battered against one springy branch and then another, turning end over end. He dropped his sword.

Trying desperately to grab something, anything, he found himself now crashing through leaves. Whatever lay below—or was it above?—the treetops, he doubted it would be soft ground. Then all at once he stopped and found himself dangling in utter darkness. Elastic webs clung to his legs and torso.

"Pinocchio!" Lazuli screamed from above.

"I'm all right," he called back. "At least I think I am."

"I am too," Maestro said, fluttering around his face. "Thanks for your concern."

The luminous aleya swooped down next to him and made a chime of relief. In her light, Pinocchio saw tree limbs and debris broken away by his fall caught in the torn sheets of webs sagging below. And just out of reach, his sword hung in a tangle of strands. Beyond that was nothing but a yawning void. He shivered.

A series of shrill cries sounded from up in the leaf canopy. Then Rion's voice rang out: "Monsters from the prison! We're under attack! Everyone take defensive positions. Prester Lazuli, behind me. Sop—"

"I'll give the orders," Mezmer snarled.

Pinocchio's heart jolted.

There was a swish of arrows. The clunk of swords hitting wood. And more shrieks from the creatures flying about. The aleya trembled next to Pinocchio.

Several creatures burst from the leaves above, flapping around Pinocchio. They were moving so rapidly he could barely tell what they were, but they had far too many wings—certainly more than two. And their gruesome faces were spiderlike with four glistening black eyes and furry fangs.

Maestro squeaked in terror before clawing his way down Pinocchio's shirt.

Pinocchio eyed his sword. If only he could reach it! He grabbed a web connected to the tangle around his sword and began pulling it toward him. The spider-bat monsters—whatever they were—swirled around him furiously.

His sword was almost in his grasp when Pinocchio saw something move in the broken branches caught by the web. It was small, no bigger than his hand, and seemed at first like a mushroom. But then the stem split, becoming a pair of legs and a pair of arms. The creature turned its mushroom cap up to him. It had a tiny face on the gills.

"P-Prester?" it gasped. "Are you the prester?"

Pinocchio couldn't imagine that this tiny creature was one of Diamancer's monsters, but he kept pulling his sword until the hilt was almost in reach.

The mushroom saw this and looked in panic from Pinocchio to the flapping creatures.

"No, Your Majesty, please! Don't hurt them! The arachnobats mean no harm!"

One of Rion's arrows sailed into the darkness. The shouts of Mezmer, Sop, and Lazuli echoed through the forest. A squeal of pain sounded, then another.

Pinocchio realized now that the flying spiders—no, arachnobats—weren't attacking, but simply flying wildly as if in fright. These weren't Diamancer's monsters.

"Mezmer!" Pinocchio bellowed. "Stop! Stop your attack. They're harmless!"

From above came a thump and a grunt followed by a feline hiss. "Hey, ow! What's that about, shorty!"

"Leave the arachnobats alone, you big brutes!" a little voice cried.

There was shouting and then arguing, but moments later Mezmer barked for them to be quiet.

Kataton's reptilian face emerged from the branches above Pinocchio, his tiny eyes swiveling in his protruding lids. "Are. You. All. Right. Your. Majesty?" He reached out a hand.

"Yes, thank you," Pinocchio said, grabbing his sword and then Kataton's hand. The chimera hoisted him up into the branches, out from the sticky strands, and helped him back up to the others.

Pinocchio saw a standoff between his friends and a small mob of mushrooms. The one in the front, who was quite a bit larger than the others—almost knee-high—had his fists raised and was glaring fiercely at Sop.

"Harmless, you say?" Sop spat, rubbing his stomach. "That one head-butted me!"

"You were attacking our herd, you blooming bully!" the mushroom said, black eyes narrowed beneath his red-speckled cap. "Keep it up and I'll rearrange your kneecaps!"

The mushroom that had fallen down with Pinocchio emerged beside him. He seemed older, bent slightly with age, and had a green cap. "Calm down, Goliath. This is our prester."

The mushrooms all looked at once at Pinocchio, eyes bulging. Then they fell to their knees. *"Your Majesty!"*

Pinocchio still felt embarrassed when his people did this.

"Prester Lazuli is here also," he said, gesturing to Lazuli, who was sliding her sword back into her sheath.

The mushrooms drew a breath in unison. *"Your Majesties!"* they exclaimed, bowing again to Lazuli.

"We're sorry the arachnobats frightened you, Your Majesties," the elder mushroom with the green cap said. "I know they can look terrifying."

"They're monsters!" Rion snapped, an arrow still notched in his bow.

The elder mushroom held up his hands. "No, sylph sir, really they aren't. Their webs are for catching the fruits that fall from the forest. I promise they would never have harmed any of you. But I'm afraid it's their appearance that puts them in danger from our fellow Abatonians above."

"Danger?" Lazuli asked.

An arachnobat fluttered around the elder mushroom. He reached out his tiny fingers, scratching the arachnobat's chin. Pinocchio saw now that the flapping creature definitely had more than two wings—eight in fact.

The elder mushroom said, "Centuries back, after Diamancer's Rebellion, any creature in Abaton that looked monstrous was hunted down. Our people had always been herders to the arachnobats, weaving their discarded webs into fabrics. But to preserve the herd, our ancestors moved them down here to the Upended Forest, where they could live safely."

The arachnobat flitted around Pinocchio before disappearing into the trees. The elder mushroom gave a sigh. "They look frightening, but they are not monsters."

Pinocchio smiled. He thought the arachnobats were a bit cute even, once you realized they weren't a threat.

"We owe you an apology, good herders," Mezmer said, making a bow. "I'm General Mezmer, head of the reestablished knights of the Celestial Brigade—"

The brawny mushroom Goliath leaped forward. "The Celestial Brigade! Is that a fact? My great-great-great-great-great-greater-greatest grandmother Stinkhorn the First fought right alongside General Mezmercurian."

"Did she, now?" Mezmer said, looking doubtfully at Goliath. "Well, we're searching for the prison where Prester John housed the rebel monsters. We have reason to believe it is hidden here in the forest."

"Yes," the elder mushroom said. "The pyramid is nearby."

Goliath waved a hand, excitement swelling in his gills. "Hurry-scurry, General! Goliath will show you the way."

With Goliath in the lead and a scampering mushroom mob around their feet, Pinocchio and the others made their way from branch to branch deeper into the forest. Arachnobats flittered by on occasion, and the aleya had nearly gotten to the point where she didn't hide every time she saw one.

"Have you seen any monsters?" Lazuli asked. "Have they been escaping?"

Goliath shook his cap. "Prison's been mum as a tomb, long as our ancestors have been in the Upended Forest."

"But we've only just returned from our annual mustering," the elder mushroom said. "We've been away from this part of the forest for months."

"Ah, here we are, Your Majesties," Goliath called.

Pinocchio saw no signs of a prison. Only more upside-down trees and an increasing number of flittering arachnobats.

"Where's the prison?" he asked.

"Down this one." Goliath patted a stubby hand to an enormous tree trunk.

As Pinocchio looked closer, he saw it wasn't a tree trunk but a thick, ancient tangle of vines that disappeared into the leaves below.

Goliath jumped from his branch and clung to the vines as he disappeared down.

Mezmer put a hand to Rion's shoulder, as he was already heading for the vine. "I'll go first, my good knight."

Rion gave a stiff nod and stood aside.

One by one, they started down. Pinocchio followed Lazuli, with Sop behind them. The huge tangle of vines had shoots jutting out to allow easy holds. Tangles of arachnobat webs had also collected along it, adding a helpful stickiness.

Once through the leaf canopy, Pinocchio saw only the empty, dark void he'd seen when he'd fallen. As the glowing aleya drifted ahead, he could make out where the thick mass of vines was leading. He gave a gasp.

The prison was as he remembered from Regolith's memory—an enormous pyramid of weathered wood. It was suspended over the black abyss by the vines, swinging side to side ever so slightly. It almost looked like one of the decorative lanterns back at the Moonlit Court, but on a massive scale.

Once they reached the top of the pyramid, the knights spread out along the sloped sides, inspecting the structure. Centuries of fallen arachnobat webs coated the surface, making it easier to hold on to, but Pinocchio imagined that one misstep could send any of them tumbling down into the dark chasm below.

"It's bigger than I imagined," Mezmer said, breathing hard as she came back up to meet Pinocchio and Lazuli. "But I don't see any signs that the walls have been breached."

"So how do we get in?" Pinocchio asked.

"Your Majesties," Rion called, a few steps down one side of the pyramid.

The sylph pointed to a square of gold, set into the wood. As they knelt to inspect it, Pinocchio saw that in the center of the square was a handprint, as if someone had pressed their palm into the gold when it was still soft. It was the only part of the prison that didn't look dingy with age.

"What is this?" Rion asked.

"The keyhole to unlock the prison," Lazuli said. "Dr. Nundrum said the prester's hand would open the entrance. Let's see if he was right."

Lazuli cut Pinocchio only the quickest glance before pressing her palm into the impression. He knew what she was thinking. If it didn't work for her, Pinocchio would have to try, even if that meant drawing on the Pearl's powers.

Lazuli's thin fingers didn't quite match the size. But then the sides shrank, fitting to her hand before golden light glowed at the edges. A sharp crack resounded on the pyramid face below them. Pinocchio let out an exhale of relief.

"There's a door," Sop said. He pulled away the webs and grasped the edge of the wood with his claws, tugging it open.

Pinocchio followed Lazuli down to face the doorway. Stairs disappeared into the darkness inside. He tilted his head.

"I don't hear anything," he said.

"Are the prisoners still sleeping, then?" Rion asked.

"Only one way to find out," Lazuli said, stepping forward.

"No," Rion said, taking her by the arm. "I think it best if only Prester Pinocchio, General Mezmer, and I inspect the prison. If all is safe, then—"

She looked down at his hand holding her. "I'm coming," she said, and jerked her arm free.

"Lazuli," Rion said. "Be reasonable."

She narrowed her eyes at him. "I think you forget your place, Rion! I am your prester."

"But, La . . . Prester Lazuli, what if the monsters down there really are a danger?" He scowled. "We wouldn't want to lose both presters. Would you risk Abaton's safety to prove your bravery?"

Lazuli's eyes flashed. But Mezmer stepped forward.

"Rion, darling," Mezmer said. "First of all, you are out of line speaking to your prester this way. Secondly, let me remind you that *I'm* the general of the Celestial Brigade, not you."

She turned to Lazuli, her orange fox eyes softening. "And as head of the Celestial Brigade and the one responsible for the safety of Abaton and her presters, I'll have to insist that you remain up here, dear. I'm afraid Rion's right. It's not prudent for both our presters to head into potential jeopardy."

"What?" Pinocchio snapped. "Lazuli has to go!"

"No," Mezmer said. "She doesn't."

"You command the powers of the Pearl, Prester Pinocchio," Rion said.

To the others, Lazuli's face was a mask of royal serenity. But Pinocchio knew her well enough to see all the little nuanced flitters and flicks of her eyes and lips. In the end, she simply lifted her chin and said, "If you insist, General Mezmer. I defer to your judgment."

"I'll stay with you, Prester Lazuli," Maestro said, leaping from Pinocchio's shoulder to Lazuli's. His decision certainly had more to do with self-preservation than gallantry.

Mezmer turned to the mushroom people. "Will you stay

with Prester Lazuli? Listen out. We'll call if we run into trouble. And if we do, see that Her Majesty reaches the surface safely. We have kirins waiting."

"Of course," the elder mushroom said with a bow of his green cap.

"Kataton—" Mezmer began.

"I'll. Come."

Mezmer gave a sigh. "Very well. Down we go, darlings. Rion, would you lead the way?"

The sylph, who had been scowling a moment before at the reprimands, flashed an eager smile now. He notched an arrow in his bow and stepped through the low doorway.

Pinocchio glanced back at Lazuli before following Rion. He patted the Sands. "See you soon."

She crossed her arms and gave a stiff nod. "Good luck."

13.

Fog and Flame

The interior of the prison was steeped in an unnatural cold.

Following the others down the steps, Pinocchio felt the racing of his heart. A thousand sleeping monsters lay somewhere below. And if they were awakening and attacked, how was he to use the Sands to put them back to sleep? Especially if he wasn't supposed to draw on the Pearl's powers.

At each turn of the stairs, the next flight got a little longer. Pinocchio realized this was due to the prison's pyramid shape. Between Rion's glowing sylph eyes and the aleya's light, Pinocchio saw how the walls had begun to split with age. The stairs beneath their feet creaked ominously.

A sharp crack rang out, and they spun toward the sound.

Goliath rubbed his head, where he'd butted it against the wall. "This place is crumbling to pieces."

Mezmer scowled. "Where did you come from?"

"Me?" The mushroom pointed a stubby finger up. "Well, from the Upended Forest, General. Don't you remember? I'm Goliath."

"Yes, but I thought I asked you and your people to stay with Prester Lazuli!" she grumbled.

"Oh, they're watching over her. You could use my help, you could. No need for a knight like me to have armor—with a head like this one!" He rapped on his mushroom cap.

"You're not one of my knights." Mezmer sighed.

Pinocchio grinned. For someone who'd always dreamed of leading a glorious band of knights, Mezmer seemed to be getting her wish little by little, even if they weren't as glorious as she'd imagined.

"General!" Rion called.

The stairs ahead detached from the walls, jutting out like a rickety, downward bridge over empty darkness. Below, the hollow interior of the prison loomed.

"What's holding those stairs up?" Sop asked, eyeing the precarious path.

"They're connected to the other wall," Rion said. "I'll check to be sure it's stable."

He descended several steps and knelt to examine the structure.

Sop peered into the depths. "How far down do you think the floor is?"

"Far," Mezmer said, "judging from what we saw outside."

"Why don't you go check it out for us?" Sop said to the aleya.

The little creature made a worried chime and flittered back.

"The monsters are sleeping, you cowardly bubble," Sop snarled.

"Looks fine, General," Rion called. He stood and motioned for them to continue after him down the staircase.

"Onward, darlings," Mezmer urged her crew.

Pinocchio followed Rion, but he hadn't taken more than a few steps when he felt the staircase shift ominously. "Wait!" he cried, throwing up a hand.

A loud *pop* sounded beneath his feet, followed by a low groan and the unmistakable sound of the wood beginning to break. Pinocchio only had an instant to react if he was to escape the collapsing staircase. He leaped forward toward Rion, boosted by his seven-league boots. He nearly collided with the sylph, which could have been disastrous if it had sent them over the edge. But Rion caught him, and they tumbled against the stairs.

Pinocchio glanced back in time to see a section of the groaning stairs come loose and plunge into the dark. His heart nearly stopped. Mezmer was still on it.

Something green flashed from the far side of the gap, leaping onto the falling staircase. It snatched Mezmer and bounded with a powerful spring at the last instant before disappearing from Pinocchio's line of sight. Black claws caught on the edge of the staircase before him.

Pinocchio lunged forward. Kataton was dangling one-handed, his other arm wrapped around Mezmer.

"A. Little. Help. Your. Majesty," the lizard groaned.

Pinocchio reached out for Mezmer and tugged, glad at that moment to have his automa strength. Mezmer stepped on Kataton's shoulder and climbed up. Kataton then pulled himself up after.

"Darling," Mezmer gasped, her orange eyes swimming as they took in the sight of Kataton, "that was marvelous."

"I. Told. You. I. Could. Be. Fast," Kataton said. "When. Necessary."

"Yes, the moment was exceedingly necessary." She spun back to the missing section in alarm. "Were any others on it?"

"We're fine, Mez!" Sop bellowed from the far side of the gap with Goliath and the hovering aleya.

Mezmer gave a sigh of relief. She got to her feet and surveyed the distance. There was no way back across.

"Better stay there," she said. "Except for you, our shining aleya. Come over. We'll need your light."

Sop nodded, but Goliath backed up several steps with a determined grimace. "There in a jiffy, General."

By the time Mezmer and Pinocchio had both shouted a united, "Wait!" Goliath had already flung himself headlong across the gap like a mushroom rocket. It was fortunate the stairs he was aiming for were lower than where he'd leaped. It was also fortunate Kataton reacted with another burst of speed, especially since Goliath hadn't judged the distance right. The lizard caught him.

"I ordered you to stay put!" Mezmer snarled as Kataton set Goliath down.

"Sorry, General, not leaving you and His Majesty. Knight's duty and all." He clapped his hands together. "So . . . going down, are we?"

Mezmer gave an irritated tap of her foot, but Pinocchio hadn't missed the twinkle of admiration in her eye at her reckless new recruit.

The aleya drifted forward, and Rion gestured for the others to follow. The stairs soon reached the far wall, where a new expanse zigzagged across the cavity of the prison, weaving back and forth, lower and lower into the dark depths.

Sop was soon lost from sight, but Pinocchio knew his keen eye would be following their progress by the aleya's light. Rion cautiously tested each section, but since he was a sylph, the real measure of its strength came when the others descended. To their relief, the stairs held, although they occasionally creaked worryingly.

Pinocchio kept looking over the edge, but the aleya's light didn't reach the bottom. He listened intently for any sound of monsters—sleeping or not.

His hand brushed against his satchel, and he remembered that Riggle was in there, tucked away in his box. He wondered how the little worm was doing after all of the tumbling in arachnobat webs and leaping across collapsing staircases.

He pulled the box out and whispered to the lid, "Are you all right in there, Riggle?"

A tiny muffled reply sounded. "A bit dizzy, Your Majesty. But managing."

Pinocchio tucked it back away and continued on.

When at last the bottom came into view, it seemed to be filled with a thick fog. Were the monsters sleeping beneath it? They stepped off the final stair. Mezmer waved a hand to part the fog.

The floor was empty. No monsters. No sands. Only a thick layer of dust and the ruins of the broken stairs. Pinocchio couldn't believe it! This wasn't as he'd seen in Regolith's memory. Were they too late?

"Where are they?" Mezmer asked.

"They have to be here!" Rion said. "Spread out and search!" He drew up his bow and disappeared into the fog.

"I'll give the orders," Mezmer snarled, but halfheartedly. She too was so perplexed and desperate to find the sleeping prisoners, she simply added, "Look for them, darlings! And look for an opening. Maybe they broke through somewhere down here."

Pinocchio ran through the fog until he reached a wall. He followed it, tracing a hand across the ancient wood, to the corner and on around the perimeter. The walls were intact, with no signs of any breakout, which added to his worry because he knew they too would have to find a way to escape the prison eventually, especially with the stairs above broken.

He stumbled back toward the middle of the floor to wait for the others, his mind racing with a swirl of questions. If the prison was empty, how had the monsters gotten out? And if the monsters weren't here, where were they? A thousand escaped monsters! Wouldn't they have attacked by now? Abaton would surely be in grave danger. Maybe it already was. Maybe, while they were down here, back at the Moonlit Court—

A black shape swooped out of the gloom and snatched Pinocchio by the shoulders.

He was lifted off the ground. He gave a cry of alarm and had only an instant to spy Mezmer below, turning to him and rearing back with her spear. But whatever had him pulled him up fast.

Pinocchio scrambled to draw his sword and had barely gotten a grip before the creature dove into a tunnel halfway up the wall of the tall chamber. The creature released him, and Pinocchio tumbled end over end. When he landed, the creature pounced once more. Hot breath filled his face and then the thing was off him again. Pinocchio leaped to his feet and twirled around, reaching . . . His scabbard was empty.

He heard his sword clank to the floor. Standing over it was the manticore.

In the narrow tunnel hung with tendrils of illuminated fog,

the manticore looked much bigger than she had at the banquet. Her batlike wings scraped against the ceiling beams. She gave a smile, showing her mouthful of fangs. "Prester Pinocchio," she hissed. "Delivered."

"Very good," a voice whispered behind Pinocchio. "This makes amends for your failure at the banquet."

Pinocchio turned to see a dim square glowing in the fog at the back of the tunnel. A hooded figure stood shadowed against the thin light.

"Who are you?" Pinocchio said. But even as he said it, a shard of fear pressed into the pit of his stomach. "Diamancer!"

He couldn't see the crimson face beneath the hood, but a faint laughter lilted out.

"The others are awake?" Pinocchio asked. "You've found a way out of the prison?"

"Yes, but this is not the prison, Prester Pinocchio. *This* is a trap."

Ice filled his veins. "No."

"Oh, indeed it is. And your knights aren't here to protect you." Diamancer tsked scornfully. "Not that they'd be much good. What a pitiful lot they are."

Pinocchio could hear Mezmer and Kataton and Goliath's voices echoing around the chamber outside, calling his name.

"I don't need them to protect me," Pinocchio said fiercely, casting an eye back at the sword by the manticore's clawed feet.

"But they need *your* protection, Your Majesty. Because if you do not give me what I want, they will perish."

In Pinocchio's mind, he could almost see the monsters surrounding Lazuli outside. He started breathing harder. There was no doubt what Diamancer wanted. The Ancientmost Pearl.

"You can't have it," Pinocchio said.

"Very well." Diamancer lifted a hand. "We'll start with General Mezmer's group."

A blast resounded outside the tunnel. Voices cried in alarm. Falling debris smashed to the floor. Pinocchio charged toward the manticore to get past her, but she swatted him like a monstrous kitten, knocking him back before giving an amused smile.

"Shall we try again?" Diamancer whispered.

Pinocchio lay panting, desperately weighing his options. "I can't give it to you. It's impossible!"

Diamancer started to raise a hand.

"Wait!" Pinocchio shouted. "Even if I wanted to, I can't give you the Pearl. It's . . . it's inside me."

The manticore growled.

"I'm telling the truth!" Pinocchio shouted.

Diamancer tilted his hooded head. "How can the Pearl be *inside* you, Prester?"

Pinocchio hesitated, unsure how—or even whether—to explain this. He had to escape. That was the only option. Even if he had his sword, it would be useless against the hulking manticore and whatever magic Diamancer possessed. If he was going to fight his way out, he had no other choice.

He focused on summoning fire, and his gloved hand began to glow with rising heat.

"He's using the Pearl!" Diamancer shouted.

The manticore pounced, landing on Pinocchio's back, her claws scratching him and her fanged maw opening.

But then a blue light streaked through the tunnel, striking the manticore squarely on her face and bouncing around like an angry hornet.

The aleya!

The manticore leaped back, releasing Pinocchio and swatting at the agitated, tinkling orb.

Pinocchio rolled to one side and snatched his sword. Springing to his feet, he dashed past the manticore down the tunnel. "Come on!" he cried to the aleya.

"Stop him!" Diamancer cried.

As the aleya streaked past, an alarm seemed to go off in Pinocchio's head—although he might flee, Diamancer could still harm the others. Pinocchio spun around and threw out his blazing hand, feeling his legs tingling.

The fire was not the little ball of flame this time. It was as if all his anger and all his fear for his friends had ignited into an inferno. Great sheets of fire rushed down the tunnel. The manticore's eyes widened and she turned.

"Send me back!" she screamed, charging at Diamancer. "Send me back!"

Before she reached him, glass shattered as if the manticore had run into a window. Diamancer disappeared, but his voice cried out unnaturally loud, "Finish destroying the building! Once they're dead, we'll dig the Prester's corpse from the ruins and take the Pearl."

But oddly, the manticore vanished in a plume of fog, much as she had at the banquet. There was no time to wonder. The flames had caught upon the wooden walls and began engulfing the tunnel.

Pinocchio spun around and hurtled through the tunnel, launching out the opening.

He fell.

The aleya spun around him as he plummeted, chiming rapid terrified notes. Pinocchio hit the floor hard, coming down on his hands and knees. It would have broken his bones. A fall that far should have! But the automa wood in his arms and now in his legs had saved him.

"Pinocchio!" a voice shouted.

He rolled over, groaning. Lazuli's face peered down at him.

"What are you doing here?" Pinocchio murmured.

"Rescuing you," she said.

"How . . ." Pinocchio stood, the muscles in his back stiff from the fall. "How did you get down here?"

"I jumped," she said, helping him to his feet. "My landing was a lot lighter than yours."

"Where are—"

"Over here, darling," Mezmer said, emerging from the fog with Kataton and Goliath. "When Sop told Lazuli about the bridge collapsing, she thought we needed help. She arrived just before that other set of stairs came down. Lucky for us."

Pinocchio screwed up his brow, unsure why that was lucky.

"I called up a wind," Lazuli explained.

"We would have been crushed!" Goliath looked at her, amazement sparkling in his tiny eyes. "It was just *wow* and then *whoa*. Incredible, Your Majesty! I had no idea a sylph could summon such a wind!"

Mezmer gave Pinocchio a displeased look. "This is twice now you've run off to fight that manticore without me, darling. Look, I'm the general and I keep missing the glorious combat. It's my job—"

"I didn't run off," Pinocchio began. "That thing grabbed me—"

A sharp crack rang out from somewhere above. Flames bloomed in the upper recesses of the pyramid. Broken timbers began toppling down.

"Watch out!" Mezmer shouted.

While the others hurled themselves to one side, Lazuli threw out her hands. A wind rose, much more powerful than anything he'd seen Lazuli do before. She reached with her hands as if physically taking hold of some invisible ribbon and twisting and shaping the air until she sent the debris crashing to one side.

"How did you do that?" Pinocchio gasped.

She dropped her hands to her knees, gulping deep breaths. "Ever since I became prester . . . I've noticed . . . my powers . . . are getting stronger." But the effort had clearly cost her.

Flames from the tunnel were now lapping along the interior while new flames emerged higher up. The entire pyramid groaned.

"Listen," Pinocchio said to Lazuli. "We can work together. If we both summon wind—"

"No!" Lazuli said, grabbing him by the arm and flinching with worry as her fingers found wood. "You mustn't! I'll handle this. Help Mezmer find a way out."

Already more beams and sections of the staircase were coming down. Taking a deep breath, Lazuli threw out her arms. The wind was like a tornado, pulling up pieces from the floor and hurtling them against the falling debris, before crashing over to the side.

Mezmer grabbed Pinocchio by the wrist, pulling him away. "I don't see how we'll get out."

Goliath jabbed a finger at the wall. "We break our way through."

"With what?" Mezmer gasped.

Goliath made a fierce face. "With me." He smacked a fist against his mushroom cap. "Take me by the arms and legs! Use me like a battering ram."

Pinocchio and Mezmer exchanged shocked expressions.

Only Kataton seemed unbothered by his outlandish suggestion.

"You heard me," the little mushroom said, leaping into Kataton's arms. "Start smashing!"

Mezmer took him by his other arm and leg, and swinging him back, they brought his rock-hard head against the wall. A crack resounded. Pinocchio hoped it was the wall and not Goliath. But the little mushroom only bellowed, "Oh, you call that smashing? Keep it coming! Harder now! That wall is thick. Goliath is thicker!"

As Mezmer and Kataton pounded Goliath against the wall, Pinocchio pried away the broken wood. From the corners of his eyes, he saw the fires growing brighter and smoke rapidly filling the room.

More debris fell. Lazuli threw out her arms, blasting the smoldering timbers away. The pile was growing ominously closer to them.

"How's it coming?" she called.

"I think . . ." Mezmer grunted as she hammered Goliath. ". . . we're getting . . ." They swung him once more. "Through!" Goliath's head punched into the splintered wall.

Pinocchio grabbed the edges of the jagged hole and, with automa strength, wrenched back hunks of broken wood until he opened a hole wide enough for them to climb through.

"Go!" he shouted.

The aleya shot through first. Mezmer snatched Lazuli by the elbow and they scrambled out. A thundering of beams came down. Pinocchio shoved Kataton and Goliath and dove after them, landing on the sloped side of the pyramid's exterior and quickly grabbing the sticky webs to keep from rolling.

Flames had made their way through the walls of the pyramid, dancing against the dark like sinister foes. Clinging to the arachnobat webs, they scrambled up the side, working their way higher and avoiding the maze of crumbing, smoking holes that were forming.

"To the vine!" Mezmer cried. "Hurry, darlings! Kataton, speed is now necessary."

Up at the top, Sop was racing around frantically by the door and screaming their names. Pinocchio hoped the mushroom people and Maestro were safely away. The stupid, faithful cat. He should have gone with them!

When Sop spied them, he wailed, "There you are! Do you realize the prison is on fire?"

"We noticed," Mezmer panted.

The fact that the pyramid was becoming a flaming ruin wasn't their only problem. As Pinocchio looked up, he saw the situation was so much worse.

Flames engulfed the tangle of vines holding up the suspended pyramid. Not only was their only escape back to the Upended Forest blocked, the whole structure was about to break. Once those vines burned through, the pyramid would fall. And they'd be on it.

He had to put out the fire. Holding out his hands, Pinocchio summoned water.

"Don't, Pinocchio!" Lazuli cried.

But they had no choice. His father had said *life or death*. This was life or death. The water curled in sheets like a torrential storm, hissing against the flame. But the vines were snapping rapidly, spraying soggy ash. The pyramid jolted beneath his feet, once and then again, each time dropping lower as the remaining vines screeched under the strain.

"It's going to break!" Goliath howled.

From out of the billowing smoke above, a swarm of

arachnobats descended, circling around them. Pinocchio was about to shoo them back to safety, but then he saw the streams of webs they were ejecting.

"Grab hold of them, Your Majesties!" the elder mushroom's tiny voice sounded from above.

The others took hold of the webs trailing up to the forest.

Pinocchio felt the pyramid give way beneath his feet. Bounding on his seven-league boots, he caught a web, feeling the elastic pull under his weight. Looking down, he watched as the enormous flaming pyramid went crashing into the gloom below.

Dazed, Pinocchio began pulling hand over hand up the sticky web, until he joined the others in the upside-down trees. They all collapsed against the twisted trunks, coughing and heaving for breath. Maestro sprang on Pinocchio's nose, trembling with happiness to see him and at a rare loss for words. The mushroom people gathered around, relief swimming in their little eyes.

"Thank you," Pinocchio gasped to them.

Mezmer peered around at Kataton, Goliath, and the aleya with tears of pride welling. "My dearests, you might not look like knights, but if I had a hundred more like you, the Celestial Brigade would be unstoppable."

Grins spread across their faces. Except for the aleya, who bobbed about brightly.

Lazuli jolted up. "Where's Rion?"

Mezmer's smile faded. "After the explosion and the prison began to collapse, we never saw him again. . . . We . . . Oh, no."

14.

The Superfluous Worm

The mushroom people sent out arachnobats. The aleya shot into the darkness toward the smoldering ruin of the pyramid far below. Even Maestro searched. From the branches, the others all called Rion's name over and over until their voices grew hoarse. But soon the cold truth of the situation settled over them.

Mezmer sank to the branch, her fox face awash in shock. "I can't believe . . . our glorious archer Rion . . ." She made a terrible grimace, so full of pain that Pinocchio couldn't bear to watch her. "I snapped at him. For not following my orders. But all he wanted was to be a brave knight. Why did I have to chastise him for that?"

She covered her face, and Sop put a paw to her back. The cat had a patchwork of singed spots on his fur from the pyramid.

Pinocchio wrapped himself in his arms, bent forward as tears filled his eyes. He didn't know what to do, didn't know what to feel.

Back when he'd been a foolish, curious automa peeking into the graves of Geppetto's wife and son, he'd first learned what death really meant. He'd thought nothing was more horrible than what he'd seen there. But when Prester John died, Pinocchio had decided that sometimes death was not a bad thing. Lazuli's father had lived so long and was ready for his ancient life to come to a close.

But it was different with Rion. Rion was young. He wasn't ready to die. He was the first person Pinocchio had actually known who had lost his life in such a tragic way.

The thought of Rion never living again was too horrible to contemplate. He wanted nothing more than to be back with his father, back in the bright safety of the Moonlit Court with its gentle breezes and sweet-scented gardens. Anywhere but in this gloomy tomb of a cavern.

He wiped his face and looked over at Lazuli. She sat motionless on a branch. Her eyes stared vaguely ahead like she wasn't seeing anything at all. She hadn't shed a tear. Wasn't she upset? Surely she was. But why wasn't she showing it?

"Lazuli?" he whispered, breaking her from her trance.

For the barest instance, her face began to contort, but then she closed her eyes and fixed her expression in that royal mask.

"Your Majesties," Goliath said, "I think I know what caused the explosion inside the prison." He loped over with something cupped in his hands. "On the floor of the chamber, after the first explosion knocked down the stairs, I found these."

They looked like broken-open shells.

"What are they?" Sop asked, picking one up to inspect.

"Thunderfruit seeds," Goliath said. "There are a few of the trees deep in the forest. We have to be careful to avoid them, because if the arachnobats bite the fruit . . . well, *munch*, *crunch*, BAM!" He made a dramatic wave of his hands. "The seeds erupt when broken. Gruesome business. Really quite disgusting."

"I've heard of thunderfruit trees," Lazuli murmured. "There's an orchard in the Mist Cities. I remember my aunt warning me not to pick the fruit."

"She was wise," the mushroom said.

"I only hope Diamancer was still in the pyramid when it came down," Maestro said viciously.

Pinocchio shook his head. "I'm not sure he was even there at all. Diamancer seemed to be behind some sort of glass. At first I thought it was just a protective shield, but when it shattered, he was gone. And the manticore vanished as well. Like she did back at the banquet."

"So they have some means of disappearing," Mezmer said. "Have you heard of this magic, Lazuli?"

She shook her head.

"But it's certainly possible," Maestro chirped. "I've never learned much of the details around Diamancer's ascent to power. But surely he commanded strange magic."

"Whatever happened down there, what's important now is the safety of Abaton," Mezmer said, rousing herself from her grief. "Diamancer and his monsters are free, so Abaton is in grave danger." She got to her feet. "We need to get back to the Moonlit Court, darlings, before—"

"Wait!" Pinocchio said. "Hold on just a moment. Diamancer knew we were coming. It was a trap. But how did he know we'd be *here*?"

Lazuli shook her head. "Maybe he knew we'd seek Regolith and find the memories about the pyramid."

"But that's not how we learned about the Upended Forest," Pinocchio said. "Dr. Nundrum told us about it."

"And turns out, he was wrong," Mezmer said. "This might have been the prison once, but obviously the prisoners were moved at some point in the past to a new prison. It was too dusty. No one had been in there for centuries."

"Or they escaped long ago," Sop said, scratching his face.

"A thousand escaped monsters hiding all this time and Prester John didn't know?" Maestro squeaked. "Not possible!"

"Well, they've obviously escaped now," Sop argued, "and nobody seems to know where they are!"

Maestro fluttered. "But Prester John—"

"Stop!" Pinocchio said. "What I'm trying to say is— whatever's happened with these prisoners escaping—Diamancer knew we'd come here. How did he know? Someone must have told him. Or worse . . . what if Diamancer wanted us to come here and had someone send us into this trap?"

Lazuli frowned. "But Dr. Nundrum was the one who told us. Are you suggesting he's helping Diamancer?"

"Maybe," Pinocchio said. "We don't know."

"Preposterous!" Maestro said. "He's served in the Moonlit Court for ages."

"Who better to convince us to go into this trap," Sop said, whiskers bristling. "Don't you remember how that little flibbertigibbet was so insistent that we *leave immediately for the Upended Forest*!" He did the last part in a mocking version of Dr. Nundrum's flittery speech.

"He was scared of the monsters returning," Maestro said. "He just wanted the matter resolved."

"Or he wanted us to fly blind into a trap," Sop said.

Lazuli shook her head. "I can't believe it would be Dr. Nundrum."

Sop waved his arms around. "Well, Pinocchio's right! For Diamancer to pull this off, he needed someone close to the presters to get us to go to the Upended Forest. If it wasn't that overwrung owl, it was somebody in the Moonlit Court who fed Dr. Nundrum the information about the Upended Forest. Somebody!"

Lazuli looked up with a stony expression. "My aunt said that the other three high nobles wanted Pinocchio and me replaced with a regency council."

"There you go!" Sop said, jabbing a claw. "I always thought that Lord Smoldrin looked devilish. Well, all djinn do a bit, but you know, more devilish than most."

Pinocchio's thoughts went to the banquet, to how the nobles had seemed skeptical of him and Lazuli as the presters. But to help Diamancer? Surely they couldn't have been part of this.

"Until we know, it's all speculation." Mezmer's eyes narrowed. "But I agree, Diamancer can't be acting alone. And really, there's no telling who else could be involved. So . . . well . . . what do we do?"

"Hide," Maestro squeaked. "Somewhere Diamancer won't find us."

"Which would be where, exactly?" Sop asked, tightening his eye patch behind his head.

"My father is at Grootslang Hole," Pinocchio said. "We could go to the gnomes."

"First, we need to find out if Diamancer's monsters have attacked anywhere," Lazuli said. "I'll contact my aunt Sapphira."

"And I'll use Riggle to speak to my father," Pinocchio said.

"I'll make sure the kirins are ready to go," Mezmer said. "We shouldn't stay here any longer than possible, in case Diamancer comes back. For now, he might think Pinocchio is dead. We don't want to be around if he brings more monsters than that manticore."

Mezmer began barking orders at her knights to post watches before she set off toward the falls.

Lazuli took the small mirror from her bag and moved off to a branch to speak to her aunt. Left alone, Pinocchio dug the box containing Riggle out from his satchel. Maestro perched on his shoulder, listening as Pinocchio opened the lid.

"Riggle, I need to speak with you."

The worm's little pink head poked up from the dirt. "Yes, Your Majesty?"

"We're in danger and—"

"I heard! I'm glad you escaped, Your Majesty!"

"You heard?" Pinocchio asked, impressed that the worm could hear that well buried inside his box down in the satchel.

"Yes, everything. And I've already gotten your father's attention. He's here with me. He's quite worried."

"Has he heard any news from the Moonlit Court?" Pinocchio asked. "Is there any word whether Diamancer's monsters have attacked?"

He listened as Riggle repeated his questions, remembering that whatever the worm was saying here, he was also saying to his father in Grootslang.

"Your father says there's no news of any monsters being seen. But he says that he discovered a book that says Prester John moved the prisoners from the pyramid after Mezmercurian's death."

Pinocchio gave a jolt, thinking how in Regolith's memory

174

Mezmercurian had warned Prester John that the Upended Forest was becoming inhabited. Had he listened longer—had he endured more of the awful transformation—would he have known then that the pyramid was no longer the prison? Pinocchio cursed himself, feeling doubly angry because the escape from the pyramid had cost them so much.

"Your father doesn't know where the prison is," Riggle continued, "but he thinks one of the primordials might have been charged with guarding the prisoners."

"Is that all?" Pinocchio asked. Riggle seemed to be listening to something on his father's end. Maestro fluttered impatiently on his shoulder.

The worm said, "No, your father says we can't be sure who lured you to Diamancer in the pyramid. He fears it could be anyone. Whoever it is might be using Diamancer or Diamancer might be using them . . . either way, someone is trying to take the Ancientmost Pearl and usurp the throne. He wants you to find somewhere safe to hide while he finds out more about who is behind this."

"What about Grootslang?" Pinocchio asked. "Should we come there?"

Riggle repeated the question to Geppetto.

"Your father says that while he trusts Chief Muckamire, he might be wrong to do so. For now, he thinks you should be suspicious that anyone could be involved in this plot."

A dagger of fear ran through Pinocchio. He suddenly remembered that Chief Muckamire was the one who had given him Riggle. Could he have kept a part of Riggle as well?

"Riggle," Pinocchio breathed. "Is Chief Muckamire listening to you speak now?"

"Yes, Your Majesty."

Pinocchio felt frozen. "Can I talk to you without anyone else hearing?"

"Whatever you say, only I hear," Riggle answered. "But whatever I say to you, my other selves say it as well."

Pinocchio realized he had to be careful with his words. "Riggle, do you know if Chief Muckamire is involved in this plot against me?"

"I can't—"

"Don't say Chief Muckamire's name!" Pinocchio said. "I don't want him to know that I'm aware he's listening."

The worm nodded and continued again. "I can't be certain, Your Majesty. I am not always in his company."

Pinocchio hoped the word *his* would be interpreted as referring to his father.

"Your father has come to the same conclusion as you, Your Majesty," Riggle added. "He just said so to me. He says we should speak no more now, and that you should not tell him where you are going."

Pinocchio realized why. His father would be desperate to know, but he couldn't risk Chief Muckamire discovering it as well.

"He says to tell you he loves you," Riggle said. "He's put me away, Your Majesty."

"Thank you," Pinocchio said.

He closed the lid over Riggle; icy panic threatened to envelop him. Was his father in danger at Grootslang Hole? Surely the kindly gnome lord wasn't involved in this plot. But hadn't Lazuli warned him that even friends could become enemies? Chief Muckamire, Lord Smoldrin, and Raya Piscus had wanted him and Lazuli off the throne. They'd urged Lady Sapphira to support their plan to form a regency council of the high nobles to rule Abaton.

When Lady Sapphira had refused, maybe the other three high nobles had continued plotting in secret. Maybe they had awoken Diamancer. Maybe they . . .

Pinocchio tried to remember every word Riggle had just said, wondering if there was anything that would have put them in danger.

The only thing that came to mind was that if Diamancer was working with Chief Muckamire to steal the Pearl, then they would now know that Pinocchio had survived the pyramid's collapse. They had to leave immediately.

But as he got to his feet, another concern grew in his mind.

Pinocchio put down Riggle's box gently on the branch and crossed a few limbs to get out of earshot. He could hear Lazuli over a short ways, speaking to her aunt in the mirror.

"Maestro," Pinocchio whispered. "How do we know we can trust Riggle?"

"I was thinking the same thing," the cricket replied. "At any time, he could be passing information from what he's hearing to Chief Muckamire . . . or possibly to any other person who has a piece of Riggle. We can't know how many Riggles there are!"

"Should we leave him here?" Pinocchio asked, looking back at the box.

"What if your father needs to contact you? What if he comes to some danger?"

Pinocchio sighed. He would have to hang on to the worm. "What if we wrap the box in something so he won't be able to hear?"

"It might keep us from hearing Riggle if your father is call-ing for you," Maestro said. "No, I think I have a better idea. I'll stay in your bag. I managed before. And if Riggle is speaking to anyone, I'll know."

Pinocchio nodded. It seemed like the best solution. "Thanks, Maestro."

He climbed back to the branch with the box, and placed it in the satchel with the Sands of Sleep. Maestro looked up at Pinocchio, made a little assuring nod, and then climbed in.

Lazuli was still speaking to her aunt. Pinocchio paced along the tree trunk, eager for her to finish so they could talk. He found Kataton standing nearby.

Surprised, he asked hurriedly, "What are you doing here?"

"Standing. Guard," Kataton said with a roll of his eyes. "Over. You. And. Prester. Lazuli."

Pinocchio smiled weakly. Riggle's conversation had shaken him. It had sown seeds of such uncertainty about who to trust. But surely he could trust Kataton. He was a true knight—as loyal and good as any hero who had ever served in the Celestial Brigade.

"Kataton," Pinocchio said. "When you rescued General Mezmer, you were so incredibly fast, faster than I've seen anyone move. How did you do that?"

"I. Have. Always. Been. Told. I. Am. Slow," he said. "Others. Made. Fun. Of. Me." Kataton shifted his stance, the reptilian frills on the sides of his face expanding. "But. I. Do. Not. Think. Of. Myself. As. Slow." He tapped a claw to the side of his head. "If. You. Believe. In. Here. That. You. Are. A. Certain. Way." He smiled. "Then. You. Will. Be."

Pinocchio rubbed a hand along his arm, feeling the wood beneath his shirt. He wished Kataton was right. He wished it was that simple.

"Pinocchio," Lazuli said behind him.

He took hold of a branch and climbed over to meet her, out of earshot from Kataton. He quickly told her about what had happened with his father and Riggle, about the concern that Chief Muckamire or the other Noble Houses could possibly be involved in this plot.

Lazuli listened with that same stony gaze. She nodded as he spoke, but her eyes looked distant and unblinking. When he finished, she said nothing, simply stared ashen-faced into Pinocchio's eyes, but it was as if she wasn't seeing him.

"Are you all right?" he asked. He'd never seen her like this.

Her eyes flicked to Kataton. Then she said in the barest whisper, "I don't know what to do."

"Me either," Pinocchio said.

"But . . ." Her lips trembled momentarily before she brought her face back nearly to perfect composure. "I'm supposed to."

"No one expects that!" Pinocchio said.

"My father did. When I put the Pearl back inside you down in the Deep One, after I brought you back to life, he told me it would be up to me to keep Abaton safe. To help you rule. But that while you were to protect the Pearl, I was his daughter, Abatonian royalty, the one he expected to look after Abaton."

Her face seemed on the verge of shattering into a thousand pieces.

"Rion . . ." she said. "He wanted to be my friend. You make friends so easily, Pinocchio, but I never knew whether I should. I was his prester. I've always been told I should . . ." She put a hand over her eyes. "He's dead and he died trying to protect us and Abaton. I never should have let him die."

"You didn't know where he was!" Pinocchio said. "It was chaos down there—"

"But I'm the prester! I'm the one who is supposed to protect my people! But these monsters keep coming and we've no idea how to stop them and we've lost . . ."

For a moment, Pinocchio thought she might at last allow herself to cry. But then her eyes danced off Kataton, and she drew in a shuddering breath before looking back at Pinocchio.

"I can't lose any more," she said.

Lazuli had lost her father. Their friend Rion. Now Abaton itself seemed dangerously on the verge of being lost.

Her lips trembled. "Promise you won't let that happen? Promise I won't lose you too."

How could she ask him to promise that? Not when the safety of Abaton might depend on his using the Pearl. Not when she knew he'd made a promise to Wiq that he hadn't been able to keep.

But the look of pain and desperation straining against her face brought a lump into his throat.

It was all so infuriating. Why was the Pearl affecting him in this way? It didn't seem like it should, from all his father told him about Prester John and how he contained the magic of Abaton inside the Pearl. Why couldn't he just command it the way Prester John had?

But he couldn't. And Lazuli knew he couldn't. But she clearly needed some reassurance that her whole world wouldn't be swept away.

"We'll find another way to stop Diamancer," he said.

She smiled a shaky smile that faded nearly as soon as it formed. "I need my aunt," she said. "I . . . we need to go to her in the Mist Cities."

Pinocchio hesitated before asking, "Do we know we can trust her?"

"The other High Nobles and Dr. Nundrum might have turned against us. Who knows if they're helping Diamancer? We don't know who's against us and who's not!" Lazuli narrowed her eyes. "But if there is anyone I trust in Abaton, it is my aunt. She's only ever wanted the best for me, even before I was prester. She'll know what we should do."

Pinocchio gave a nod. Then he said, "Lazuli?"

"What is it?"

He wasn't sure what he wanted to ask. He was thinking how Lazuli had warned him that sometimes friends could become enemies. And he would never have suspected before that Dr. Nundrum or Chief Muckamire or even Riggle could be his enemy. But now he wasn't sure.

But what if *he* was really their enemy? What if the ones they'd been suspecting hadn't done anything wrong, but he was the one doing something bad—by keeping his secret from the people of Abaton, for withholding what the Pearl was doing to him even though that was putting them all in danger.

"How do you know whether someone is a good person or a bad person?" he asked.

Lazuli tilted her head, searching his face. She didn't look like she had an answer, and already Kataton was coming their way across a branch.

"General. Mezmer. Is. Ready. Your. Majesties," he said.

Lazuli brought her chin up confidently. Pinocchio was amazed at how quickly she transitioned. Amazed and a bit sad.

"Lead the way," she said.

They followed Kataton, scrambling along the wild tangle of branches through the Upended Forest until the three of them reached the others waiting at the falls. The kirins were poking their horned heads through the curtain of water.

The mushroom people had gathered, not only to see off their presters but also Goliath, who was officially joining the Celestial Brigade. The fierce little mushroom pumped a fist in the air before leaping onto Pini. Pinocchio and Lazuli said their good-byes, offered their thanks, and climbed onto the kirins, along with the others.

Back above, the desert was washed a dim purple with the approach of dawn. Pinocchio looked around at the empty lakeshore. "Where's Quila?" he asked Wini.

"She disappeared sometime in the night, Your Majesty," the kirin said.

Pinocchio wondered what had become of the poor griffin but was too exhausted to think any more about it. He hoped there was a way to sleep while Wini flew. Kataton would hold him on.

Mezmer rode on Fini's back with Lazuli. She pulled out the map. "So where do we go, dearests?"

"To the Mist Cities," Lazuli said, laying her weary head between Mezmer's shoulder blades.

The aleya raced ahead. Pini, with Sop and Goliath on her back, came into formation beside her sisters. Kicking their hooves, the kirins rose into the star-strewn sky and left the Upended Forest.

15.

The Mist Cities

By afternoon, the Caldera Desert had given way to jagged, snowcapped mountains. This range, according to Lazuli, was inhabited by few creatures except clans of yetis, a race of giants composed of living snow. Pinocchio peered down from Wini as they passed over range after range. He spotted what at first seemed like a snow-crowned peak until black eyes blinked up at him from a massive frosty face.

"He's huge!" Pinocchio said. "Couldn't we ask them to join our army?"

"Yetis are incredibly slow," Lazuli said. "They move at literally a glacial pace. Besides, if they came down off these mountains, they'd melt."

Pinocchio waved at the yeti. By the time it waved back, it was a mere speck on the distant mountain.

The mountains rose higher and higher, almost like an enormous flight of spiky stairs. The group was shivering with the cold—all except Lazuli—as their kirins soared upward. Frost crackled across Wini's scales.

Soon the tops of the mountains seemed to have broken loose, scattered like dandelion pods and hovering in the sky. The ground below came to an end. What lay beneath the floating islands was a steep mass of fog, looming like a fortress and blocking from view whatever was underneath.

"The Mist," Lazuli called to the others. "We must keep above it. They say if you fly into the Mist, you'll never fly out."

Pinocchio leaned forward against Wini as the kirin rose sharply. The Mist looked denser than any cloud he'd ever seen. It almost appeared solid, except for little whipping tendrils at the edges. Although the wind barely blew where they were flying, the interior of the Mist seemed to contain a ferocious storm, swirling like a massive leaden cyclone.

"How far until we reach the Mist Cities?" Mezmer asked.

"There!" Lazuli pointed.

Beyond the barren airborne islands and above the Mist, tiny specks took shape in the crystal-blue sky. As they drew closer, the specks grew into a series of shimmering cities. There were a dozen or more in total, and each of the cities rested on floating slabs of rock. Pinocchio couldn't believe what he was seeing. The cities were like perfect jewels with their lacy towers and onion domes of turquoise and quartz. And each was connected to the others by narrow, elaborately carved bridges.

Kataton swiveled his eyes in wonder. Goliath gasped, "Sweet mother of mushrooms! They live up here?"

The kirins banked side to side as they passed one city after another. Curious faces watched from windows, balconies, and along the many bustling avenues. Children playing, mothers carrying babies, elderly couples walking arm in arm, merchants and vendors, whether humbly dressed or in brocaded silk tunics, all stopped what they were doing to gaze at the trio of kirins passing by.

"Which city are we going to?" Pinocchio asked.

"The last one," Lazuli replied. "My aunt's Opaque Palace is there."

The Opaque Palace was not connected to the rest by any bridges. It was far more majestic than the others, the sides of the city crisscrossed with broad avenues leading up to a domed palace of the palest blue marble. Lady Sapphira was waiting for them in a sunlit courtyard at the foot of the palace, along with a great crowd of finely dressed sylphs.

Wini, Pini, and Fini circled the palace dome before landing in the courtyard.

Lady Sapphira curtsied as footmen helped them down from the kirins. "Your Majesties, welcome to the Mist Cities."

Lazuli looked for a moment like she might throw herself into her aunt's arms, the relief so heavy on her face. But she composed herself and took her aunt by the hands, accepting a kiss on her cheek.

Sapphira scanned the party with an amused smirk and turned to Mezmer. "I see the Celestial Brigade has gained recruits, General."

Mezmer stiffened. "And lost the finest among our numbers, my lady."

"Yes, Prester Lazuli told me. My condolences. But you'll be pleased with what I have to show you."

Sapphira waved to the palace steps. The sylph nobles who had gathered in the courtyard to greet the presters parted. Pinocchio's eyes widened. Row upon row of the uniformed sylphs stood at attention. They wore polished armor and each held a long bow of white wood. Quivers of perfect arrows hung at their belts.

Lazuli had said her aunt had been preparing defenses, but Pinocchio had never imagined this.

"These are real soldiers," Mezmer said breathlessly.

"I have dubbed them my Sky Hunters," Sapphira said with a proud tilt of her head. "My people have long excelled at the sport of archery. I selected the best for you, Your Majesties. The bravest. The strongest. They will help defend the Moonlit Court."

Pinocchio thought with longing how these archers could also help to rescue Wiq and the others in Venice, if only Lady Sapphira and the nobles could be persuaded.

Mezmer couldn't stop herself from hurrying toward the Sky Hunters, eyeing each one up and down with unabashed admiration.

"Lady Sapphira," Pinocchio said. "We can't thank you enough."

"Of course, Your Majesty," she said. "But they are not the only reason I invited you to the Mist Cities." Sapphira bundled Lazuli's arm in hers and started up the palace steps.

"What is it, Aunt?"

"Come. We must first—"

A shadow passed over them. Sapphira shielded her eyes to look up when one of the Sky Hunters cried out, pointing to the dome of the palace. "Wyvern!"

Perched atop the peak was a long, sinuous dragonlike creature, glossy green-black like a beetle. The wyvern clung to the marble with two muscular hind legs. Its forearms were leathery bat wings, tipped with curling claws. The wyvern swung its barbed serpentine head side to side before locking eyes on Pinocchio and Lazuli. It emitted a piercing shriek.

Mezmer and Sop launched themselves at once in front of the presters and Lady Sapphira, weapons out. The lieutenant of the Sky Hunters began barking commands, and the archers fired a volley of arrows. The wyvern kicked off from the dome, disappearing behind the palace, as the arrows clanked harmlessly against the marble.

The courtyard erupted in screaming panic, the crowd of sylph nobles running in every direction. The aleya spun circles around the cowering kirins. Even Kataton and Goliath looked uncharacteristically anxious. Only Sapphira's archers remained calm.

"Where did it go?" Pinocchio asked, scanning the skies.

All too abruptly, the answer came. The wyvern wasn't alone.

Rising up on flapping wings from every side of the floating island, hordes of monsters appeared. Some were wyverns, others Pinocchio recognized from his father's book as drakes and nagas, but most were monsters he knew no name for—spirits of ash and flame, demonic flying nightmares, ghoulish riders mounted on enormous bats or skeletal birds. He searched the skies for Diamancer among them.

All the air seemed sucked from Pinocchio's lungs. The monster threat—when it had been the lone manticore rampaging in the gardens at the banquet or even a dozen attacking remote villages—might have been stopped with a decent troop of knights. But as he saw the multitude of monsters darkening the skies all around them, he realized the danger was beyond anything he'd feared, beyond what their inexperienced Celestial Brigade could handle.

But what about Lady Sapphira's Sky Hunters?

"Defend the presters!" Mezmer shouted to her knights.

The ragtag warriors pulled the shields from the sides of the kirins and formed a circle around Pinocchio, Lazuli, and Sapphira.

The monstrous horde attacked. Dark forms streaked across the courtyard. Drakes sprayed fire, and wyverns smashed the heavy tips of their tails against the palace walls as if the aim was not just to kill them, but to destroy the entire city. The sylph archers spread out into strategic formations, firing arrows at the darting attackers.

"Now's the time, dewdrops!" Sop shouted at the kirins. "We need those horns."

The kirins looked from one another to the monsters. But then Wini narrowed her eyes and said, "For the presters!"

The other two shook their manes and clopped their hooves. "For the presters!" They shot into the sky screaming, "SURRENDER, FOES, OR PREPARE TO BE IMPALED!"

Pinocchio lifted his eyebrows in surprise. Who knew they had that kind of ferocity inside them? Certainly not Sop, who watched with a great grin speading across his face.

Pinocchio and Lazuli locked shields with Mezmer, Sop, and Kataton until they formed a domed turtle shell against the monsters' assault. Goliath poked his rock-hard head into a gap. Pinocchio's first impulse was to get out and fight, but whenever he tried to rise, Sop pulled him back.

"Stay down!" the cat hissed, taking a blow to his shield that buckled his knees.

The quarters were so tight, Pinocchio couldn't even draw his sword or reach the Sands of Sleep in his bag. From the shadows of the shield dome, he could hear masonry cracking on the palace walls, screaming voices from the panicked nobles, the *whizz* and *thunk* of the Sky Hunters' arrows, and sinister peals of laughter from the monsters swooping overhead as if it were all a happy game.

"Prester Pinocchio," Sapphira screamed. "You have the Pearl. Protect us!"

Pinocchio's eyes met Lazuli's. He saw the uncertainty and fear welling in them. "Not yet," she whispered.

"Then when?" he said.

"Prester Pinocchio!" Sapphira cried.

"No." Lazuli's eyes glowed. Then she shouted, "Mezmer, get us into the palace."

"All right, darlings. Hold formation. Shields together as we move up the stairs."

Pinocchio wrestled with what to do, terrified at using the Pearl and terrified at what might happen if he didn't.

"One step at a time, darlings," Mezmer ordered. "No gaps. Keep those shields tight."

In an awkward cluster, they inched up the steps. Sapphira hunched beside Pinocchio, squeezing Lazuli's hand and trying to peer through the cluster of shields covering them.

One of the monsters gave a high-pitched shriek: "The presters! Stop the presters!"

The shields were pounded with heavy thumps and the shrill scrapes of claws.

"Keep going!" Mezmer barked.

But then bright light blazed as a section of the shields was torn away. The formation fell apart. Mezmer rushed forward to jab her spear at a drake trying to slash Lazuli with its claws. Kataton, Goliath, and Sop fought back the monsters coming in low, while the kirins dove and jabbed and kicked at the ones in the air. The sylph archers unleashed arrow after arrow. Pinocchio slashed with his sword while Lazuli held her shield over her terrified aunt.

An explosion sounded overhead. Pinocchio had an instant to look up as several wyverns battered full force against the palace walls. Crumbling marble rained down in blocks of heavy stone.

"Watch out!" Pinocchio cried.

Kataton, swinging his ax in the thick of battle, hadn't seen the falling rocks. His lightning speed wouldn't save them now. Neither would the kirins or any of the others. And Lazuli was caught in her frightened aunt's clutches.

Pinocchio threw down his shield and flung out his hands, knowing it would take more than mere wind to stop the weight of all that stone coming down.

What he summoned was as if several elemental forces had fused together. It gushed from his fingertips like water and wind, and solidified in a protective dome like translucent lava. The falling rock met it explosively, pieces breaking and tumbling from the side, striking the palace doors.

Pinocchio released the magical shield. Already he felt the wood creeping across his shoulders and up his chest. He grew dazed, his head filling with that awful, familiar fog.

He'd saved Lazuli and Sapphira from being crushed, but now the doors to the palace were blocked by the boulders.

The monsters that had seen what he'd done stared in amazement, but only momentarily. As their eyes fell on the presters, they gathered for a final assault.

Lazuli tore herself from her aunt and leaped to Pinocchio's side, drawing her sword from her belt. "We have to protect my aunt! We fight, but not with the Pearl. Do you understand?"

He shook his head. There was no way they could fight off this many monsters without it.

Lazuli's lip quivered. "You promised me, Pinocchio."

"I know and I'm sorry," he said. "But we both know what I have to do."

She was about to argue, but he said fiercely, "Listen! When I'm done . . . when I'm an automa again, take the Pearl from my chest. You can use it. You can save the others."

"No!" she cried. "I can't—"

But the monsters were already descending. Lazuli, as if to prove to him that they could fight off the horde, launched forward, swinging her sword at the swooping, shrieking beasts.

She fought desperately, ferociously, and Pinocchio knew she was fighting for him as much as for Abaton. But it was not going to be enough. He couldn't worry about broken promises or the pain his choice would cause. He had to act. He had to act now.

Pinocchio raised his hands. White-hot fire plumed from them. The closest monsters were blasted aside and others coming down banked to escape the inferno.

Pinocchio felt the wood growing, consuming his skin, encasing his chest, creeping up his neck and into his face. His thoughts were growing dimmer, like pools of shadow seeping in from the edges of his mind.

He saw Mezmer mercilessly battling with her spear. And over there, Sop was back-to-cap with Goliath. Kataton's arms moved with blurred speed, although his face remained absolutely placid. Wini and her sisters were screeching war cries and charging through the air at the darting monsters, horns lowered. Even the aleya was dashing about, popping up in the faces of bats and wyverns, trying to blind them.

None of the knights were cowering in fear. In those final moments, he had to admire how bravely they were fighting—just as Mezmer had always hoped. But even with all the sylph archers volleying their arrows, the battle was hopeless. The monsters were too numerous.

Pinocchio staggered back a step, the flames that had been pouring from his hands dissipating into smoke. He was no longer a boy. He was an automa. And any second now, the last of his thoughts would sift away like grains of sand in the wind.

He collapsed, wood clattering against stone. He reached for his shirt and tore it effortlessly with his wooden hands. His fingers fumbled against the latch on his chest. Once he opened it, Lazuli would be able to take the Pearl. It would be hers to use.

He hesitated, thoughts clinging desperately to the traces of his mind. He had wanted so many things that now he would never have. He wanted to swim in the glass-green lagoon and see the undines' city below. He wished he had plucked a wild spice-berry out in the deepest heart of the jungle. He wished he could have had years and years and many happy years in the Moonlit Court with his father. With Wiq. With Lazuli.

Lazuli . . . He rolled his head to one side, searching for her in the mayhem.

How he hated leaving Lazuli. She had lost so much. Her mother and her father. Her friend Rion. Now she would lose him. And he would be lost to her.

But the Pearl would be in better hands. That was all that mattered. If anyone could save Abaton, it would be Lazuli.

He opened the latch on his chest, felt the smooth surface of the Ancientmost Pearl inside. Lazuli had to take it. Where was she?

In the blur of his fading vision, he found Lazuli collapsed on the ground beside him, her eyes fluttering, then closing. A trickle of blood came down from her hair. Had she been struck? Injured by one of the monsters?

Lady Sapphira knelt beside Lazuli, pulling her cape around protectively. Then she gazed at Pinocchio. Her eyes met his, glowing with surprise at what she saw.

She threw her cape out and it expanded, the fabric swirling into Mist, encompassing Pinocchio. Everything went dark.

Lady Sapphira materialized in the darkness of her chambers, deep below the palace. The enchanted cape settled back into form across her shoulders. Heavy curtains were drawn over the windows, but she could still hear the muffled sounds of battle above.

She waved a shaking hand. A candelabrum illuminated with a flickering violet light. She took a deep breath, steadying her racing heart.

Her niece lay unconscious on the floor. Sapphira stepped past her and circled around the wooden boy beside Lazuli. Wooden lids were closed over his eyes. She'd heard what he'd said to Lazuli, although she could hardly believe it, could hardly believe what she was now seeing.

Prester Pinocchio was no human boy. He was an automa. An alchemy contraption. A vile mockery of gears and wood assembled into the shape of a boy.

Sapphira narrowed her eyes. Lazuli must have known what he was—what *it* was. And yet, her niece had hidden this truth from her.

The panel in the automa's chest was empty, and for half a moment, Sapphira felt panic. Had one of the monsters—but no, she saw the wooden boy's hand at his side. She saw what was still clutched in it. A globe of inky black.

The Ancientmost Pearl.

She pulled it from the stiff fingers. The wooden boy didn't move.

A tentative knock sounded at the door.

With a sweep of her long cape, she marched over and opened it. The captain of her guard stood in the doorway.

"I've come as you requested—" His eyes fell on the Ancientmost Pearl in her hands. "Your Ladyship, wh-what do you have?"

"The Pearl," she said. "It is safe. And see what we have saved it from."

She stepped aside to reveal the lifeless automa lying on the floor.

"Is that . . . ?" The captain's eyes glowed. "That can't be! He's . . ."

"Our prester is an automa," Sapphira said. "Abaton has been deceived."

"But . . . but . . ." The captain turned from Pinocchio to Lazuli. "Your niece?"

"I'm afraid she has been a part of this deception, Captain."

The captain frowned. "You feared something was amiss with the boy. But . . . this! We never imagined this!"

Sapphira nodded. "No, we didn't."

The captain knelt next to Lazuli. "What happened to her?"

"She took a blow to her head in the battle. She's unconscious. Put her in the bed."

As the captain lifted Lazuli from the floor, Sapphira took out a small bottle from a cabinet. Lazuli would be upset when she woke. Upset to learn that her secret was now revealed. Sapphira set the potion on the table by the bed. It would help calm her niece during the difficult discussion they were going to have.

"Your Ladyship," the captain said, giving Pinocchio a look of disgust. "And what of the automa?"

Sapphira walked over to where the wooden boy lay on the

floor. It still resembled the prester in many ways, although what had once been smooth skin now showed the grain of wood. His hair was chiseled to look like curly locks. Seams showed at his neck, wrists, and knuckles where the mechanisms inside allowed him to move. *Would* have allowed him to move. This automa would not move again. Not without the Pearl or whatever the alchemists put inside these contraptions to animate them.

The automa that had once disguised itself as a human boy, that had fooled them all into believing it was their prester, was finished.

"That," Sapphira said in a near whisper, "does not belong here. Get rid of it."

"As you wish."

The captain pulled the sword from Pinocchio's belt and let it clatter to the floor. He slipped the satchel off Pinocchio's shoulders. Grabbing the wooden boy by the ankles, he dragged its body across the room and drew back the curtain. After opening the window, the sylph grunted as he hoisted Pinocchio over his shoulder.

Sapphira watched as her young captain leaned over the ledge and dropped the lifeless automa into the swirling Mist below.

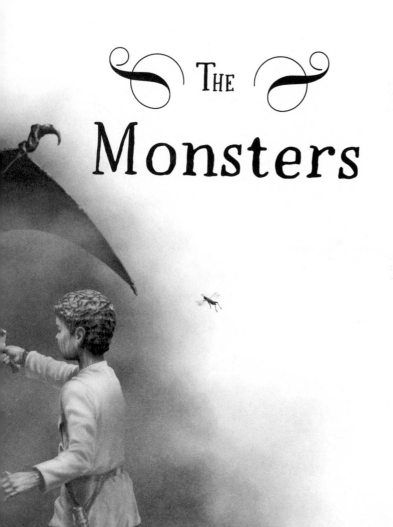

PART THREE

The Monsters

16.

The Traitor

Lazuli woke to a ribbon of moonlight curling across her face. She felt so groggy she nearly fell back asleep. But then she was startled by a flood of memories: the monsters attacking the palace, Pinocchio fighting them and turning back into an automa, and then the blow to her head—the last thing she remembered.

She sat up, rubbing the knot behind her ear. It was tender to the touch, and her head throbbed. She was so sleepy as well, unnaturally so. She reached out in the dark, feeling around to discern where she was. She touched an empty glass vial on the table by her bed.

"A sleeping potion," a voice said. "You were hurt and needed to rest."

A candelabrum glowed to life, casting a faint violet color

around the room. A shadow stood before the light, turning to face Lazuli.

"Aunt Sapphira," Lazuli breathed. "Where am I?"

"Safe in my palace," Sapphira said, still standing in front of the candelabrum so it silhouetted her. "Or what is left of my palace after the attack."

"The monsters . . . ?"

"Driven back by my Sky Hunters. For now."

Lazuli felt the briefest wash of relief, but then another jolt of fear arrived. "And Prester Pinocchio?"

"Yes, Prester Pinocchio," Sapphira said softly. "We need to discuss Prester Pinocchio."

"Is he alive? What about Mezmer and Sop and my knights?"

"Slow down, my dearest niece."

Lazuli hated when her aunt spoke to her like this, like she was a child.

"Let us first address Pinocchio." Sapphira had her hands laced behind her back as she made her way to the foot of the bed, the violet light flickering across her face. Her expression was calm and lovely, as always, but Lazuli knew her aunt well enough to recognize anger masked behind those pleasant features.

"You have been keeping secrets from me, Lazuli."

"What do you mean?" She didn't feel awake enough to tackle whatever her aunt was accusing her of and struggled to rouse her brain.

"You did not tell me our prester was no mere human boy. You have allowed him to deceive us. All this time his new subjects thought him the son of Geppetto, thought him a human child of Venice. But he is not, now, is he?"

"I don't know what you're suggesting."

"I *suggest* nothing!" Sapphira snapped. "I know. I saw him

with my own eyes. He is some sinister wooden contraption built by the Venetian alchemist to pose as our ruler and protector!"

Lazuli's heart was racing, pumping dread into her every pore. "What have you done with him?"

"Have I not always looked out for you, my niece and prester?" Sapphira said. "I could not have your subjects see what he was. I have spared you the awkwardness of having to clean up the mess you made."

"Where is he?" Lazuli shouted. She leaped out of the bed but immediately found the world spinning. She toppled onto the mattress.

"Rest, my dearest," Sapphira said, coming around to pull back the covers.

But Lazuli had no wish to be treated like a sick little girl. She needed to see Pinocchio. Poor Pinocchio, wherever her aunt had locked him up, he was probably back to being a thoughtless automa. But if she could only get to him, maybe she could help him remember. He would turn back to his true self, as he had after the Deep One.

"My father . . . he knew what Pinocchio was," Lazuli said, drawing sharp breaths through her nose, wishing they would clear the dizziness. "He saw what made Pinocchio special. He gave his blessings for Pinocchio to keep the Ancientmost Pearl. He accepted him—and me—as the new presters."

"But your subjects have not accepted you, child," Sapphira said wearily. "As much as I tried to persuade them. Even when they thought Pinocchio just a Venetian boy, there were those who feared children could not handle the responsibility."

"But my father—"

"His Great Lordship could not have predicted what difficulties Abaton would face. The return of these monsters. The threat of Diamancer. Had he known this, he would have placed a more experienced ruler on the throne." Sapphira sighed. "I had hoped under my guidance that you would be capable, despite your inexperience." A flash of anger illuminated the lady's eyes. "But *you* . . . you kept secrets from me! You didn't trust me."

"It wasn't that I didn't trust you," Lazuli said. "Truly it wasn't, Aunt. I feared you wouldn't understand about Pinocchio."

Sapphira scowled. "What was there to understand? It was an automa!"

"Pinocchio is my friend!"

Sapphira's lips tightened. "Your father was too great to bother with trivialities like friendships. I have none as well. A great ruler has more important responsibilities. You let down your kingdom, Lazuli. More so, you have betrayed us. You must decide what you will do now."

"What do you mean?" she asked.

"Your people need the responsibility and safety of our homeland entrusted to a ruler who can lead them, someone who can handle Diamancer and his monsters, someone our people will rally behind."

Lazuli knew who her aunt meant. And she had always believed Sapphira would make the best prester. But Lazuli's concern for Pinocchio was coursing through her with white-hot ferocity. What had her aunt done with him?

"You can't be the prester," Lazuli said. "You don't have the Ancientmost Pearl. Pinocchio does, and wherever you've got him, the Pearl will turn him back—"

Sapphira brought her hand from behind her back. The Ancientmost Pearl lay cupped in her palm.

Lazuli's heart felt like it had stopped. The Pearl was not in

Pinocchio! Her aunt had taken it from him. But that would mean . . .

"Where is Pinocchio? Tell me!"

"Without this," Sapphira said, lifting the Ancientmost Pearl, "that deceiver could no longer function. There was no need to distress you with the sight of what it became. It's gone. And the Pearl is back where it rightfully belongs. With a true Abatonian."

Lazuli couldn't breathe. It was as if she'd been punched in the chest. Grief and shock welled into anger. She tangled the sheets in her furious grip. Tears scalded her eyes, but she fought to keep from crying in front of her aunt. She would never give her the satisfaction of proving to be the weak, sobbing little girl.

But . . . Pinocchio! How could her aunt have done this to Pinocchio?

"Don't pout over broken toys, child," Sapphira chided. "You are Abatonian royalty. And there is still hope that you can be the one to help me rule. Maybe one day, when you are ready. But now our homeland is in danger from these monsters. I fear the Moonlit Court will be attacked next, and I am readying my archers to fly to our capital and defend our people."

"The warden . . ." Lazuli said.

"What about the warden?" Sapphira asked.

"Why isn't the warden able to keep the prisoners from escaping?" Lazuli asked. "Maybe the warden is freeing them on purpose! And the prison . . . Master Geppetto believes one of the primordials is guarding—"

"Dear, dear, child." Her aunt shook her head. "You are focusing on the wrong things. Abaton is in danger! What is most essential is to protect our people from the imminent threat of these monsters. And this time, my Sky Hunters won't simply drive them back. No! The monsters will not escape. We will destroy every one of Diamancer's rebels and be done with this threat."

"You mean to kill them?" Lazuli whispered.

"They are monsters. For the sake of Abaton, they do not deserve our mercy." Her aunt reached out a hand. "Will you come with me, my niece? Will you renounce your claim on the throne and declare to your people that I should be the new prester?"

"You cannot be the prester," Lazuli said.

"I do this not for my own glory, but for Abaton. I have the Pearl. I can stop these creatures."

"But, Aunt," Lazuli said. "Don't you remember why my father refused to execute Diamancer and his monsters?"

Sapphira narrowed her eyes impatiently.

Lazuli said, "Diamancer and his monsters might have rebelled, but they were still his subjects, still children of Abaton. My father imprisoned them rather than killing his people. A real prester—a true prester—would never kill her own subjects. It would be a betrayal of all that Abaton is."

Sapphira frowned. "You have a kind heart, Lazuli. A sentimental heart. It is why you will never be a true prester."

The words stung as painfully as a poisoned thorn. But Lazuli knew her aunt was probably right. She had no wish to be the sort of prester Lady Sapphira wanted her to be. Nor the sort of prester her father had been—remote, friendless. But she had thought—hoped—she and Pinocchio could have been respected rulers.

"I ask again," Sapphira said. "Declare me prester so that I might protect Abaton. Do this and your mistakes will be forgiven."

Lazuli fought against the images of Pinocchio rising in her mind. Not as a blank-faced wooden automa, but as he'd been when he was alive. Laughing with that crooked smile when she joked with him. The sparkle in his eyes whenever his father entered the room. The determined furrow in his brow when he spoke of how he'd live up to his promise to save Wiq.

"I can't," Lazuli said.

Sapphira looked down at the heavy Pearl cupped in her hands. She said nothing for several long moments. At last, with a sigh, she said, "You disappoint me, niece."

With a sweep of her cape, she marched to the door and opened it. A trio of hooded Sky Hunters stood waiting in the hallway.

"Guards," Sapphira said. "You are aware of how my niece conspired to put that wooden boy on the throne. She is quite mad. The grief over her father's death has been too hard on her. We must not have her undermining our mission. Carry her to the dungeon and lock her up. Then let us depart for the Moonlit Court."

The sylphs nodded. One marched toward the bed.

"You're imprisoning me?" Lazuli gasped at her aunt.

"You have admitted to being a traitor," Sapphira said.

"I'm not a traitor. I—"

"Take her away," her aunt said.

The guard lifted Lazuli in his arms. She wanted to beat her fists against him, to scream at them that they were mistaken about Pinocchio, but she knew they would never believe her.

They carried Lazuli down flight after flight of stairs, down to the lowest levels of the palace, down to where they must have been in the rock that supported the hovering city.

When they reached the end of a darkened hallway, a guard

removed a set of keys, unlocked the door, and swung it open. Lazuli was carried inside and placed on the cold stone floor. The guard left, locking her inside.

Lazuli sank to the floor, shaking uncontrollably. Her aunt was right. She had failed her people. "Father," she murmured. "I'm sorry."

At last, no longer able to help herself, she let the hot flood of tears come rushing out.

17.

The Sleeping Thousand

The automa fell into the Mist. His limp body flipped end over end, toppling through wisps of cloud so dense they soon slowed his fall. So when he landed, it wasn't with a crash, but with a dull puff of vapor.

He lay motionless. The mists surrounding him painted everything a uniform murky gray. The cricket crawled out from his collar, making his way up onto the wooden forehead.

"No," he peeped. "No, Pinocchio. You incorrigible scamp, you can't be dead."

Maestro had never sounded so distraught. He made pitiful shudders, his antennae falling across Pinocchio's wooden head in misery.

"I couldn't stop them," Maestro whispered. "How could I,

small as I am? They saw what you were and I couldn't do anything to stop them. I . . . I'm sorry, Pinocchio, I couldn't save you."

The droning howl of wind swelled, but the surrounding Mist didn't seem touched by the storm, as if the wind was somewhere farther, out there beyond the gray and murky landscape surrounding the two.

But something growled. Maestro spun on his six tiny legs.

Out of the Mist, a dark form emerged. No, dark *forms*. And they were gathering. Some crept. Some flapped on leathery wings. Others slithered forward. Shapes menacing and ominous.

Monsters—each and every one.

Maestro trembled with such terror against Pinocchio's wooden head it was like a clock ticking overly fast, something wound tight and ready to burst. The cricket was little. The monsters were big. Maestro was doomed.

"Where am I?" Pinocchio murmured.

Maestro leaped straight up, his wings fluttering manically before he landed back on Pinocchio's face.

"D-did you just sp-speak?" the cricket chirped.

Pinocchio rolled slowly over onto his side, wood and gears creaking. The fog was clearing from his mind. "Of course I did."

"But . . . but . . ." Maestro stammered, crawling across his wooden ear now.

The growls grew louder.

"Stay quiet," Pinocchio said.

"Im-impossible. I don't know how you're speaking, but . . . you shouldn't be!"

Pinocchio started to sit up. "Neither should you, so hush before anything discovers us."

Glowing eyes blinked to life all around them.

"I think they already h-h-have," Maestro peeped.

Pinocchio leaped to his feet, turning in a circle. The Mist gathered so thick about his legs that he couldn't tell what exactly he was standing on. "Where are we, Maestro?"

Maestro trembled from the top of his head. "I th-think we w-were thrown into the Mist below the sylph c-cities."

"What lives in the Mist?"

"I thought n-nothing did," Maestro managed.

A fiery demon rose from the murk, making a lunge for Pinocchio's head. He ducked just in time.

"I guess you were wrong," Pinocchio said.

More creatures appeared out of the ghostly landscape, their snarling faces fixed hungrily on him. Each had the diamond brand on its forehead. Pinocchio shook his head in confusion. These were Diamancer's monsters. What were they doing here? Hadn't Lazuli said nothing that enters the Mist could ever get out?

Pinocchio reached for his sword at his belt, but realized he didn't have it. Typical.

"What do you want?" he called.

A horned creature with a matted, hairy face strode forward on scaly legs. "We are monsters," it growled. "We want what monsters want."

"We want to devour things," slobbered a gruesome toadlike monstrosity.

"We like to destroy!" a voice like crackling embers hissed.

"And butcher," a skeletal ghoul said, tapping a sword against its bony palm.

Something oozing and larvalike rumbled, "We want to suck the guts out of living things until they won't ever live again."

Pinocchio blinked woodenly. "Oh," he said. He searched the terrifying horde, trying to find Diamancer. Maestro flattened on his head, his trembling having accelerated to full velocity.

A green-skinned maiden skulked around him, eyeing Pinocchio up and down. One moment she appeared perfectly pleasant, but then the next her features morphed into something hideous with far too many teeth. "You look familiar, boy," she hissed.

Pinocchio drew back in alarm. "I am the prester!" he said, mustering as much ferocity as he could.

But then he touched his chest and felt the partially open panel. Slipping his hand inside, he found it empty. The Pearl! He'd taken it out to give to Lazuli . . . But how was he moving and thinking without it? He didn't even have a springwork fantom to animate him.

"We were told to kill the boy prester," the ghoul said. "You look strange, boy. Are you sure you're the prester?"

Pinocchio wondered how best to answer this. If he stuck to his claim that he was the prester, he would be inviting them to kill him. But if he said he was no longer the prester, would that mean giving up any sort of royal authority he might be able to use? He doubted he had any authority over these monsters in any case.

"Who told you to kill the prester?" he asked, playing for time to see if he could figure out a way to escape—although it looked utterly hopeless. There had to be a hundred menacing shadows surrounding them.

"The warden," the ghoul with the sword rasped.

The warden? At Regolith, Pinocchio had seen that Prester John was preparing to pass the wardenship from Mezmercurian to someone else. That had been centuries ago. He wondered again about Dr. Nundrum. He had sent them to the Upended Forest. He had been a close adviser to Prester John, just as Mezmercurian had been.

"The warden promised us tasty things to eat," the ghoul said. "Fancy castles to ruin. A few moments of freedom, if only we killed the prester." Pinocchio couldn't tell if it was grinning or if that was just how skeletal-faced ghouls always looked.

"You won't be killing anybody!" Pinocchio growled.

He plowed his shoulder into the ghoul, knocking the jangling sack of bones to the ground. He snatched the ghoul's sword from its grasp.

As Pinocchio whirled around brandishing the weapon, he was met with rumbles of laughter. "We at least have something to kill," the toad monstrosity slobbered.

A wyvern charged, flapping its wings to gather speed. For an instant, Pinocchio felt like he was back in Al Mi'raj's theater, when he'd battled other automa to entertain the people of Siena. His warrior instincts sprang to life. Lightning quick, he dodged the wyvern's jaws, rolling across the spongy mist-ground and coming back on his feet.

"I don't want to hurt you," Pinocchio warned.

But the monsters didn't seem concerned. From all sides they launched themselves at Pinocchio. Maestro sprang from his head in escape.

His sword met one scaly or leathery hide after another as he leaped and spun. The surface of the Mist beneath his feet was squishy and uneven. Pinocchio had trouble finding his balance as he rounded from one attacker to the next.

A drake sprayed fire, which he barely managed to dodge,

although his singed backside was left smoking. Claws raked his wooden arms. Teeth cracked against his wooden shoulder. He was grateful for his automa armor, but the assault came too fast, too relentlessly. There were far too many opponents for him to keep up.

Something thudded against Pinocchio's chest, followed rapidly by several other thuds. Pinocchio staggered back. Foot-long spines were lodged in his wood. Pinocchio looked up at the monster that fired them.

A midnight-blue face smiled down at him with jagged fangs. It had a black lion's body, with bat wings, and a tail tipped with a cluster of spines.

It was her! The manticore who had attacked during the banquet, the same one he'd faced in the tunnel. She slashed out with her heavy claws, catching his sword and knocking it from his grasp.

Pinocchio crouched, searching for the fallen sword. But as he turned, head bent, the monstrous toad sprang, its huge mouth enveloping him to his waist. Pinocchio kicked as the thing tried to chew on his wooden legs before slurping him down in a slimy gulp.

He'd been swallowed! The surprise of this appalling turn of events was matched only by the shock of how dark and constricting the squishy interior was. He couldn't move. He was only glad he didn't have to breathe, because he wasn't sure he'd have been able to.

This had gone from bad to worse. Utterly, horrifyingly worse.

He tried to twist, but only slid deeper into the tight, slimy cavity. Was this it? Was this his end? Dissolving in a monster's stomach and never seeing his father or Lazuli or any of his friends again? And Wiq! Poor Wiq—who must think after so long that Pinocchio was never going to fulfill his promise to rescue him—would remain a slave to the Venetian Empire. Pinocchio had let them all down, and there was nothing he could do anymore to change that. He stopped squirming as all hope was squeezed out of him. . . .

But then he remembered Maestro. He was still out there. Tiny as he was, there was only so long the cricket could flutter around before one of those nasty monsters would spot him and snap him up as a pathetic snack.

NO—he couldn't let that happen! Pinocchio had to get out.

He wiggled side to side, trying to worm his way back up the gut. He banged elbows and knees. He dug his fingers savagely into the mushy interior. He bit something unthinkably disgusting.

"Lut me ut of ere!"

Spasms shook the walls of the gut surrounding him. With a slosh of liquid and a series of retching noises, he found himself spewed from the monster's mouth. He landed with a splat in a pile of sour slime.

The toad monstrosity backed away from him, still heaving, as the monsters laughed.

"Maestro!" Pinocchio cried, climbing to his feet.

As he did, his foot kicked at something solid down in the murk. The ghoul's sword.

"Pinocchio!" Maestro's tiny voice piped.

Pinocchio saw the cricket streaking toward him from out of the fog. But closing in fast on Maestro was the wyvern, wings wide and jaws open.

Pinocchio snatched up the sword and made a bound off the

toad monstrosity's head. With one hand, he caught Maestro. With the other, he slashed with the sword. The wyvern tried to veer, but the blade drew a bloody gash across its side. The wyvern shrieked and crashed down into the gloom.

As Pinocchio landed, a howl of wind rose up, stirring the gray stillness into a storm. The Mist whipped ferociously, spinning round and round.

The monsters crouched in fear, muttering to one another and taking cover against the gale that was plastering down their wings and fur. The sound of the storm swelled louder and louder, drowning out the howls of the monsters.

Pinocchio huddled, cupping Maestro close. "What's happening?" he asked. The cricket only trembled against his wooden chest.

With a great upward whoosh of wind, the storm expended itself. For the briefest few seconds, the Mist overhead parted. A clear night sky was visible. Bright stars blinked against the black. The moon—only a half-moon but glowing a brilliant bone white—threw down a lance of light from over the high walls of mist.

The light flooded against the upturned faces of each and every monster, from the manticore to the wyvern, whose side was weeping blood where Pinocchio had slashed it. They all stared transfixed, mouths agape with wonder at the moonlight.

Pinocchio lost himself momentarily in the sight. The expressions of the monsters were almost tender—terrifying and horrible, yes, but clearly touched by the lovely vision of the night sky. As if they hadn't seen stars such as these in so long.

Then the mists folded back in, blocking out the moon and starlight, and drifting back down in thick grayness once more.

The monsters were silent. But their eyes fell on Pinocchio again.

The manticore strode toward him, her wings unfurling and her spiny tail slashing side to side. Pinocchio held up his sword, and Maestro scrambled onto his shoulder.

The manticore stopped a few paces from them, her feline eyes glowing jade green. The other monsters gathered, but didn't seem ready to attack again—at least not yet.

The manticore growled. "What did you do to the prison?"

Pinocchio cocked his head to one side in confusion. "The prison?"

"The Mist!" she said. "It never parted that way before. How did you do it?"

"I didn't do it," Pinocchio said. "I don't know how it . . . Wait! This is the prison?"

He glanced around at the gray gloom, at the monsters surrounding him with the diamond brand of Diamancer on their foreheads.

"You're still in the prison?" Pinocchio struggled to understand. "But I thought you escaped?"

The manticore stared at him, jade eyes narrowing.

"You've been attacking around Abaton," Pinocchio said. "Tonight, even—I saw you attack the Opaque Palace. Why are you now back in the prison?"

The manticore snarled, showing a mouthful of sinister fangs. "The warden can release us from the prison when we're needed. And the warden can send us back."

Pinocchio thought how the manticore had disappeared into a strange cloud of mist at the banquet and in the pyramid.

"We were asleep for so long," the manticore continued with a hiss, "but the warden woke us and promised us the chance to do what we love best."

"To devour," the monstrous toad croaked.

215

"To attack." A ghoul laughed.

"To destroy," the manticore finished.

"Yes, I gathered that you like all that," Pinocchio said.

But he had not forgotten the look on their faces when they saw the open sky. He wondered if they liked that too.

"But why?" Pinocchio asked. "Why would the warden do this? Didn't Prester John give the warden the responsibility of watching over you?"

"At first, the warden wanted to know if you really possessed Prester John's Pearl," the manticore spat. "I was released to attend your lovely banquet, to test your powers, which you proved, although not especially impressively. Now the warden has bigger plans for us."

"What plans?" Pinocchio asked.

"What do we monsters care?" The manticore sneered. "We simply do what the warden bids, until the day we win our freedom."

Pinocchio scanned the dismal surroundings, ready in case any of the monsters attacked. "And the warden's going to free you and Diamancer?" he asked.

The manticore gave a low chuckle. "No," she replied. "The warden is smart enough to know better than to awaken something like Diamancer. Our general sleeps still, not far away, with the others. The warden only awoke one hundred of the Sleeping Thousand."

The monstrous toad croaked, "You ought to see the others. Our sleeping brethren are much worse than us." It chuckled.

If these terrors weren't the worst, Pinocchio had no wish to meet the other nine hundred. His mind raced with thoughts. Diamancer wasn't awake, so that couldn't have been who he'd seen in the tunnel in the pyramid. Whoever had been shrouded beneath that cloak must have been the warden.

The monsters began getting restless. They edged in, snarling and clacking their teeth. But Pinocchio saw how they eyed his sword. The wyvern he'd slashed hadn't risen from where it lay in the Mist.

Pinocchio backed a step, keeping the sword steady. "Who is the warden, then?" he asked. "Is it Dr. Nundrum?"

The manticore lashed her spiny tail. "Can you part the Mist? Can you release us from the prison?"

"I told you. I don't know how," Pinocchio said. Although if he did, he certainly wouldn't set these monsters free.

"But he's the prester, en't he?" a cobralike monster asked, swiveling its hooded head toward the manticore.

Maestro was creeping down into the back of Pinocchio's shirt. "Let's go!" he peeped.

The manticore was watching Pinocchio expectantly, waiting for his answer. Pinocchio wasn't even sure. Was he the prester? He didn't have the Pearl, and now he'd become an automa again. . . .

The manticore smiled. "If he was the prester, he'd have escaped already. No, he's just a wooden boy." She surveyed the blood on Pinocchio's sword. "A deadly wooden boy. A deadly wooden monster, even."

Pinocchio winced. He hadn't meant to harm the wyvern so badly. He'd been scared for Maestro and only trying to protect him.

The manticore turned, folding her wings against her back. "He's one of us now. Let the newest prisoner and his tasty cricket friend settle in. There will be more time to play with them later."

One by one, the monsters began to depart, disappearing into the gloom. Several cast longing eyes at Maestro, but they seemed willing to do as the manticore had said—for the time being.

"Can we get away from them, please?" Maestro asked.

"And go where?" Pinocchio whispered.

"Anywhere but here."

Pinocchio slipped away into the Mist.

18.

The *Lionslayer*

Moonlight spilled through the lone barred window.

Lazuli lay on the stone floor of the cell, the tears still wet on her face. She had wept with shame at how she'd failed as prester. She'd wept with frustration that she was locked in this dungeon. But mostly, her tears had been for Pinocchio.

His death was her fault. Her aunt had been the one who'd taken the Pearl from him and done what with his wooden body? Destroyed him? But Lazuli felt it never would have happened if she'd only explained about Pinocchio earlier, trusted her aunt with the truth.

Now he was gone, no matter how badly she wished she could go back and do things over again. She'd not just failed Abaton as prester—she'd failed Pinocchio as his friend.

A small chime interrupted her thoughts. Lazuli looked up,

first at the door and then around her cell. The chime sounded once more. From the window. A bubble was glowing against the moonlit sky. The aleya!

Lazuli sprang to her feet and ran to the window, grasping the bars. "What are you doing here?" she gasped. "How did you escape?"

The aleya pressed against the bars, squeezing until she looked like she might pop, and then came through into Lazuli's cell. She made a proud tinkle.

"But General Mezmer . . . the others, where are they?" Lazuli realized she wouldn't be able to understand the aleya, so she tried a different question, something the aleya might be able to answer for her. "Are they safe?"

The aleya bobbed up and down.

"Good! Have they also escaped?"

The aleya swiveled back and forth.

"They're locked in another cell?"

She bobbed swiftly.

Lazuli sank back to the floor. "There's nothing I can do. I'm trapped in here. I probably deserve to be . . ." she murmured. But Mezmer didn't. Nor did her other knights who had fought so bravely.

The aleya made a sharp noise and streaked toward the window. She made several motions like she wanted Lazuli to follow her out.

Lazuli sighed. "I want to help the others escape, but how?"

The aleya flew to Lazuli's hands and then made a rush at the door. She repeated it a few times until it dawned on Lazuli what she was suggesting.

"I already tried summoning the strongest wind I could against the door, but . . . well, this is a sylph prison." She got back to her feet and wrung her hands together. "If I could only get the keys . . ." She looked at the aleya. "But no, you don't have a way to pick them up."

The aleya made urgent bobs up and down.

"You can?"

Of course! She remembered when the aleya had delivered the spiceberry to Pinocchio when their ship had been stranded over the jungle.

"Then you can get the keys from the guard!"

The aleya flew over to the door. There was no keyhole on the inside.

"Oh," Lazuli said. "We need another way. If there was something that could knock the door down . . ." She spun around to face the aleya. "Wait! Let me think." An idea struck her.

She was in the Mist Cities. She'd been visiting here since she was a child. She'd roamed all their neighborhoods. But there had been one place she'd been warned not to go. To the orchards where . . .

She was getting ahead of herself. The plan wouldn't work if she didn't have a way to handle the guards.

"All right," she said, taking a steadying breath. "I know what you can get. Two things, actually."

The aleya bobbed eagerly.

"It might be dangerous," Lazuli said. "Are you afraid?"

The aleya hesitated momentarily and then swished back and forth.

Lazuli smiled. "Good. They might be tricky to locate, but listen . . ."

While the aleya was gone, Lazuli began to gather stones. The cell had been carved out of the solid rock of the city's foundation, but a few spots around the door frame and window had begun to chip. It would have taken years to break away enough to escape that way. However, with a bit of prying, Lazuli managed to collect enough small pieces of rock for her purposes. She only hoped they would be big enough.

When the aleya returned, she hovered outside the bars, her chimes sounding closer to grunts than Lazuli had previously heard.

"You found it!" Lazuli said.

The aleya made an exhausted droop, the strap of the heavy bag hanging from her slightly misshapen body.

"Well, come on then. Bring it in."

The aleya pressed to the bar and then bounced back, giving a grumble of a chime.

"Sorry, I didn't realize," Lazuli said. She reached through the bars and took Pinocchio's satchel, working it through the narrow opening.

Once she had it, she said, "Did anyone see you take it?"

The aleya, now back to her normal round shape, swiveled back and forth.

"Great, now go to the orchard on the far side of the city beyond the Opaque Palace. Do you remember which tree I said? The ones with the purple leaves. The thunderseed fruits will be growing out over the edge of the city, for obvious reasons."

The aleya gave a bob of understanding before rocketing off.

Lazuli ran to the window, calling in a strained whisper, "And please, please, be careful with it!"

She hoped the aleya heard her. Settling back to the floor, Lazuli dug into the satchel and pulled out the sack with the Sands of Sleep that Pinocchio had gathered from Regolith.

Pinocchio. The thought of him brought a sharp pain to her

heart. She blinked hard, forcing back the tears. She had to stay focused.

Untying the sack, she looked at the shimmering white sand inside. She'd have to be careful not to touch it. But then she remembered she had touched it before. When they'd found Regolith. The Sands hadn't affected her then. Why?

She'd not had time to ponder the reasons before, but now she wondered if she and Pinocchio had been able to touch the Sands of Sleep at Regolith because they were the presters. Why else would she have been immune to their effects?

But she was no longer the prester. Her aunt was.

Wasn't she?

Slowly, Lazuli pressed a finger into the Sands. A faint tingling rose inside her. For half a moment, she thought the Sands were going to put her to sleep. But she didn't remove her finger, and the Sands didn't make her sleepy.

She furrowed her brow curiously. She cupped a handful of the Sands experimentally. Except for that faint tingling, nothing was happening.

Some magic was at work here. Lazuli couldn't help but wonder if it wasn't too late for her to atone for her failures as prester.

The aleya made a chime outside the window. She was trembling slightly.

"I know, I know," Lazuli said, reaching out. "This was so brave of you."

The aleya deposited a small purple fruit in the palm of her hand. Lazuli brought it through the bars. It was about the size of a lemon and roughly the same shape.

Unburdened of her load, the aleya pushed her way through the bars and hovered over Lazuli's shoulder.

"Now to open it," Lazuli said. "I've never done this before, so you might want to back away."

The aleya went to the far side of the cell and then seemed to reconsider, heading out the window instead.

Lazuli dug her nails into the thick skin of the thunderfruit. She held her breath. As gingerly as she could manage, she pried the fruit open. Nothing exploded. Thankfully.

Inside, the fruit had only a shallow layer of juicy flesh, but the core was a nest of tiny dark seeds. Carefully, one by one, she plucked them out and started a pile at the base of the door.

She had no idea how many she needed. Not enough and she'd only manage to alert the guards. Too many of the seeds and . . . well, she didn't want to think about that. She settled on half.

Then moving all the way across the room, she picked up a rock. She looked to the window. "Wish me luck."

The aleya made a tiny, apprehensive *plink*.

Lazuli tossed the stone. It missed the seeds, bouncing against the door before rattling to one side. Lazuli blew a hard breath and picked up the next stone.

She adjusted her aim and tossed it. The stone missed. "Come on!" she told herself.

Lazuli remembered Rion's archery lesson, how he'd "let his arrow find the target" simply by making subtle manipulations of the wind. Taking another stone, she squinted and made a throw—sending a bit of breeze to guide it.

She could see in that fraction of an instant before the stone landed that she had done it. Throwing herself to one side, she covered her face as the seeds erupted in a thunder crack of explosive force.

Pieces of debris rained down on her. A few chunks hit her in the back. Her ears were ringing fiercely, but otherwise she seemed to be in one piece. What about the door?

She shot up and saw the bottom of the door had been blown to splinters. Only the top half hung on its hinges, and even that fell away with a crash a second later.

"Quick!" she shouted at the aleya. "Go out in the hallway and listen for the guards."

The aleya popped through the bars and disappeared around the corner. Lazuli scooped a handful of the Sands of Sleep from the pouch. She slowly walked toward the door. When she was just a step away, she stopped and waited.

The thundering of her heart in her ears was almost as loud as the ringing. Then the aleya shot back to the cell, tinkling. Lazuli could hear the guards shouting and running down the hall. She drew a deep breath.

When they sounded almost to the door, she stepped out and summoned a wind, sending the Sands of Sleep scattering across the half-dozen surprised sylphs charging her way.

One after the other they dropped to the floor. Lazuli watched them a tense moment, waiting to see if they were really asleep. When none of them moved, she listened for whether more guards were on the way. She heard nothing. But then a faint banging came from down the hall. The aleya made a shrill note and whipped down the long hallway, bobbing up and down outside a door toward the far end.

Lazuli ran after her. At the little barred window in the door, she was met by the fox's flabbergasted face.

"Lazuli?" Mezmer gasped.

"I'm getting you out," Lazuli said.

She ran back toward her cell. She still had half the seeds, but with a quick glance, she spotted a ring of keys in a sleeping guard's hand. That would be easier. And safer.

"Thank you very much," she whispered to the guard, snatching his keys.

It took her several tries before she found the right key. With a turn and a pull, she had the door open, and Mezmer threw her arms around her. "Good work, my clever prester."

Over Mezmer's shoulder she saw the beaming faces of Sop, Kataton, Goliath, and the three kirin sisters.

"Now," Mezmer said, letting go. "Which way is out?"

"I think that way," Lazuli said, pointing to the snoring pile of guards.

They raced down the hallway past the ruined door of Lazuli's cell.

"Wait!" Sop said. "Where's Kataton?"

The chimera lumbered slowly down the hall after them. "Coming."

"Um, Kataton, old pal," Sop called, waving urgently with his paws. "Now might be one of those times—"

Voices echoed from the stairwell up ahead.

"More guards!" Mezmer snarled. "And we've got no weapons."

Lazuli pushed them into her cell. "We've got one weapon at our disposal." She carefully picked up the remaining pile of thunderfruit seeds. Stepping back into the hallway, she waited until the guards appeared.

"The princess has broken out!" the first shouted when he saw Lazuli. "Get her!"

"I'm not the princess," Lazuli grumbled. "And don't come a step closer."

The guards seemed about to continue their charge, but then their eyes fell on their sleeping comrades sprawled across the floor. Lazuli held up one of the seeds, giving them a meaningful look. The seeds hadn't put them to sleep, but Lazuli figured these guards didn't need to know all the details. As long as the threat kept them back.

"Drop your arrows," she commanded.

"What do we do?" one of the guards hissed.

"Drop them," the first guard said to the others crowded at the end of the hallway. Arrows clattered to the floor.

"Your Majesty," Goliath called from the cell door. "The general needs you."

Sop stepped out and held out a hand. "I'll watch these idiots."

Lazuli eased the seeds into Sop's palm. "If they come for you," she whispered, "just throw one or two of these. The bang will be enough to scare them back."

Sop cackled. "Oh, I hope they come for me."

When Lazuli was back in the cell, Mezmer said, "We need a way to get past those guards. If we can only get topside, Wini, Fini, and Pini can fly us away."

The kirins bobbed their horns in eager agreement.

"Is there more of the Sands of Sleep?" Mezmer asked.

"There is," Lazuli said, touching a hand to the pouch, "but we'll need it for—"

Goliath raised a hand to silence them. Then he tilted his head as if listening for something.

"What is it?" Lazuli asked.

"I heard a faint voice."

Kataton swiveled his eyes toward the door. "More. Guards?"

"I hear it too." Mezmer's tall ears rotated slowly. "It's not coming from outside. It's in here somewhere. Don't you hear it?"

Lazuli only heard the ringing from when she'd blown the door. "I don't—"

But then she did hear the tiniest, muffled voice say, "Your Majesty!"

"Where's that coming from?" Wini asked.

Then Lazuli remembered. "Riggle!" She had forgotten all about the superfluous worm Pinocchio had been carrying.

She grabbed the satchel from the floor and dug out the small silver box. When she opened the lid, the worm's pink head broke from the dirt.

"They have arrived, Your Majesty," he piped.

"Who has?" Lazuli asked.

"Master Geppetto," the worm replied. "I told him that you had been imprisoned. He requests, Your Majesty, that you wave a hand out the window so he can locate which room you're in."

Mezmer shoved an arm through the bars and gave a wave. "I don't see anything. Are you sure . . . Oh, wait. I can't be seeing this right!" She laughed. "Cinnabar, you ol' fire eater, darling! Is that you? What took you so long?"

"Cinnabar's here?" Lazuli tried to look through the window, but Mezmer was blocking her view.

She couldn't tell what was out there, how Geppetto and the djinni had arrived, but then she heard Cinnabar's voice saying, "Attach this grappling hook to the bars. And back up! It'll probably take out some of the masonry too."

Mezmer hustled her knights back to the far side of the room, watching the window.

"What's going on?" Sop called from the hallway.

"You'll see, darling. Just keep those guards where they are."

"Crank the winch!" they heard Cinnabar order.

There was a *click, click, click* and then the entire frame of bars pulled from the windowsill with an explosive crack, littering the floor with crumbled stone. As the dust cleared from the air, Cinnabar landed in the hole where the window had been.

"Come quickly, Your Majesty!" he urged, holding out a hand to help Lazuli up.

When she climbed through the hole, her mouth fell open at what she saw.

A flying ship was hovering outside. However where the sides of the hull and sails should have been was nothing but fog, nearly invisible against the dawn skies beyond. But there—seemingly floating in midair—was the dark, stained wood of the large deck, with several dozen gnomes all standing around. Master Geppetto's face appeared as he pulled back a chameleon cloak to reveal himself.

"Can you jump, Your Majesty?" he said, holding out a hand.

Of course she could. Gladly! She landed on the deck gracefully and squeezed Geppetto around the neck.

"What is this?" Lazuli gasped. "How did you find us?"

"You can thank Riggle," he said.

She was still holding his box. The little worm inside tipped his head bashfully.

Tiny Chief Muckamire marched up. "And as for this . . ." The gnome waved a hand to the ship. "May I present your royal vessel—the *Lionslayer*."

"The what?" Lazuli asked.

"The name was Cinnabar's idea," Geppetto said. "As were the improvements."

She glanced from the mechanical winch that had pulled the bars from the window to the massive crossbow cannons mounted at the stern and then over to Cinnabar, who was continuing to help the other knights aboard.

"Told you my gnomes would do something fine with that Venetian flying ship you left with us." Chief Muckamire laughed. "Master Geppetto, Cinnabar, and my gnomes—we've all been working on it around the clock. Starting on additional ships as well."

"But it's invisible," Lazuli said, still amazed.

Geppetto tugged on his mustache. "We've covered the hull, masts, and sails in material similar to what's used in chameleon cloaks. Made it easy to sneak up to the Mist Cities. But won't be long before they realize we're here."

The last of the kirins leaped through the window onto the *Lionslayer*.

"All aboard?" Chief Muckamire asked.

"Wait!" Kataton said, seeming to work hard to get the words out swiftly. "Where. Is. Sop?"

There was a bang, followed by several more. Then Sop, cupping his hand around the rest of his seeds, climbed up to the window and jumped on board. He was cackling with laughter.

"All right, so I threw more than two. No real harm done. I think one of those guards wet himself."

"Hoist the main," Cinnabar barked. "Let's shove off!"

The gnomes scattered around the deck to positions and soon the ship turned to fly away.

"Let's get you belowdecks, darling," Mezmer said, "in case we're spotted."

At that moment, a cry rang out from above. "The prisoners are escaping!"

Up at a watchtower sprouting from the side of the palace, a sylph guard was pointing to them. Along the walls, more sylphs appeared, staring down in shock at the half-invisible flying ship.

But none of them were armed. The Sky Hunters had all left for the Moonlit Court.

The ship sailed off, and Lazuli followed Mezmer down the gangway.

At the bottom of the stairs, Geppetto caught her arm. "Lazuli."

Her heart gave a lurch as she saw for the first time how raw his eyes were. Geppetto opened his mouth to speak, but his lips trembled falteringly. "Pinocchio?" he said. "Riggle said—" A choke stole rest of his words.

She put her arms around him and squeezed. More tears came, but this time she didn't care who saw.

When she blinked her eyes open, she found Chief Muckamire, hands laced together, watching her and Geppetto with a look of utmost sadness.

"I've long admired Lady Sapphira," the gnome said. "But she made a tragic mistake with Prester Pinocchio."

Lazuli cast her eyes to the floor. "I shouldn't have kept the truth about Pinocchio from her . . . from you and our people."

"You did it for good reason!" Chief Muckamire said. "I admit that like all our people, I have believed that the workings of Venice's alchemist were something sinister. But I feel differently now that I've been working side by side with Master Geppetto and Cinnabar. Different about Venetian alchemy and different about Prester Pinocchio."

The gnome shook his head. "If Lady Sapphira only could have known what I now know . . . how he was loved. How he cared about those that we Noble Lords have scorned. Cinnabar told me of the bracelet he wears, of the promise Prester Pinocchio made to help our brethren enslaved in the Venetian Empire. I feel ashamed. . . ." He puffed up his beard. "We must make amends."

But Lazuli was the one burning with shame. "It's my fault, what happened to Pinocchio," she said, unable to look at Geppetto. "Lady Sapphira is my aunt . . . and I should have . . ."

Geppetto gave a squeeze to her shoulder. "You only wanted to protect Pinocchio," he said. "And now you must help protect Abaton."

Lazuli couldn't bring herself to answer.

"Lady Sapphira . . . what she did to . . ." Geppetto fought to form the words but couldn't. He cleared his throat before saying, "But your aunt needs you. Abaton needs you. You have the Sands of Sleep. We have this warship. We must help your aunt stop these monsters."

Cinnabar appeared in the top of the gangway. "My apologies for interrupting, Your Majesty. But where should we go?"

Chief Muckamire and Geppetto watched her expectantly.

Lazuli drew in a deep breath. "To the Moonlit Court." She wasn't sure what her aunt would do when she saw her niece again—whether she'd declare Lazuli a traitor or accept her help. But she couldn't let fear get in the way. "How quickly can you get us there, Cinnabar?"

"How quickly?" Cinnabar gave a crooked smile. "Oh, we've made some nice adjustments to the speed, Your Majesty. A little trick I learned from the alchemists of Venice."

He called to a gnome. "Wumble, light the canisters."

"Aye, aye," the gnome said with a salute. He hurried down a gangway and disappeared through a trapdoor into the belly of the ship.

A moment later, a sound like a fiery furnace erupted from the ship's stern. With the sun rising, the *Lionslayer* gathered speed and flew past the Mist Cities, racing off across Abaton.

19.

The Legacy of Diamancer

Gray nothingness hung all around Pinocchio. If it hadn't been for the slow shifting of the thick fog, he would have felt like he was embedded in a chunk of colorless stone. Out beyond his line of sight, monsters crept through the murk, finding places to rest or fighting with one another in short, vicious battles. But these attacks sounded more like play than real. None of the monsters were seriously injured.

Except for the wyvern.

Pinocchio listened to the low moans of the wyvern with teeming guilt, like the cavity of his wooden belly had been filled with termites chewing away his insides.

For a moment, the mists parted. He spied the manticore crouched beside the wyvern with one heavy paw resting on the hollow between the wyvern's wings, whispering to the dying creature. The wyvern's long, serpentine head lifted feebly to lick at the bleeding gash that had split his scaly side. He let out a small groan before letting his head flop back to the misty ground.

Pinocchio looked down at the bloodstained sword in his hands. "He was going to eat you," he said to Maestro.

"Believe me," the cricket whispered from his shoulder. "I'm not complaining!"

"But I shouldn't have . . ." Pinocchio's voice trailed off. "I didn't mean to . . ."

"You did what you had to do to protect us both. Besides," Maestro added, "these monsters respect warriors. They don't blame you. If . . . you must realize, if you hadn't fought so well, they surely would be more keen to devour us by now."

Pinocchio nodded briskly.

The wyvern let out another plaintive cry. Pinocchio dropped his head.

"Come on," Maestro said. "Let's not listen. I don't like the idea of anything sneaking up on us, but let's go somewhere else until . . . it's over."

Pinocchio got listlessly to his feet and went deeper into the fog. Soon the sounds of the dying wyvern faded. As they went, Pinocchio stared down at his feet.

"What happened to me, Maestro?" he asked. "Back at the Opaque Palace."

Maestro shifted on his shoulder. "Lady Sapphira saw what you were. What you'd become. She was upset, understandably, I suppose. But she didn't have to throw you down here!"

What Pinocchio had dreaded since arriving in Abaton had finally happened. And just as he'd expected—just as Lazuli and his father and Maestro had all warned—once his people discovered he was an automa, they'd reacted with horror. They wanted him gone.

"But the Pearl . . ." Pinocchio said.

"You took it out," Maestro said. "Oh, why did you have to do that?"

"I was giving it to Lazuli."

Maestro sighed. "Well, Lady Sapphira has it now. And hopefully she'll return it to Lazuli. But she was upset with Lazuli too, for hiding your secret from her. Still, I can't comprehend how you're . . . this way." He flicked his antennae. "You're yourself! Except you're not. I mean, you're an automa, but you're not acting like you did the last time you were an automa. What's going on?"

Pinocchio shook his head. Maybe it had something to do with being in these mists. Or maybe it was just some last bits of the Pearl's powers clinging inside him. Would they fade? Would he lose himself again?

He missed the sensation of being human. The way this fog might have felt cool against his skin. The way the little hairs on his arms might tickle under the breeze. But this wood only felt dull and thick, and his movements as he walked throught the insubstantial world of the prison felt clumsy and stiff. He longed for his old body, his old self, his true self. Or was this his true self?

A new sound rose beneath his feet. Not the soft squish of the Mist's floor, but a light crunch.

Pinocchio stopped and waved a hand to part the fog. Lying before him was a blackened face as big as a tree stump. Maestro squeaked. Pinocchio reared back. But then he realized the monster's eyes were closed. Part of its face was buried in silvery sand, along with its shoulders and torso. A low snore rumbled from its tusked mouth.

"It's asleep," Pinocchio said. "It's . . . one of the others."

Pinocchio crept around it, waving a hand as he went. There were more, half-buried under the Sands of Sleep, trapped in their centuries-long enchanted slumber.

The toad monstrosity was right. These others were much more terrifying than the one hundred that had been awakened. Humongous beasts covered in jagged spines or thick, leathery plates. Some were humanoid—horned ogres or demons with multiple heads or a multitude of eyes. Others bore a passing resemblance to animals of the humanlands—vultures, wolves, crocodiles, or insects—but grotesque and full of vicious claws and fangs.

Pinocchio eyed the clusters of sleeping monsters with curiosity. Maestro, however, was shaking with terror in his collar.

"Maybe . . . maybe this isn't the best place to be."

"They can't hurt us," Pinocchio said. "They're sleep—"

He froze. Ahead, rising out of the tendrils of Mist and mounds of sand-covered monsters, was a block of polished obsidian. A humanlike figure lay atop it on his back, arms folded across his waist. Sand clung to him like ancient mounds of dust.

Maestro jittered uncontrollably. "D-D-Diamancer. Th-that's Diamancer."

"I want to see him."

"No, don't—" Maestro began, but Pinocchio was already weaving through the sleeping monsters, taking care not to stir the sand from any.

When he reached the edge of the obsidian block, he looked down at Diamancer. In some ways, he seemed the least monstrous of any in the prison. He had no claws, no fangs, no horns or wings. He simply looked like a man, except that his skin was a deep bloodred.

But what was disturbing about Diamancer's appearance were those missing eyes, the way his skin ran smooth and unblemished where his lids should have been. It was hard to tell whether Diamancer was really sleeping. His face beneath the scattered sand had an odd expression as if he were about to smile. Pinocchio half expected him to sit up. It sent a shiver through his gears.

Trying to drive the fear away with brave words, Pinocchio said, "He doesn't look so menacing."

Even as he said it, he wished he hadn't. What if Diamancer could hear him? What if he took this as some sort of challenge? Pinocchio felt certain that if Diamancer had commanded these monsters' loyalty, if he had rallied them to a nearly successful rebellion against the immortal Prester John and his army, he must have had qualities that were much more dangerous than fangs or claws.

"Why did they follow him, Maestro?" Pinocchio asked. "Why do you think they turned against Prester John?"

"I couldn't say," the cricket chirped. "They're monsters. They like destruction. I suppose Diamancer gave them an excuse to act the way they want to act."

"But monsters lived in Abaton long before Diamancer came along," Pinocchio said. "I haven't heard anything about them causing problems before the rebellion."

"Well, I suppose," Maestro said. "But they weren't really monsters back then."

"Right, so why are they called monsters now?"

"Just look at them, Pinocchio!"

Pinocchio frowned. "Back in the Venetian Empire, when I saw the djinni Al Mi'raj for the first time, I thought he was a monster too. But here in Abaton, he'd be one of the noblest races."

"Djinn are elementals," Maestro argued. "Not monsters."

"That's what I'm trying to say. . . . Djinn aren't considered monsters because elementals are part of the ruling class. Who's a monster and who's not seems nothing more than the opinion of a bunch of so-called noble lords, not because of any real truth."

"What does it matter?" Maestro said with an irritable flutter of his wings.

"Because it's not fair! Just because you look a certain way doesn't mean you're a monster. But when you call someone a monster, then they start to act like one."

He remembered what Kataton had said about why he never took heed when others called him slow.

"It's because of the Noble Houses' treatment that these monsters rebelled," Pinocchio said. "It's because of that sort of prejudice that Diamancer was able to convince these . . . creatures to turn against Prester John."

Maestro grew silent. He crawled out onto Pinocchio's wrist and turned around to face him, flicking his antennae. "When you say *look a certain way*, would that include being an automa?"

The anger drained from Pinocchio. He hadn't realized it until Maestro said it, but yes, it was true. He had been so afraid for so long that his subjects would see their prester as something despicable and unworthy if they learned he was an automa.

But at this moment, he was not nearly as ashamed of being an automa as he was at what he'd done to that wyvern. Sure, he'd been defending Maestro, but he should never have hurt him so badly. And now he was dying. It was his fault. What sort of monster did that make him?

Guilt churned, searing through Pinocchio's gearworks.

"I can't let him die!" Pinocchio leaped to his feet and dashed past the bodies of the sleeping monsters.

When he reached the manticore, she cracked her eyes, her head resting on the wyvern's back. "Back so soon," she hissed.

Several other monsters began gathering, eyeing Pinocchio menacingly.

"This is a bad idea," Maestro peeped from his collar. "They're going to eat us. Well, I think they've realized you're not so digestible, but what about me?"

Pinocchio ignored the cricket, as well as the monsters. Looking from the manticore to the wyvern, he asked tentatively, "Is he—"

She croaked, "Dead, most likely. Azi has lost too much blood."

Pinocchio looked at the wyvern's face. He walked down his long body, past the crumpled wings lying half-buried in mist, until he reached the gash his sword had made. Dark blood still dripped from the wound.

"His name was Azi?" Pinocchio asked.

The manticore narrowed her eyes at Pinocchio before giving a nod.

"What's your name?" Pinocchio asked.

She frowned before answering, "Khora."

"Khora," he said. "We have to save him."

The manticore shook her head. "I have no means of closing the wound."

Pinocchio squeezed his hands together in desperation. If he only had the Pearl, it might have saved Azi. But then his eyes fell to his wrist—to the bracelet of jasmine Wiq had given him.

Although the leaves and flowers had long fallen from its vines, the wood had remained supple. It might work. It just might.

"Khora, give me one of your spines," he said.

"What are you doing?" Maestro whispered.

"I can save him."

Khora rose to her feet, her jade eyes widening. "Why would you?"

"Because he was a creature of Abaton," Pinocchio said. "And it was wrong of me to kill him."

"We monsters kill," Khora said.

"I'm not a monster," Pinocchio said. "And neither was Azi. He didn't have to be. None of you do."

Khora's eyes flashed with confusion.

"May I have one of your spines?" he asked again, urgency cracking his voice.

The manticore swung her tail around to Pinocchio, and he pulled one of the sharp needles loose. He bit down on the blunt end, breaking through with a crack. Holding it up to inspect, Pinocchio was glad to see it had done as he hoped. A rough hole had opened through the spine.

He locked a wooden finger around the jasmine bracelet, fighting against the regret burning inside him. "I'm sorry, Wiq," he whispered.

He snapped it loose. Quickly he uncoiled the long vine Wiq had woven together.

"You intend to sew it shut?" Khora asked. "It is too late for that, wooden boy."

Pinocchio hoped beyond hope it wasn't. He had to try. And he realized more than Azi's life depended on it. Pinocchio might not have had the Pearl, he might not have been worthy of being the prester, but the responsibility of protecting Abaton had been given to him all the same. If Azi died by his hand, then Pinocchio felt he truly belonged in this prison of traitors.

Knotting one end of the vine through the needle's hole, he

pinched a portion of Azi's thick skin. Pressing the spine to it, he knew if he had not been an automa, he never would have had the strength to push it through—he might never have been able to slash the wyvern's tough hide either. The spine pierced the skin, but Azi didn't stir.

The monsters watched silently as Pinocchio threaded the jasmine vine through, over and over, again and again, pulling closed the horrible, oozing wound. Warmth tingled in his wooden arms as he sewed, but Pinocchio's whole attention was fixed on stopping the bleeding, stopping the wyvern from dying.

The mists began churning. A few of the monsters grumbled anxiously. Others slunk away.

When Pinocchio at last tied off the end of the vine, he watched the wyvern's face, hoping, pleading . . .

Azi didn't move. He didn't waken.

The mists swirled in a sudden storm—not as ferocious as the one earlier, but a swift gale that extinguished in an instant.

As the mists descended again, a solitary feather as large as a man's arm floated out of them. Khora watched it, drifting back and forth, until Pinocchio reached out to catch it. He clasped it in his wooden hand. The feather was the same steely gray as their surroundings, but with the barest hint of sky blue at the tip. Then it faded, evaporating into mist.

"What was that?" Pinocchio asked, feeling a slight tingling in his fingers where he'd touched the feather.

Khora tilted her feline head. "I've no idea."

Pinocchio looked to Azi. He'd hoped desperately the feather might have brought some enchantment that would save him. But as he watched the wyvern, he didn't stir. His eyes remained closed. He was still as stone.

"I told you," Khora said, with a strange note—was it tenderness?— in her voice, "it was too late."

She rose to her feet and slowly padded off into the gloom.

Pinocchio ran a wet hand across the wyvern's skin, tracing a finger over the pointless stitch he'd sewn to close the gash. The woody thread that had been Wiq's gift—the bracelet and promise—could not be taken back now. It was lost, just as Pinocchio was, just as the hope that his friend would be freed from the Venetian Empire was, and as Abaton soon would be.

Resting on Pinocchio's forearm, Maestro stared up as if he expected another of the phantom feathers to fall. "What is this place?" the cricket murmured.

Pinocchio's thoughts were still on Azi, but he answered dully, "The Mist."

"Yes, but . . ." Maestro twitched his antennae. "What is the Mist, really?"

Pinocchio sighed. "I don't know why you're asking me. You know more about Abatonian—"

"The eye," Maestro interrupted, still looking up. "The mouth. The seed. And the feather. Those are the symbols of the four Primordials who guard Abaton."

Pinocchio sat up straighter. When he'd been on the lowest street of Grootslang Hole, he'd seen those symbols on the shrines. The eye had been for Regolith, the primordial of earth who guarded Abaton's memories. The devouring mouth was the Deep One, the primordial of water and guardian of Abaton's shores.

Understanding began to dawn on Pinocchio. "Maestro, what's the primordial of air?"

"I've only ever heard it called the Roc. An enormous elemental bird, but this Mist . . ." The cricket turned to face Pinocchio.

"When Prester John moved the prisoners from the pyramid, he moved them here. Not just to the Mist. But to the Roc. The Roc was given to Diamancer's traitors to guard! So this place . . . the Mist, we're inside the Roc! Don't you see?"

Pinocchio shook his head in disbelief. "But . . . why did that feather just fall?"

"As a sign from the primordial guardian," Maestro said. "To you! You're the prester."

"But I'm—"

"You tried to save Azi," Maestro urged. "A prester's greatest responsibility is to protect his people."

"But I didn't. I killed him!"

Maestro gave an impatient flutter of his wings. "Accidentally, trying to protect me. But you felt remorse and you tried to make up for your actions. Even though Azi was a monster, you saw him with the eyes of a true prester."

Maestro snapped his tiny head around. Light was blooming from the Mist nearby. Monsters were moving through the gloom, clustering around the bluish glow.

"Do you see that?" Pinocchio asked, climbing to his feet.

"What is it?" Maestro asked.

The silent shifting monsters were blocking their view. Pinocchio pushed his way through the ones at the back to see what had drawn their attention. Resting on a wooden stand was a tall, oblong pane of glowing glass that he had not noticed before among the drifting mists.

"It looks like a mirror—" Pinocchio started to say.

A face appeared in the glass. A hooded figure.

Pinocchio ducked down behind the back of the toad who had eaten him. In the pyramid, when he had thought Diamancer had trapped him, that had been a mirror as well, the glass shattering when he summoned the flames. But now he knew: it hadn't been Diamancer then. And this wasn't Diamancer either.

"Our esteemed warden." Khora made a slight bow of her head toward the mirror.

"Are you and your monsters ready to be released again?" the warden whispered.

Pinocchio peered around the toad, trying to see the warden's face, but Khora had stepped in front of the mirror.

"We are ready," she replied.

"Good," the warden said. "I am planning to open a portal for you. You will find yourself not far from the Moonlit Court."

Monsters chuckled and growled.

"We're to attack the palace, then?" Khora said.

"Eventually," the warden whispered. "First, I want you to watch the skies for a flying ship that is headed for the capital. It carries the traitor Lazuli aboard. The ship will be difficult to spot, as the gnomes have been dabbling in human alchemy to make it nearly invisible to the eye. But I trust that you and your monsters can spot it."

Pinocchio stiffened. Lazuli was aboard the ship! And if the gnomes were there, then his father might be too.

"And when we spy this flying ship?" Khora asked.

"Destroy it," the warden said. "It must not reach the Moonlit Court. There can be only one prester. And it will not be Lazuli. Do you understand?"

"Of course," Khora said.

Pinocchio felt awash in fear. He needed to warn her, to help her, but how could he, trapped in this prison?

"Once you have finished with the ship, your monsters may attack the Moonlit Court. As before, I want more menace than massacre. Frighten the people of the palace. Tear off some balconies. You may even have some chimera servants if it makes you happy. But in the end, you will allow my forces to drive you back. I will be seen as the victor and Abaton's savior."

Pinocchio couldn't believe what he was hearing.

"I understand," Khora growled. She paced a few steps sideways. "Warden?"

The warden's face, shadowed beneath the hood, peered out from the mirror. "What is it, Khora?"

"I assume you mean us to stop the prester Lazuli so—"

"She is not the prester," the warden snapped.

"But *you* intend to be," Khora said, coolly. "Our attack will persuade the gentle people of Abaton that you are their only chance for protection. And after you do, you'll ask to be named their prester."

The warden was silent. Then a moment later, a hand held up a dark, dull orb.

"I already am the prester, Khora," the warden said. "I have the Ancientmost Pearl. Not Prester Pinocchio. And not my niece."

Niece? Pinocchio staggered a step, the realization of what the warden was saying dizzying him.

"Then after we help you, my prester," Khora said. "Will we be rewarded?"

The warden leaned closer to the mirror, the hood drawing back slightly to reveal a lock of blue hair and Sapphira's crystalline gaze.

"You and your kind are monsters," she said. "There is no place in Abaton proper for monsters. But if all goes well, if you carry my demands out to the letter, you might still be rewarded. I can make sure that you never have to return to this prison again. Would you like that?"

Khora dipped her head.

"Very good, then. Destroy the ship before attacking the palace. And enjoy what you do best." The light from the mirror dimmed, Sapphira's face vanishing into cold black.

Pinocchio could scarcely believe this. Lady Sapphira was the warden! Lady Sapphira was sending these monsters against her own people. Pinocchio understood why she had taken the Pearl from him when she thought he was an automa. But this was something else entirely. She had been plotting against him and Lazuli all along, probably since their arrival in Abaton. And she was willing to put the lives of her people in danger to trick her way onto the throne.

Pinocchio ran toward Khora. "You can't help her!"

She rounded on him with dagger-slit eyes. "We are not helping her. We are helping ourselves."

"Attacking, destroying, these won't help you."

"But they're fun," the gruesome toad croaked.

"Look around," Khora said. "What have we to live for here? And if the warden fails to live up to her promise, if she tries to send us back, then I swear I will put a spine through her heart. We will be free!"

This threat was met with monstrous cheers from the others.

Pinocchio looked back to Khora. "But Prester Lazuli . . . you can't attack her! You can't—"

A fierce wind rose, whipping the mist into a whirlpool turned on its side. An opening formed at the center, bathing the gloomy prison with golden sunlight and a dizzying view of the jungle near the Moonlit Court, although from a vantage high in the sky.

"To battle!" Khora cried, throwing out her wings and charging toward the portal. She sailed through, disappearing into the sunlight beyond.

The rest of the ninety-eight monsters bellowed great growls

and cackles and cheers. The ones with wings took flight. The ones without leaped onto the backs of those who could fly. A drake swept down to grab the monstrous toad's thick folds in its talons before soaring out.

Pinocchio ran to the portal and looked down. Wherever this opened, it was unbelievably high in the air. If he jumped through, he'd come to a horrible, wood-splintering end.

"What are we going to do?" he asked Maestro.

"What do you think?" the cricket chirped. "We're stuck here. Besides, I have absolutely no wish to see the Moonlit Court decimated, nor to see those monsters devour Prester Lazuli."

"But we have to—"

A raspy croak sounded behind them. Pinocchio spun around. Azi was lumbering to his feet, his crimson eyes blinking from his dark serpentlike face. He was alive! Pinocchio gaped in amazement. Azi turned his gaze down at the stitched wound on his side. Pinocchio spied tiny white flowers blooming from the jasmine vine.

The wyvern threw out his leathery wings and rose into the air. He circled around the mists before launching himself toward the portal.

"Wait!" Pinocchio cried.

The wyvern's claws clamped around his shoulders, jerking Pinocchio off his feet and rocketing him and Maestro through the opening.

He looked first down past his wildly kicking legs at the jungle far, far below. Then he snapped his head around to peer at the wyvern's shiny beetle-black underbelly.

Azi stretched out his neck and pumped his great wings as he flew.

"He's going to drop you to your doom!" Maestro shrieked.

With a squawk, Azi cut a ruby eye at them. There was a hint of something playful in the wyvern's look.

"I don't think he is," Pinocchio said.

Azi let go of Pinocchio. He and Maestro plummeted straight down. Pinocchio screamed and flailed, but an instant later, the wyvern swooped beneath them, catching Pinocchio squarely on his back.

Pinocchio sat in disbelief half a moment before adjusting his legs around the wyvern's shoulders to give him room to flap.

"I . . . I told you he wouldn't drop me," he said.

"He did drop you!" Maestro protested.

"Not to my doom," Pinocchio said. "He's carrying us."

"Where?"

"I don't know."

Azi turned his head and rasped, "Just tell me where, my prester."

So wyverns spoke! One of these days, Pinocchio was determined to figure out which Abatonians did and which didn't.

"Look for Lazuli's ship!" he said, leaning forward to find a better grip on Azi's scaly neck.

The wyvern banked sideways in a stomach-lurching twirl. The rest of the monsters were scattered across the sky, searching for the flying ship. Faint cries of panic carried on the wind. Down at the Moonlit Court, tiny figures were emerging into the gardens, pointing at the sky. The streets of the Crescent Port around the harbor began to swell with curious and then alarmed citizens.

"They've seen the monsters," Pinocchio said. "They think they're under attack."

"Aren't they?" Maestro said.

"Not if I can help it."

Pinocchio scanned the skies, looking for any sign of Lazuli's ship. He wasn't sure what Sapphira had meant by a *nearly invisible ship*. Was it translucent or painted a sky-blue color? Or was it cloaked in some way so that it was almost impossible to spot? He hoped the latter. Maybe Lazuli could slip past Khora's monsters.

Some of the monsters were getting impatient with the search and swooping nearer to the towering Moonlit Court. Pinocchio heard squawks of pain as a few were hit by arrows from the Sky Hunters. Archers were appearing from balconies and windows to defend the palace. Others mounted griffins and took to the skies.

Cries of panic rose as those outside began flooding back toward the safety of the palace or into their homes and shops down by the harbor.

A sharp voice rang through the mayhem. Sapphira emerged on the palace steps, calling out orders to her archers. Dr. Nundrum, the djinn lord Smoldrin, and the undine lord Raya Piscus huddled in the palace doorway watching. The captain of her Sky Hunters came down to stand in front of Sapphira, defending her.

Pinocchio almost fell from Azi when he saw the captain. Over his suit of white, he wore gleaming armor and a helmet covering his long blue hair.

Pinocchio couldn't believe what he was seeing. Rion was alive.

The shock wave of understanding made Pinocchio dizzy. Rion hadn't merely survived the destruction of the pyramid, he'd escaped. Sapphira might have gotten Dr. Nundrum to convince them that the prison was in the pyramid, but Rion had been the one who led them there, knowing it was a trap, knowing he'd escape and thinking they wouldn't. The explosions—had Rion caused them? Of course he had. Why else would Rion have been so insistent that Lazuli not go to the Upended Forest, not enter the prison? He'd known what waited there for them.

Lady Sapphira had sent Rion to join their mission to protect Lazuli. She hadn't wanted harm to come to her niece. But she had for Pinocchio. To get the Ancientmost Pearl from him. To declare herself the prester.

Pinocchio narrowed his eyes at Rion. He'd thought Rion was their friend. He'd admired Rion, trusted him! Pinocchio cursed himself for being such a trusting fool.

But all the people of Abaton were trusting too. They trusted Lady Sapphira. As she stood on the palace steps holding the Ancientmost Pearl high, Pinocchio knew they believed only she could save them from this threat. This false threat. This deception.

The monsters—as dangerous as they might be—were not the real enemies here. Sapphira was.

Pinocchio shored up his grip on the wyvern. Time to set things straight.

"Azi," he called. "How good are you at dodging arrows?"

The wyvern gave an assuring croak. Giving another glance around, Pinocchio saw no signs that the monsters had spotted Lazuli's ship.

"Bring me down to those steps."

Azi flattened his barbed head and fell into a steep dive. As they sped nearer to the Moonlit Court, shocked, terrified faces watched them. Rion shouted orders to the Sky Hunters. Volleys of arrows were released. Azi turned out to be quite skilled at evading them. He tucked his wings and spun sideways in wild curlicues that might have sent Pinocchio flying if he hadn't gotten his knees locked tightly beneath the base of the wyvern's wings.

But as they streaked closer to Sapphira, the close-range shots were hard to avoid. Most of the arrows broke against Azi's thick hide, but a few embedded themselves with sharp *thwacks*. Azi reared back as he landed, beating his wings to blow aside the attacks. Pinocchio leaped off, landing at the bottom of the palace steps.

Half a dozen arrows thudded into his wooden chest and arms. More concerned for Azi's safety than his own—being wood had its advantages at such a moment—Pinocchio roared for the wyvern to get away. Reluctantly, Azi took back to the air.

"Lower your bows!" Pinocchio shouted, raising his hands. "I'm here to talk. I mean you no harm."

Maestro huddled at the back of Pinocchio's neck, shaking with terror.

Sapphira stood behind Rion, who had his bow drawn, shielding his mistress. Lord Smoldrin huddled back, the green seaweedy face of Raya Piscus and the wide eyes of Dr. Nundrum peering out from behind him. Frightened servants stared from the palace door and windows.

"M-mean us no harm?" Raya Piscus managed. "But you and your monsters are . . . Wait, who are you?"

Lord Smoldrin's eyes flamed as they took in the wooden boy. "Prester Pinocchio? But you're . . . alive?"

"He's not alive!" Sapphira said, from behind Rion. "Can't you see? He was never alive. He's some sort of wooden device—built by the alchemist Geppetto to allow Venice to claim the throne. We've been tricked! And now he's gained control of the imprisoned monsters as his army."

"This is a lie," Pinocchio said. "Sapphira is the one who tricked you . . . tricked us all!"

Lord Smoldrin rose to his feet, his yellow face contorting in confusion. "But at the Opaque Palace . . . everyone there said the monsters killed the presters."

"My dear niece . . . Her Majesty, our Prester Lazuli, she was killed," Sapphira said. "But not this *thing* masquerading as our prester. See my archers' arrows in him. He is made of wood. Wood enhanced by alchemy. Wood that cannot be broken or destroyed. This is a machine of murder, and it killed my niece!"

"I didn't kill Lazuli," Pinocchio said. "She's not dead. Lady Sapphira made it look like we were killed. She's the one who commands these monsters."

"How can you say that when you rode down on one of them?" Dr. Nundrum cried, pointing to Azi, who was circling out of range of the Sky Hunters' arrows.

"I saved that wyvern's life," Pinocchio hurried to explain. "He's helping me. But I don't control the others. Sapphira has been the warden of the prison all along. She's the one who's been releasing them to make you afraid, to trick you into crowning her the prester so she can save you from their attack."

"Then where is Prester Lazuli?" Raya Piscus bubbled.

"She's on the way," Pinocchio said. "But Sapphira's monsters are waiting up there to stop her. That's why they aren't attacking the Moonlit Court yet."

Dr. Nundrum and the noble lords threw up their hands and flinched as a shadow passed over the balcony. Pinocchio turned to see one of the skeletal birds with a ghoul rider sweep down before being driven back by a volley of arrows.

"But they are attacking!" Lord Smoldrin growled.

It was true—more than half of the monsters had begun to descend on the palace, their patience stretched thin as they longed to destroy something.

"We've heard enough of the automa's lies," Sapphira said.

"He lied about what he was to get on the throne. And now he lies about his involvement with these monsters. Captain Rion, stop this contraption."

Pinocchio looked Rion in the eye, hoping to see some hint of the old Rion who he'd believed was his friend.

Rion drew back his bow and launched an arrow. It sank with a crack into Pinocchio's shoulder. The arrow couldn't hurt him as an automa, but Pinocchio felt wounded all the same.

Other archers began firing. This was hopeless. His attempts to convince any of them that Sapphira was the traitor had utterly failed.

He turned to find Azi, but as he did, Maestro gave a squeak of alarm. Rion's griffin, Quila, stood behind Pinocchio, blocking his retreat. All at once the griffin pounced, knocking Pinocchio to the palace steps and pinning his arms with her powerful talons.

"Azi!" he started to call.

But up above, he saw griffins descend on the wyvern, locking him by the wings. They fought and snapped at one another, all the while tumbling from the sky until they disappeared into the gardens below.

"Now," Sapphira said, standing over Pinocchio. Her eyes flashed. "What to do about you . . ."

20.

The Warden

Cinnabar cut off the *Lionslayer*'s engines out over the ocean. They had followed the coast up to the capital and now that the Moonlit Court was in sight, he sailed the ship inland across the sparkling lagoon.

Lazuli watched from the sun-drenched decks. Monsters swarmed thickly in the skies around the palace, unleashing flames and howls and thunderous blows against the white marble walls. Cries of terror echoed all around. Whether inside the palace or trapped out on the grounds, her people were in danger, including her aunt.

Lazuli touched the pouch that held the Sands of Sleep. She hadn't used much on the guards at the Opaque Palace. But was there enough for all these monsters? It didn't matter. All that mattered was protecting her people as best she could. But to do that . . .

"If you're ready, Your Majesty," Chief Muckamire said. He looked a little queasy as he stared at the battle. Many of the gnomes around him were visibly shaking.

"I'll sail us down swiftly," Cinnabar said from the helm.

"Very good, darling," Mezmer said. "We'll have the element of surprise as we—"

"We can't," Lazuli said.

Cinnabar cocked his head like he'd misheard. "*Can't*, Your Majesty? Can't what?"

"Attack," Lazuli said. "Not down there. Not with so many of our people in harm's way."

"But what else is there to do?" the djinni asked.

As dangerous as the monsters were, Lazuli knew they were her people too. Her aunt might have been willing to kill, but Lazuli wasn't. She might not be the prester, but she couldn't do that to a child of Abaton. She just needed a way to trap the monsters so she could put them back to sleep. And the best way to do that was to draw them all to one spot.

"Fire the alchemical cannons," Lazuli said.

Cinnabar scowled. "But that will alert them to us."

"Exactly," Lazuli said.

Cinnabar and Mezmer exchanged confused glances.

"B-but . . ." Chief Muckamire blinked rapidly. "If the monsters attack us here, we won't have the sylph archers to help us. We'll have . . . we'll have to . . ."

"Face the monsters alone," Lazuli finished for him. "Yes, I'm afraid so, Chief Muckamire. We need to draw the monsters to our ship—get them all in one place so we can bind them, capture them, whatever we can do to stop them long enough to get the Sands of Sleep on them."

She turned to Cinnabar. "Do you have nets? Snares?"

"Yes, Your Majesty," he said. "We've got billow-nets that can be fired from the cannons, but—"

"Load them," Lazuli said. "Nothing lethal."

"Your Majesty," Chief Muckamire pleaded. "Are you sure about this approach?"

She turned to the gnome lord, doing her best to keep her uncertainty and worry from showing. "It has to be this way, my lord. You've helped us bravely, and I thank you. If you and your gnomes wish, I can have Cinnabar bring the ship down to the harbor so you can be let off."

Chief Muckamire looked around at his gnomes, furrowing his brow as he thought. "We are historians. Scholars and protectors of ancient knowledge. But we gnomes helped with the *Lionslayer* and I hope we will be remembered now as great builders too. What say you, my gnomes? Should we also go down as valiant warriors?"

"By *go down*," one gnome squeaked, "d-do you m-mean—?"

But already the expressions on the rest of Chief Muckamire's gnomes were changing one by one from apprehension to scowls of determination.

"For Abaton," one barked.

The others took up the rallying cry, even the gnome who hadn't been sure whether he was committing himself to going down in the history books or dying some horrible, heroic death— or possibly both.

"Very well," Mezmer said, giving a twirl to her spear. "Glorious battle it is. Cinnabar, the cannons."

The djinni raced down belowdecks, followed by several of the gnomes.

Geppetto stepped up next to Lazuli. He'd been quiet throughout the journey from the Mist Cities, lost in a fog of mourning for Pinocchio.

She reached out to touch his hand. "It's not too late for us to take you down, Master Geppetto. You have nothing left to hold you here to Abaton. You could find a way to return to Venice. You could carry on Pinocchio's wish to help those enslaved to the empire."

Geppetto's eyes were rimmed with misery as he stared out. "I've been a hunted traitor. I know that life. I have no wish for it again. I don't wish it for you either, Prester Lazuli. That might still be your fate here."

She winced at the title, uncertain she still deserved to be called prester.

"It's not too late for all of us to escape," he said. "We could leave Abaton and go where we would never fear—"

Lazuli shook her head. "I can't. This is my home. If we ever hope to rescue our people from the Venetian Empire, we need a home—a safe homeland—for them. For all of us."

Geppetto nodded. "Pinocchio wanted many things that have not come to pass. But he was your loyal friend, and he would not want me to abandon you now. I am with you to whatever end finds us."

An eruption sounded from belowdecks. The ship rocked as a fountain of fire shot out from a hatch. The aleya made a nervous chime as she spun several circles around the deck.

Lazuli gripped the railing, her knuckles turning white. The swarm of monsters attacking the palace grew still.

Cinnabar fired another cannon. The noise echoed across the jungle.

The swarm rose from the palace, gathering in a dark mass. The monsters had discovered them. And now they were coming.

Mezmer took Geppetto's shoulder. "Cinnabar will need your help belowdecks, darling."

He nodded and headed for the gangway.

Mezmer remained at Lazuli's side, watching the monsters' approach. "How will we get them back to the prison?" the fox asked.

"After we capture them—if we capture them—we'll deal with discovering who the warden is." Lazuli nodded to the Moonlit Court. "He's down there. I'm certain."

Cries and shrieks were already reaching the ship. The mass of charging monsters grew larger.

Lazuli called to Chief Muckamire. "Have your gnomes gather the ropes. Any that land on deck, we'll drive your way. Bind them."

Chief Muckamire barked orders at his gnomes as they scattered to get ready.

Lazuli drew her sword. The knights and gnomes took positions across the deck. Wini and her kirin sisters stomped their hooves against the boards. The aleya started to bob up and down. Goliath pounded his fists against his mushroom cap, talking to himself under his breath with little "Come on, beasties! You want a taste of Goliath? You don't know who you're dealing with here." Kataton blinked his extended eyes, looking more like someone about to take a nap than a warrior facing a horde of bloodthirsty monsters.

The sound of the monsters swelled like a storm. The bright tropical skies darkened ominously as the howling, darting forms surrounded the ship.

"Get ready!" Mezmer cried.

A drake swooped down, dropping a cobra-headed naga onto the deck, followed by several ghouls who leaped off skeletal birds. The knights charged, clashing swords with the landing monsters. Lazuli threw out a hand, sending a gust of wind into the naga, who flipped over the railing.

Cannons erupted, not with flames, but now with the hiss of projectile nets that flung out, encircling clusters of monsters. Cables attaching the nets to winches spooled out, until the monsters dropped beneath the ship's hull in bundles.

More monsters were landing on the decks. Mezmer's orders cut through the mayhem.

"Don't hide behind your shields, darlings. Fight! Sop, drive off that nasty toad that just landed at the stern. Nice jab, Pini. You really are getting quite vicious with that horn! Kataton, behind you! Yes, darling, hold that thing down while Wumble binds him! Here comes another . . ."

Mobs of gnomes had tied up several of the attacking monsters, but more kept coming. Lazuli spied a creature that seemed like nothing more than a green-skinned maiden slithering over the railing. It hardly looked threatening, but as Lazuli hesitated, the creature opened its mouth, revealing a mass of long, foul teeth. Its face morphed into something misshapen and hideous. Its nails grew into ragged black talons.

Lazuli summoned a gale to blast the thing away. But the creature screamed—the force of its wailing cut through the elemental wind and sent Lazuli tumbling back. The creature launched at her, snapping that mouth of hideous teeth.

But when it bit down, it found the pole of Mezmer's spear in its jaws.

"Get back, darling!" Mezmer shouted.

Lazuli scrambled to her feet. The creature splintered Mezmer's spear and rounded its face toward her.

Lazuli reached for the pouch at her belt holding the Sands of Sleep. She'd only need a little. But before she could pull loose the string, the creature wailed once more. The blast picked Lazuli and Mezmer up off their feet, sending them skidding against the gangway hatch.

"Your Majesty," Mezmer said, reaching for Lazuli.

"I'm fine," Lazuli said, shaking off the dizziness.

The aleya shot at the wailing creature, chiming angrily and spinning around its face to distract it from her prester.

"But you won't be for long," Mezmer said, pulling Lazuli to her feet. "None of us will be. There are too many monsters."

Wini and her sisters joined the aleya, surrounding the wailing creature and driving it toward a group of gnomes with coils of rope in their shaking hands. But the knights were outnumbered. More monsters kept coming.

And with a heavy thump, a great batwinged lion with a midnight-blue face and a barbed tail landed on the quarterdeck. Lazuli recognized her immediately—the manticore from the banquet.

"We've got to get belowdecks," Lazuli said to Mezmer.

The fox shouted, "Pull back, my glorious knights!"

The gnomes flooded down first. Kataton had lost his ax, but had begun using Goliath instead, ramming him against the monsters to defend the others as Lazuli and her knights retreated.

Once they were below, Lazuli ordered the others behind her. She opened the pouch with the Sands of Sleep and dug out a handful. A mob of monsters was pushing its way through the hatch. Lazuli scattered Sands across them and instantly the monsters collapsed in a heap, their bodies blocking the door. Snarls and shoves came from behind the sleeping pile as the monsters on deck tried to get past.

"That might hold them back for now," Lazuli said to Mezmer.

Cinnabar appeared through a trapdoor in the floor. "Your Majesty, we've exhausted our nets, and unfortunately they've done little good. The smolder spirits burned through the ropes. I think they're starting to set alight the hull."

Glass shattered next to them. A skeletal bird pecked its beak through the window. Several gnomes squeaked, along with the aleya.

Sop leaped forward. His sword cracked against the enormous bird's gruesome beak. The creature croaked and pulled back. But a moment later they heard wood crunch.

"It's pecking through the planks!" Cinnabar growled.

Up at the gangway hatch, Mezmer, Kataton, and Goliath had their shoulders against the sleeping monsters, desperate to hold back the monsters trying to push their way inside.

Chief Muckamire squeezed his way through the tide of bodies to reach Lazuli. "They're tearing the ship apart, Your Majesty! Maybe we should surrender."

Cinnabar narrowed his yellow eyes. "I doubt these monsters are interested in us surrendering, Chief Muckamire."

"Then what should we do?" the gnome lord cried.

Lazuli looked around at the gnomes and her knights. They were trapped and hopelessly out of options.

"The monsters are retreating," Lord Smoldrin gasped.

On the steps of the palace, Sapphira watched the monsters with the barest hint of a smile forming at the corners of her lips. The others, with their faces turned in puzzlement to the horde flying away, might not have seen. But Pinocchio had.

He wrestled against the griffin's hold. Despite his automa strength, he was twisted at such an angle—arms pinned by his sides, knees locked together—that he couldn't get enough leverage to push the griffin off.

"Lazuli!" Maestro squeaked in his ear.

"It's Prester Lazuli's ship!" Pinocchio shouted. "The monsters left because they've spotted it. They're attacking her!"

"My high nobles," Sapphira said, "do either of you see a ship?"

Raya Piscus shook her head in her sloshing shroud. Lord Smoldrin, however, said, "But what made those explosions? Something drew them up there. They're attacking . . . something."

"They are monsters—creatures of chaos and mayhem," Sapphira said. "Whatever has attracted their attention won't interest them for long. They'll be back and I want all my archers ready. This time we show no mercy."

Pinocchio grunted beneath Quila. He had to help Lazuli. His father and all his friends were up there being attacked. The griffin dug her lion claws deeper into the wood of his legs, grasped her talons more tightly around his arms.

"But first, Captain Rion," Sapphira said, turning back toward Pinocchio. "Have your griffin finish with the puppet."

Rion nodded at Quila. The griffin locked her powerful hooked beak onto the sides of Pinocchio's face and began to tug.

Maestro gave a terrified squeal. "Let go of him, you overgrown chicken!"

Pinocchio grunted, fighting to get an arm or a leg free. He could feel the gears in his neck straining under the griffin's pull.

How could they so callously do this to him? But in their eyes, Pinocchio was a thing, not a person—something foreign and despised, something to simply be disassembled and discarded.

Any moment, he felt as if his head would come free. He squeezed his eyes shut.

Then all the pressure, all the force of the huge griffin, was gone. Pinocchio thought his head must have come loose and now he could no longer feel his body. But his head wasn't in her beak. Quila was off of him, tumbling across the steps and scattering the high nobles and Rion and Dr. Nundrum.

Azi stood over Pinocchio and issued a furious roar. His hide was bloodied, torn, and clawed in places from his fight against the other griffins. He looked absolutely terrifying.

Maestro clung to Pinocchio's shirt. "Get on!" he piped.

Pinocchio grabbed the wyvern's wing and hoisted himself onto his back. Arrows began raining down, but Azi drew up on his hind legs and beat his wings, carrying them into the sky.

"Hurry, Azi!" Pinocchio said. "We've got to save our prester."

Lazuli was trapped in the middle of the galley, surrounded by her knights and the gnomes who were desperately defending her. But monsters were nearly through the sleeping mass clogging the gangway and were breaking through the windows and walls. She shut her eyes, holding Master Geppetto's hand, readying herself for . . .

A high, piercing screech cut through the howls up above.

The monsters around them froze. "Azi?" one of them murmured. They looked at one another curiously.

In the silence that had fallen, a voice carried from up on deck. ". . . Khora, call them off!"

Lazuli knew that voice! And as Geppetto's mouth fell open, she knew he recognized it as well.

"Pinocchio?" she breathed. "He's . . . alive?"

The monsters began drawing back through the holes. Lazuli

couldn't wait any longer. She pointed at the pile of sleeping monsters in the hatch doorway. "Get them out of the way!"

Mezmer, Kataton, Sop, and Goliath began pulling the monsters, dragging them by arms and legs until an opening was cleared. Lazuli clambered through into the bright sunlight on deck.

The others were scrambling out behind her. Shielding her eyes, Lazuli was struck first by the terrible state of the decks. Rails had been torn away. Boards splintered. Most of the sails hung in tatters. Cinnabar gave a distraught whimper.

Mezmer and her knights surrounded Lazuli, taking defensive positions, although many were badly injured. Monsters clung to every side of the ship, but they hardly seemed to notice Lazuli or her defenders. Their gazes were fixed on a wyvern hovering several yards off the stern.

The midnight-blue manticore was facing the wyvern, their wings beating in alternating time.

Lazuli shook her head in disbelief. Pinocchio was an automa and yet his eyes were ablaze with determination that no automa could ever have shown. Stranger still, he was sitting on the wyvern's back. Was she really seeing this? Had he tamed the monster? And why weren't the other monsters tearing Pinocchio apart, as they had the ship?

"Azi was dead," the manticore hissed. "How can this be? I saw the last of his heart's blood spill. And yet . . . you saved him?"

Pinocchio nodded. "And now Azi has saved me."

The wyvern made a low croak at Pinocchio: "Twice."

"Well, now," Pinocchio said, "that first time you dropped me, so really—"

"How have you done this?" The manticore narrowed her jade-green eyes.

Pinocchio shook his head. "I don't know. I don't even know

how I'm this way. . . . It doesn't matter. I do know that you are no longer the real traitors to Abaton. The warden is. Your warden is the real monster!"

Lazuli blinked. Had Pinocchio discovered who the warden was?

"We are monsters too," the manticore replied.

"Only if you believe you are," Pinocchio said. "Khora, you and the others were made to believe that, by Diamancer and by how your kind were treated all those centuries ago. You claim you only like to destroy, but I saw your faces when the mists parted. Don't you want to be part of Abaton again?"

Lazuli couldn't believe Pinocchio was offering to free these traitors. And more so, she couldn't believe that he was able to hold the monsters at bay with only his words. While many of the monsters looked impatient, many others were listening, especially the manticore Khora.

"The warden promised we would not have to return to the Mist," Khora said. "We would never return to our prison."

Lazuli drew back with surprise at the realization that the Mist was the prison.

"You trust her promises?" Pinocchio asked.

Many of the monsters gave low growls. Khora curled her lip, showing her fangs.

"Prester John spared your lives after Diamancer's Rebellion," Pinocchio said. "He covered you in the Sands of Sleep and locked you in the prison until the time came that you were ready to repent for your treason. Today is that day! You aren't monsters. You're Abatonians, like the rest of us. Today you can win your freedom."

"You cannot give us our freedom, wooden boy," the manticore said. "Your promise is empty. You are not our prester."

Hard as it was for Lazuli to comprehend, Pinocchio seemed to feel something for these monsters. Hadn't that always been Pinocchio's way? From the arachnobats of the Upended Forest to Gragl and her barnacle people in the belly of the Deep One, Pinocchio was able to see them not as monstrous, but as they really were. As a prester should.

"But he could be!" Lazuli shouted. "He could be your prester!"

Khora brought her narrowed green eyes around to Lazuli.

"He's just a lad of lumber, a timber tot." A ghoul laughed from the back of his darting bat. "Nothing more."

"He is your prester," Lazuli said firmly.

"He does not have the Ancientmost Pearl," Khora said. "And neither do you, daughter of Prester John."

"Enough talky-talky," one of the drakes growled. "Let us destroy something, Khora."

Khora did not reply, her eyes wandering between Pinocchio and Lazuli.

"The warden ordered us to destroy the ship," a cobra-headed naga hissed. "We should finish it, so we can get to demolishing the Moonlit Court!"

"Yes! Yes!" others cheered.

Lazuli knew that Khora must be weighing Pinocchio's words, but she could read nothing from the manticore's dark expression to give her any assurance.

"If you won't help me," Pinocchio said, "that is your choice. But I won't allow you to harm Lazuli or any aboard this ship."

Many of the monsters laughed.

"Don't listen to him, Khora," a smolder spirit called. "We saw the warden holding the Ancientmost Pearl. She has the powers of the prester. He can do nothing to stop us."

Lazuli startled at those words. The warden had the Pearl? But no, that couldn't be. Her aunt had the Pearl. . . .

"I don't know what powers you possess," Khora said, staring fiercely at Pinocchio, "but you brought Azi back to us. You returned his life."

The wyvern cast his writhing neck back at Pinocchio.

"It is for that I will honor your request," Khora said. "We have had enough fun here. We have stopped their ship from reaching the Moonlit Court as the warden commanded."

Several of the monsters grumbled.

Khora gnashed her teeth at them. "I say we have done enough! It is time to move our revelry to the Moonlit Court. Azi! You will come with us. Leave the wooden boy."

The wyvern gave a weak croak. But Pinocchio patted his neck and Azi swooped past Khora, landing on the deck of the *Lionslayer*, where Pinocchio leaped off.

One by one, the monsters clinging to the sides of the ship let go, taking to the skies. Khora was the last to follow. She gave Pinocchio an inscrutable look before throwing out her wings and flapping toward the Moonlit Court.

Geppetto rushed at Pinocchio, taking hold of his face and drinking in the sight of him nearly nose to nose. "My boy! My boy! Is this true?" He engulfed his son in a fierce hug.

Mezmer, Sop, and the others pressed in, reaching for Pinocchio, seeming to need to touch him to believe he was real.

Lazuli forced her way through the throng. "You're really alive!" Joy shot through her as she said the words, barely believing they were true.

Pinocchio smiled around at all his friends, but then the smile faltered as cries and screams rose from the Moonlit Court. The palace was under attack once more.

Lazuli suddenly remembered what Khora had said about the warden. "Pinocchio, how did the warden get the Pearl from my aunt?"

Pinocchio looked at her with confusion. "But . . . don't you know? Your aunt . . . she's the warden."

Lazuli felt her knees start to buckle. Pinocchio grabbed her by the arm. Her head was swimming, fighting against the words Pinocchio had spoken. They couldn't be true. Not her aunt. She wasn't the warden.

"You're wrong," she murmured.

Pinocchio shook his head as if he wished for all the world he didn't have to say the words. "She is. I saw Lady Sapphira in the prison, speaking—"

"No," Lazuli choked.

"She's the warden," Pinocchio said. "All along, she's the one who's been working against us. The attack at the banquet. The trap at the pyramid." He waved a hand toward the Moonlit Court. "All this! It's part of her plan to become the prester."

Lazuli squeezed her eyes shut, shaking her head. When her aunt had taken the Pearl from Pinocchio and spoken so pitilessly about how she'd gotten rid of him, Lazuli hadn't wanted to believe she could be capable of such deceit. She'd thought her aunt hadn't understood about Pinocchio—that she'd simply done this terrible act for what her aunt believed was a good reason.

Lazuli looked at Pinocchio through tear-blurred eyes.

"I'm sorry, Lazuli," Pinocchio said. "I tried to tell them. I reached the palace and tried to explain that . . . But I failed. They wouldn't believe me." He looked at his wooden hands with frustration. "But why would they? They saw what I am."

Cries carried up from the palace, along with the sounds of breaking stone. Lazuli looked away from the white tower rising up from the jungle surrounded by swarming, swooping monsters. She couldn't bear to watch. "Is there no way to stop this?"

"It will stop soon," Pinocchio said. "Lady Sapphira doesn't intend for the palace to be destroyed. She just wants to frighten everyone, and make it seem like she saved her people—"

An explosion sounded. Lazuli pressed against the railing with the others. Several more bright explosions flashed in the sky, sending monsters plummeting into the gardens.

Lazuli strained her eyes to see what was happening, but Sop, who always saw the best with his one good eye, said, "Exploding arrows. They're using some sort of exploding arrows. Now, where did they get those?"

"Thunderseeds," Lazuli murmured. Of course, from the orchards of the Mist Cities. "My aunt doesn't intend to send the monsters back to the prison," she said. "She told me as much, although I was too foolish to understand completely at the time . . ."

"But Lady Sapphira promised Khora and the others," Pinocchio said, "that they'd never have to see the prison again."

She looked at him, realizing that if her aunt was the warden, then at the banquet and at the battle in the Mist Cities, Sapphira had simply been able to send the monsters back to the prison when they had wreaked enough havoc. But this time . . .

"My aunt wasn't promising them freedom. She intends to kill them. All of them. And she has the Pearl. With that . . . none of the monsters will escape."

21.

The Assault on the Moonlit Court

Lazuli could see Pinocchio tremble as he gripped the ship's railing. "Your aunt told our people you were dead," he said. "That I killed you. If we could only reach the palace . . . we could show them you're not!"

Lazuli felt cold with fear. How could she face her aunt again? She loved her aunt dearly, this woman who had been her mother's sister and the high noble to her mother's people. She couldn't bear to look into Sapphira's eyes knowing she would now see a stranger or worse: she'd see her aunt as she really was, her betrayal and treachery unmasked.

But if this was to end—if her people were to be saved—she would have to. Even if it broke Lazuli's heart to pieces, Abaton needed her to be brave.

She turned to Cinnabar. "Is there no way to get the ship down? The alchemical canisters? The—"

"Gone." The djinni waved a claw helplessly toward his beloved *Lionslayer*. "The ship can't go anywhere, Your Majesty. I'm sorry."

Lazuli felt something butt against her arm. She turned to see Wini. "I can carry you, Your Majesties."

The kirin and her sisters had been injured in the battle with the monsters. Fini and Pini lay on the deck, licking their wounds.

"But you're hurt, Wini," Lazuli said.

Wini forced her pearly horn high. "A knight of the Celestial Brigade serves to the end. It would be my honor."

Mezmer clutched her chest with pride.

But Geppetto shook his head ferociously. "This is madness. Even if Wini could carry you down, how would you get past those arrows?"

Cinnabar reached over the side of the ship's railing and gave a heavy tug that sounded of ripping fabric. He held something in his hands that looked like nothing more than open sky. "The chameleon cloth," the djinni said. "It masked the ship. It can mask Wini."

Pinocchio gave him a grateful grin as he took one side of the cloth. "I'll help you cover them," he said to the djinni.

"You're coming with me," Lazuli said.

Pinocchio blinked his wooden eyelids. "What? But they know what I am."

"So we don't have to fear that anymore," Lazuli said. "We are the rightful presters, Pinocchio. It's time we show our people who we are. It's time we show them who my aunt is! When they see the truth, they can decide for themselves which prester they will follow."

Geppetto grabbed for Pinocchio's hand, an argument already on his lips. But Lazuli said, "Master Geppetto, I know you've only just gotten Pinocchio back. You're afraid for him. I'm afraid too. But we can't let our fears hold us back any longer."

Pinocchio exchanged a worried glance with his father and then with Lazuli. "Are you sure?" he asked her.

Lazuli climbed onto Wini's back and held out a hand.

Pinocchio gave the chameleon cloth back to Cinnabar and got on behind Lazuli.

Lazuli unsheathed her sword and dropped it to the deck of the ship. This battle wouldn't be won with swords. Pinocchio seemed to understand, and with a nod, he let his sword clatter beside hers.

As Cinnabar began to drape the cloth over them, Wini glanced to her sisters. "Farewell," she called. A hole tore as the cloth pulled over Wini's horn, making a narrow opening for them to see out.

Lazuli could feel poor Wini trembling beneath her. She gave the kirin a gentle stroke. "Whenever you're ready," she whispered.

Wini shot from the deck, soaring into the sky and circling the *Lionslayer*. Geppetto and Cinnabar, Sop and Mezmer, all the knights and all the gnomes watched with somber stillness, their eyes searching but never quite spotting where Lazuli and Pinocchio were.

Wini sped across the lagoon and toward the Moonlit Court. With the palace and the battle growing rapidly closer, Lazuli felt Pinocchio hold tighter to her waist with his hard wooden hands.

Lazuli had barely had time to wonder at how inexplicable it was that Pinocchio was alive. Not just that he'd survived those monsters, but that he was an automa, and yet, he was himself.

"Pinocchio!" she gasped. Her mind began racing with more

thoughts than she could easily weave together. But a thread was forming, and it began with the realization that Pinocchio was not merely an automa again.

"How did you bring the wyvern back to life?" she asked quickly.

"I don't know. It might have had something to do with the Mist. The prison . . . the Mist, it's not what we thought. It's alive. It's the primordial of air."

"The Roc?" Lazuli gasped. Could that really be? She'd always imagined that the great bird of so many sylph legends lived somewhere high in the uppermost reaches of the sky. But of course, like Regolith at Grootslang Hole, the primordials each seemed to reside near their elemental people.

"When I saved Azi, a feather appeared," Pinocchio said. "That's how Maestro discovered what the Mist really was. So maybe the Roc was showing me that *it* had saved Azi."

"But that can't be," Lazuli said. "A primordial couldn't bring back the dead. Only the Pearl has that power."

Pinocchio's voice pitched higher. "Except I don't have the Pearl. Your aunt does!"

When her aunt had held the Ancientmost Pearl, it had been dull and colorless, as if all the light had gone from it.

"The magic must still be inside you," she gasped. "It's got to be. It's why you're this way, and not acting like a thoughtless automa. And—"The realization dawned on her with such clarity. She'd not believed it before, because she'd always thought only Pinocchio possessed the magic of the Pearl. He had been the one with the Pearl, after all.

But now she could see that the powers didn't belong exclusively to the Pearl. They belonged to the presters—the ones sworn to protect Abaton and its people.

Lazuli had that power too. It was why the Sands of Sleep hadn't affected her. It was why she'd been able to summon winds in the pyramid that no normal sylph could ever have managed.

"What?" Pinocchio asked. "What were you going to say?"

Before she could answer, Wini was weaving through the monsters and into the thick of the battle. Lazuli caught sight of the palace steps with her aunt defended by . . . Was that Rion?

But just then, as Wini dodged around a screeching drake, something exploded next to them.

The blast of the thunderseed-tipped arrow threw Wini from her course. The kirin spiraled and Lazuli, ears ringing from the explosion, thought for a moment she and Pinocchio would fall before Wini righted again. Lazuli hung dizzily against the kirin's neck. The chameleon cloak had protected them from the worst of the blast. But it now lay in tattered ruins.

The wide, surprised eyes of the Sky Hunters, as well as the icy glare of Sapphira, began locking on them.

"The automa!" she cried.

Lazuli realized the remaining pieces of the cloak were still draped over her and Wini. She couldn't imagine what the archers thought Pinocchio was riding, but from all along the balconies, Sky Hunters took aim with their bows.

"Pinocchio!" Lazuli shouted. "The powers are still inside you. And they're inside me too. We have to use them . . . NOW!"

All Pinocchio could think was that Wini was in danger. Truthfully all three of them were, but his heart felt lodged in his throat at the thought that the brave kirin was going to lose her life when that volley of explosive arrows was released. There was no time to question what Lazuli was saying, no time to wrestle with doubt.

Wini couldn't see where to go with the tatters of the chameleon cloth over her eyes. In her panic, she was speeding headlong into the archers' range. Sky Hunters were drawing back their bows.

Pinocchio held up a hand. When the marble walls of the Opaque Palace had been coming down, he had made a shield. Air and earth. That might do it.

Cascades of arrows streaked toward them.

Pinocchio couldn't feel the sensation in his arms like before. Was Lazuli wrong about the powers? But then a faint tingling gathered and—

A dome of blurry substance, almost like thick translucent glass, extended before Wini's snout. The first of the arrows met it, exploding in bright flashes of noise.

At first, the dome held against the blasts. But as more of the thunderseed-tipped arrows struck with their deafening booms, the dome began to crack.

"It's breaking!" Pinocchio cried.

Lazuli fought to pull away the tattered cloth, freeing her hands so she could extend them. Another explosion. Another crack.

With a shout, Lazuli unleashed not just a blast of wind, but more of the strange glass, more of the combined elemental magic, as he had done. The dome swelled. The cracks were gone. The Sky Hunters' volleys of exploding arrows struck, but did nothing to penetrate the shield he and Lazuli had made.

The archers, seeing their attack fail, lowered their bows.

Lazuli smiled back at Pinocchio, her eyes luminous.

"You did it!" he gasped.

Lazuli patted the kirin and pulled loose the remaining cloth. "Take us down, Wini."

Wini tipped her horn and picked up speed, diving for the palace steps. Out the windows and from hiding places in the gardens, servants and palace officials and citizenry emerged—all eyes following them. Voices carried: "Is that Prester Lazuli?" "She's alive!"

Wini landed. Lord Smoldrin, Raya Piscus, and Dr. Nundrum poured out from the palace behind Sapphira, staring in open-mouthed disbelief. Rion and his griffin, Quila, drew in front of Sapphira protectively.

"What is this?" Lord Smoldrin asked, swinging his great horned head toward Sapphira. "I thought you said the automa killed your niece?"

"Pinocchio has done nothing to harm me," Lazuli said, climbing off the kirin. Pinocchio thought he saw her hesitate, trembling and trying not to look at her aunt. "This is a lie that . . . my aunt told you. One of many lies she has used to trick you into declaring her your prester."

Sapphira's face was a mask of poise under the shocked and bewildered gazes of the nobles and servants. She shook her head slowly, almost remorsefully.

"I'm afraid I have lied to you, my people," Sapphira said. "I did not want you to know about my niece. About her treachery. How she plotted with the alchemist Geppetto to put this Venetian contraption on our throne. Yes, I told you she had been murdered by the automa. In truth, I imprisoned her in the Opaque Palace to spare you from having to learn that Prester John's own daughter has been nothing but a traitor to Abaton."

"I'm not the traitor," Lazuli said. "I—"

"You refused to help me stop these monsters," Sapphira said. "I begged you to join me, to stand with me as prester, but you refused. Do you deny it?"

"I refused to help you kill them," Lazuli admitted. "As prester, I am bound to protect the people of Abaton—all the people of Abaton. Not just the nobles or the gentle races, but also the wayward ones, the monsters, and even those who have left Abaton for the humanlands but long to return. A true prester would never do what you have done, Aunt."

"You are not the true prester," Sapphira said coolly. "I am. I have the Ancientmost Pearl." She held the dark orb aloft for all to see.

Lazuli took a step forward. She shook ever so slightly—not from fear, Pinocchio thought, but from sadness that she was having to stand before her aunt in this way.

"Use it, then," Lazuli said.

Dr. Nundrum and the nobles edged back from Sapphira. Silence had fallen over the battle. Monsters and archers alike were frozen, flapping in the air or watching from the balconies as this other battle was taking place between Lazuli and Sapphira.

Sapphira held the Pearl before her with both hands cupped around it. Her eyes closed, a furrow creasing her brow. Pinocchio could see that she was genuinely trying. She believed she might somehow be able to command its powers. But he knew, at last, where that magic lay.

Hadn't his father discovered this back at Grootslang Hole from the books in the gnomes' library? Prester John had written that the Pearl itself was not the source of his powers. It had merely been a vessel to contain the wild magic of Abaton when Prester John's dreams and fears had come to life. When that vessel had been placed in Pinocchio, the wild magic had returned. But it still belonged to Abaton's presters.

Khora's voice carried from the skies above. "She can't command it. She cannot summon the Pearl's powers!"

The monsters around her began to smile terrible smiles, eyes flaming and growls rumbling from inside them.

Khora dove toward Sapphira, and Pinocchio knew immediately what she intended to do. She had promised to put a spike in the heart of the warden. The manticore whipped around with her deadly tail.

Pinocchio threw out a hand. A translucent shield rose up. The spikes shattered against it. "No, Khora!" he shouted. "That isn't the way."

The manticore fumed, fangs grinding together as she flapped a circle over the palace steps. But then tendrils of mist began to envelop her.

"You dare to attack me," Sapphira hissed. She was pointing at the manticore.

Khora seemed trapped momentarily, her hind legs consumed by the Mist that would drag her back into the prison, her forepaws clawing at the empty air, her fangs snarling and snapping.

The nobles gasped, as if finally seeing that Sapphira did command some power from the Pearl.

"Lady Sapphira," Pinocchio said. "As prester, it's time I strip you of your powers as the warden."

"You have no authority over me, you wooden puppet," Sapphira said.

But the Mist holding Khora vanished, releasing her.

Lord Smoldrin and Raya Piscus looked at each other. Then the lady of the undines said, "Is this true? You're the warden, Lady Sapphira?"

Sapphira was breathing hard, her nostrils flared, the mask she worked so hard to present on the verge of shattering. "His Great Lordship Prester John entrusted me with the wardenship. He chose me for this responsibility."

She looked wild-eyed at all the faces staring at her. "I . . . I only . . ." She drew herself up tall, her eyes narrowing into shards of blue light. "Abaton deserves someone worthy of Prester John's mantle. You said so yourself, Lord Smoldrin and Raya Piscus!" She pointed at them. "Do you not remember? Abaton should not be *entrusted to children*! It deserves a great ruler."

The djinni lord wrung his hands while Raya Piscus backed up a step in her sloshing shroud.

"My aunt is quite right," Lazuli said. "Abaton does deserve a great ruler. And I admit, I was doubtful Pinocchio and I could be. I feared, as you must have, that we wouldn't rule with the sort of greatness my father possessed. We haven't ruled as my father did. But we have tried to protect Abaton and its people the way we thought best."

She looked around at the frightened faces of her countrymen. "I ask you, my people, to forgive me for hiding the truth about Pinocchio. I admit I was wrong—wrong to doubt that the wise people of Abaton could see Pinocchio for who he really is, to accept him despite what he was."

"*Was?*" Sapphira said. "He *is* an automa. There's no questioning it!"

Lazuli turned to Pinocchio. "Are you?"

Pinocchio tilted his head. Of course he was. But then something lit up inside him as he understood. He was only this way because Abaton's magic had brought his fears to life.

"No," he whispered. And then he gathered his voice a little louder. "No. I'm not."

A tingling rose inside him. It started somewhere beneath the dull wood, but quickly began coursing along his arms and legs until it reached the tips of his fingers and toes. The top of his head suddenly tickled as strands of hair separated and were tossed in the wind. And his skin . . . oh, he had skin again! The warmth of the sunlight and the wind and even the beads of sweat now forming were all so wonderful.

The nobles gasped. Dr. Nundrum fumbled to push his glasses up his beak. Even Rion lowered his bow slightly, transfixed by what he had witnessed.

"Can't you see this is more of his trickery?" Sapphira pointed to Pinocchio. "Alchemy has made this wooden thing look as if it is more powerful than it is. Do not be fooled."

"This is no trick," Lazui said. "You are seeing Pinocchio as he was and as he is. An automa who became a living human boy."

"But is he the rightful prester?" Raya Piscus bubbled. "That is what we still don't know."

Lord Smoldrin murmured with agreement. The nobles and servants, the Sky Hunters and monsters, all watched uncertainly.

"Good people of Abaton," Lazuli said, looking around at them all. "The Ancientmost Pearl in my aunt's hands is not the source of the prester's powers. That magic comes from Abaton itself—given to the rightful ruler who protects Abaton's people. All of Abaton's people."

Khora's gaze met Pinocchio's, her jade eyes wide.

"Pinocchio has shown that he only ever wanted to help our people," Lazuli said. "Even those that my aunt was willing to kill. Pinocchio has been given the prester's powers because he is the true prester."

"And you have them as well," Pinocchio said.

Lazuli nodded. "I do. It's time we prove to you who your rightful presters are." She turned to Pinocchio and said quietly, "Are you ready?"

For what? he mouthed to her.

"To summon it here."

"*It* who?" Pinocchio asked.

"As prester, you command the primordials. The Roc recognized you as the prester. That's why it revealed the feather after you saved Azi. Call upon the Roc now, to prove to your people once and for all."

Pinocchio stared at her, hardly believing what she was saying. She wanted him to summon the Roc . . . here?

The flash in her eyes answered him.

"Well, you're the prester too," Pinocchio said. "You've got to help me." He reached out and took her hand.

"What do we do?" Lazuli said quietly.

"Close your eyes," Pinocchio said. "We'll summon it together."

Lazuli nodded, and they closed their eyes.

Pinocchio spoke first, barely above a whisper. "Roc, primordial elemental of air, guardian of Abaton, your presters need you." When he repeated the command, Lazuli joined him. They said it together over and over, a little louder each time. And as they did, Pinocchio mustered every bit of tingling magic with the hope it would bring forth the primordial creature. He knew Lazuli must be doing the same.

"This is a farce," Sapphira said, giving a thin laugh. "The powers that belonged to His Great Lordship are gone. The Ancientmost Pearl is empty of its powers. So, my high nobles, people of Abaton, you must choose who you will have rule. Will you let these children with their games and foolishness deceive you? Or will you choose a ruler who can offer Abaton peace and security as we've always—"

Lady Sapphira's words were drowned by gasps and then cries rising all around. A wild wind broke across the palace steps.

Lazuli squeezed Pinocchio's hand and said, "Look!"

Heart racing, Pinocchio let his eyes flutter open.

Filling the sky behind the palace was the great looming wall of the Mist. The mass swirled and started to change. A spire elongated from the front. The sides flattened out into wide, feathery strands of cloud. A shape was forming.

Lord Smoldrin and Raya Piscus came down the steps to get a better look. All heads were turned to the sight.

The Mist transformed. The spire at the front became what was unmistakably an enormous raptor's head and beak, although composed of churning, steely-colored storm clouds. The sides drew up into wings so large the sunlight dimmed. A cry erupted, like no sound Pinocchio had ever heard: a piercing screech that crackled with lightning and sent rumbles across the landscape like a peal of thunder that might never end. It shook the steps beneath their feet.

Dr. Nundrum began flapping his feathered hands. "That is no trick! They've summoned the Roc!"

Pinocchio saw Lady Sapphira glower at the owl before her gaze returned to the sky.

The sheer size of the Roc—or maybe it was that the creature was composed entirely of mist—made its movements appear like time had been slowed. But as it flapped, each protracted beat sending out feathery wisps, the Roc grew alarmingly larger and larger.

Pinocchio was aware that a hush had fallen over the scene. Monsters and archers and palace servants alike were all petrified by the eerie sight. Even Wini trembled, huddling behind him.

Lazuli cried, "My good people of Abaton, we were deceived by my aunt. And our land was nearly torn apart by her plot. Sky Hunters of the Mist Cities, if you lay down your arms and promise to defend our land—even against your own ladyship—then your betrayal will be forgiven."

Rion held his weapon hesitantly, but the others began casting down their bows and spilling quivers of arrows to the ground.

Khora landed on the steps. Pinocchio thought, for a moment, that she was making another attempt on Sapphira's life, but the manticore sank to her stomach, flattening her body and her great batlike wings. She fixed her gaze at his feet. "You, Prester Pinocchio, were cast into the prison with us. Yet you did not hate us."

From the corner of his eye, Pinocchio spied Azi circling in the sky, his barbed head directed at the presters as he listened.

"I cannot speak for the others, but I would obey and serve such a prester," Khora continued. "And Prester Lazuli, who is also brave and powerful and wishes only to protect our people. My presters, you offered me my freedom if I would pledge loyalty to the protection of Abaton. It wars against my very nature as a monster, but I can change. Abaton has changed since the days when Prester John ruled. If I . . . could but beg that you . . ." She lifted her gaze a fraction. "But no, I realize I have lost my chance. . . ."

"You are right," Lazuli answered.

Khora gave a disappointed nod.

"You are right that Abaton has changed," Lazuli said. "Abaton cannot remain the kingdom it was under my father. I thought it had to be. I listened to those who said our people enslaved in the Venetian Empire did not deserve to rejoin us in Abaton, when I should have done what I knew was right, even if it meant upsetting the order of our land."

Pinocchio smiled at her, and she gave him a nod.

"It is time for a new dawn for Abaton," Lazuli said. "Time for the mistakes of the past to be forgiven. Khora, if you and any of the other prisoners are willing to help us lead Abaton into a new age, then we will forgive your past crimes."

Khora looked up with a terrifying but grateful smile. "I will, Your Majesties!"

Azi landed beside her and rasped, "I will as well."

More monsters flew down, landing in the gardens and courtyards among the anxious bystanders, until all the remaining monsters had descended, bowing and pledging to defend Abaton.

"Good," Pinocchio said. Then, looking at Sapphira, he said, "Now is the time to ask for forgiveness."

Dr. Nundrum pushed his way through the monsters in a flurry and threw himself to the steps. "She made me help her, Your Majesties! I know I was cowardly, but she threatened to throw me into the Mist with those monsters. Please believe that I regret my part in her terrible scheme. I know how wrong I was. I repent—I truly do! I beg your forgiveness!"

Pinocchio blinked down at the owl, somewhat startled. "Then you are forgiven, Dr. Nundrum."

Sapphira looked livid. "Accepting monsters back into our land. Allowing slaves who have never lived among our people to defile our kingdom. The Noble Houses will never accept this, and they will never accept children as their presters!"

"I will!" Lord Smoldrin bellowed.

"And I," bubbled Raya Piscus.

Pinocchio glanced toward the *Lionslayer* still hovering out over the lagoon. He felt certain Chief Muckamire would add his small but enthusiastic cry of agreement if he were here.

"The sylphs will not," Lady Sapphira said, edging closer to Rion and Quila. "My loyal captain, the greatest of my archers, I have fulfilled my promise to elevate you in our ranks. It's not too late for the Mist Cities to be ours."

Lazuli held out a hand in warning. "Rion, whatever glory you thought there was in following my aunt, surely you see you were wrong. You can be forgiven . . . if you choose."

The look of self-assurance that was so often on Rion's face was gone. Raw panic replaced it. He looked from Sapphira's stern face to Lazuli's pleading one. Pinocchio noticed a twitch of something almost like regret flicker in Rion's eyes as he looked at Lazuli.

But then Rion cast a powerful gust, pushing back Pinocchio and the others. With a swift leap, he was on Quila. "Fly!" he snarled. "Get us away from here!"

Sapphira reached for him, but already the griffin was taking off without her.

They were just rising into the air when Lazuli raised her hands. A blast of wind toppled the griffin and sent Rion tumbling into a group of monsters.

"Hold him," Lazuli called.

Without a moment's hesitation, the toad monstrosity opened his enormous maw and slurped Rion down in a single gulp.

Lazuli flinched in horror. "That's not what I meant!"

But Pinocchio said with a smirk, "It should be all right. He was swallowed whole. We'll let him out later."

The toad gave a nod of his gruesome bulbous head. Muffled shrieks sounded from inside him.

Lady Sapphira still clutched the Pearl tightly. The magic that had once illuminated the orb had long faded. And it seemed too that Sapphira's color was draining until she had become ashen. She had wanted the Ancientmost Pearl so badly that she had been willing to endanger her own people, her own niece even. Pinocchio couldn't help but wonder what had led her down that terrible path.

"Please, Aunt Sapphira," Lazuli said gently. A note of sadness cracked in her voice. She stepped closer to her aunt. Lazuli seemed about to draw her expression into that regal mask. But then Pinocchio saw Lazuli's eyes well and she let her tears spill onto her cheeks. "It doesn't have to be this way. I don't want it to be this way."

Sapphira tore her gaze from the Pearl. She looked defiantly around at all the eyes on her. "I will have no part in watching Abaton come to such ruin."

Pinocchio sighed and glanced over at Lazuli.

Lazuli wiped at her cheeks. She drew her face into an expression that was both confident and heartbroken, not a regal mask but as true a look as Pinocchio had seen Lazuli show before her people.

"Then you won't have to watch anymore, Aunt," Lazuli said. "Until the day when you repent for your crimes, you will no longer be free to endanger the people of Abaton."

Those words, Pinocchio remembered, were what Lazuli's father had said to Diamancer and his rebels.

Lazuli raised her hands to the Roc. "She belongs with you. Guard her well."

With an earthshaking rumble of thunder, the Roc gathered in an enormous churning storm cloud. It descended on the Moonlit Court, its titanic talons reaching out. Sapphira screamed, dropping the Pearl and throwing up her hands to shield herself.

Lazuli cast the last of the Sands of Sleep on her aunt as darkness enveloped the palace.

A moment later, the skies cleared. The Roc flapped into the distance, beyond the jungles, back to the Mist Cities. A new prisoner had joined Diamancer and his sleeping followers.

22.

A New Dawn for Abaton

Pinocchio came racing down the long, spiraling staircase of the Moonlit Court. He was late. Everyone was already waiting on him in the foyer. Pinocchio was dripping with sweat.

His father handed him a handkerchief when he came to a stop.

"Sorry," Pinocchio said, taking it and mopping his forehead. "This armor took longer than we thought to get on."

He put a hand to the shining silver breastplate, which was doing nothing to help keep him cool in the sweltering tropical heat.

"I told you, darling, you didn't need to wear it," Mezmer said. "You're going to show up your knights!"

Lazuli hadn't opted for the heavy plates of armor, but she wore a tunic of glittering mail that was woven into her blue gown. They both had swords at their belts. If Abaton was ushering in a new age, Pinocchio and Lazuli had decided they might dress the part of their kingdom's protectors.

Mezmer's snout curled into an approving smile as she surveyed her presters. "But I have to admit, you both look splendid."

"Where is Sop?" Maestro chirped from Geppetto's shoulder. "The banquet will start any moment."

"You'll get no argument from me if we go without him," Mezmer said, rolling her eyes.

The cat's boots clunked on the marble as he strolled into the gallery. He was carrying a plate heaped with spiceberry cake, which he was shoveling in his mouth with a paw.

"We've been waiting here and you're raiding the kitchens, you incorrigible cat!" Maestro chirped at him.

"And?" Sop said through a mouthful. He didn't look a bit guilty. "Did anyone want a bite?"

"No, thanks," Lazuli said.

Pinocchio's stomach gave a growl. Sop raised a brow at him. Pinocchio eyed the ruins of his favorite dessert before shaking his head. "I think I'll wait."

The aleya sounded a chime and bumped his hand. Pinocchio held it out and she deposited a ripe cluster of spiceberries in his palm.

"Thanks!" He chuckled, popping them in his mouth.

Sop licked the frosting from his whiskers. "So what are we waiting for—who's ready to eat? I'm starving."

"If you'll lead us, Dr. Nundrum," Lazuli said.

The owl made a rapid bow, fumbling to get his glasses back on his beak. "Yes, Your Majesties. Please follow me."

Dr. Nundrum had been ready to resign his post overseeing the daily affairs of the Moonlit Court. There had been quite a bit of discussion about what to do with him. Sop suggested dropping him into the Upended Forest with the arachnobats. But in the end, the owl was so repentant they decided to give him a chance to earn their trust again. Until then, he would have to carry a Riggle with him, just in case.

Maestro fluttered ahead to prepare his orchestra. A last-minute trickle of attendants and servants was hurrying out the door to the gardens when Pinocchio spied someone slinking among them.

"Cinnabar!" he called.

The djinni approached warily. "Yes, Your Majesty."

"Where are you going?" he asked.

Cinnabar kept his eyes downturned and looked anxious to go. "I . . . I was going to check over the final repairs to the ship—"

"You're not going to the banquet?" Sop asked.

Pinocchio grabbed Cinnabar by the elbow. "Join us at our table."

The djinni gave a start of surprise, glancing from Pinocchio to the others.

"B-but, Your Majesty, I . . . I'm no noble elemental," he stammered.

"It's not that kind of banquet, Cinnabar," Pinocchio said. "Those days are behind us."

"Besides, you're a hero," Lazuli said. "And Abaton won't forget it."

The djinni's face screwed up severely, but it at last settled into a smile. A real smile. The first one Pinocchio thought he'd ever seen on Cinnabar's face.

He bowed. "Thank you, my presters."

The tall doors swung open, and the glow from the setting sun flooded their eyes. As they emerged at the top of the steps, they were met by a thunderous noise. It was cheering like Pinocchio could never have imagined. Deafening cheering. Maestro's orchestra was drowned out completely, but the little cricket continued conducting his musicians with fervent flourishes of his antennae.

A sea of tables filled the lawns and garden grounds. Around them, applauding Abatonians stood by their chairs. Pinocchio couldn't believe how many were here. The cooks really had been busy!

Spread out at the various tables were servants and nobles, elementals and chimera, all mixed together with sundry creatures and even the formerly imprisoned monsters. Lord Smoldrin stood beside Kataton. Tiny Chief Muckamire stood by Goliath and many of the mushroom people from the Upended Forest—all at a smaller table. Raya Piscus and her undines clapped inside their water-filled shrouds and gave slightly wary looks to the ghouls and blazing fire spirits nearest to them.

The grounds were, if anything, better than before. Pinocchio and Lazuli had put the monsters to work cleaning up the destruction and repairing the damage to the palace. With a little magic—and some trial and error—the presters were continuing to discover all that they were capable of doing.

Pinocchio caught Khora's eye at her table with several four-legged Abatonians, including the three kirin sisters. The manticore flashed him a smile and bowed with the rest of the multitude. Azi gave a celebratory croak.

Lazuli looked over at Pinocchio. He shook his head in disbelief. "Make them stop," he whispered with a smile.

The feast went on until long after the stars came out and the moon danced its way across the night sky. Sitting beside Lazuli at their table, Pinocchio kept looking around at the joyous scene.

Laughing voices and faint toasts of "Long lives for the presters!" erupted every few moments.

Pinocchio caught Lazuli staring off across the grounds. Following her gaze, he spotted Rion at a table with several sylphs.

Rion had managed to wash most of the foul stains out of his snow-white suit after being released from the toad. But try as he might, his hair now looked more a dingy green than blue. He seemed a little shaky still, not at all his former overconfident self. It probably didn't help that the toad, who was seated at the next table over, kept belching loudly and saying, "Yum, still tastes like sylph!"

Pinocchio made a small frown. "I can't believe I ever thought he was so great."

"You want to see the best in others," Lazuli said.

"But that's not always good, I suppose," he said.

"I don't think that's true." She flashed him a smile. "You can't help being who you are."

Pinocchio returned her smile.

Chief Muckamire popped up beside them, a merry twinkle in his eyes. "I wanted to let you know, Your Majesties, that the fleet is ready."

"Fleet?" Lazuli asked.

"Yes, my gnomes have completed a dozen ships like the *Lionslayer*, ready for your departure to rescue our people in the Venetian Empire."

Pinocchio's hand went instinctively to his wrist, but then he remembered that Wiq's bracelet was gone. Several tables over, Azi made a playful croak at the aleya circling around his table.

Mezmer leaned over, planting her furry orange paws on the table. "Your Majesties, darlings. I don't mean to rain on your banquet, but while we have ships to fly to Venice, we still don't yet have an army."

"You've got your knights," Pinocchio said.

Mezmer glanced toward Kataton and Goliath, from the aleya to the kirins. "I couldn't ask for knights more glorious, it's true. But that's only eight, including me and Sop."

"The Sky Hunters are eager to show their loyalty," Lazuli said. "They've pledged their bows. Even Rion."

Mezmer gave an appreciative if not exactly enthusiastic nod. "Well, I suppose that adds a few dozen more; still, it's hardly a fighting force capable of handling Venice's army. I mean, we'll be facing legions of airmen, not to mention Flying Lions and all the alchemical might of the Fortezza Ducale!"

"You're right," Pinocchio said. "Good thing you already have new recruits."

"Recruits?" Mezmer flicked her tall ears, perplexed. "What other recruits?"

"Khora is quite excited that her crew will have an opportunity to serve Abaton."

The fox's eyes widened.

"Besides," Pinocchio went on, giving a mischievous smile, "they're monsters. They love destruction! I think it will help ease them into their new role defending our people rather than terrifying them. Don't you think?"

A wide smile broke across the fox's snout. "Yes, darling! Oh, yes! I think they will do splendidly!"

Sop clapped a hand over his belly as he broke into laughter. "I can't wait to see the look on those imperial airmen's faces when we arrive in Venice!" He wiped a finger under his eye patch. "It warms the heart."

"So when do we leave?" Mezmer said, reeling with excitement.

"In the morning," Lazuli said.

Mezmer rubbed her hands together. "Your general will be bright-eyed, bushy-tailed, and ready to introduce some Flying Lions to my Celestial Brigade. I'll be ready at dawn!"

"Glad *you'll* be," Sop said, massaging his stomach, bloated from the feast. "I might need to work this off on our journey."

Pinocchio felt excitement swell inside him. They were going. They were finally going.

Maestro landed on the table between Pinocchio and Lazuli. "Your Majesties," he said, bowing his antennae. "I wanted to let you know that I've begun a new composition."

"Have you, now?" Lazuli said, giving Pinocchio a smirk. "A new masterpiece from the Moonlit Court's renowned musician?"

"Naturally," the cricket chirped. "It's still being refined, but I envision it as a long-form piece about how Abaton's valiant new rulers, Prester Pinocchio and Prester Lazuli, led their army of Celestial Knights in a daring rescue mission back to the wicked Venetian Empire. I'll need to tweak it once the details are known, but for now, I wondered if you might like to hear the prelude?"

Lazuli and Pinocchio smiled at one another. They sat back in their seats to listen.

Maestro flexed his wings, setting them against one another to draw out the reverberating music. "It begins in Abaton. . . ."

The fleet hovered over the green lagoon the following morning. The Crescent Port docks overflowed with well-wishers gathered to see the Celestial Brigade off.

Lazuli and her knights were all aboard the ships. Only Pinocchio still stood down by the moorings next to the cheering crowd, talking to his father quietly.

"Are you sure you shouldn't come?" Pinocchio asked.

"We've already discussed this," his father said. "I'm needed here."

Pinocchio glanced across his father's shoulder to the three high nobles standing at the front of the crowd. There had been quite a discussion, but in the end, all agreed that Abaton would be overseen by a council until the presters returned, with Chief Muckamire acting as the high steward. Geppetto would serve on the council along with several chimera elders from around Abaton.

Pinocchio suspected that Geppetto and Chief Muckamire were planning some projects that might include a bit of alchemy. The gnomes were quite excited about the possibilities.

"Besides, son," his father said. "I'm a wanted criminal in the Venetian Empire."

"Well, it's not as if we're all going to be welcomed with open arms," Pinocchio said. "This is going to be a dangerous mission! Facing imperial airmen, Flying Lions, alchemy war machines!"

Geppetto clapped his hands to Pinocchio's shoulders. "Don't try telling me you're not excited."

Pinocchio grinned. "It's just . . . Lazuli thinks our powers won't be nearly as strong once we leave Abaton."

"You'll have Mezmer and her army of knights to help you."

"But I won't have you," Pinocchio said.

Geppetto's face creased into a warm smile. "You'll manage without your old father. And I'll be here when you return."

"Come on, Your Majesty," Sop called down from the *Lionslayer*. "Some of your monsters are getting impatient."

Pinocchio glanced up to see the toad gnawing on Goliath's mushroom cap. "I'm not your chew toy, you big slobbering sack!" the little knight squeaked, batting the toad away.

Pinocchio began to head for the ladder, but his father held

him in place firmly. "You've got Riggle," he asked, "in case you need to reach me?"

Pinocchio nodded.

"Promise me you'll be careful."

"Yes, of course, Father. I'm always careful."

Maestro landed on Geppetto's shoulder and flicked his antennae. "You incorrigible scamp, you know you're not!"

Geppetto laughed and pulled Pinocchio into a mighty hug. "Now go bring Wiq and the others home," he said in Pinocchio's ear.

Pinocchio felt a bit shivery as he turned to go up the ladder, with something stuck in his throat that made it hard to talk. But he managed, "I'll see you soon."

Once he was over the *Lionslayer*'s railing, he found Lazuli at the bow.

"Ready?" she asked.

Pinocchio surveyed their fleet. The decks were crowded with sylph archers and the menacing menagerie of monsters. Over on the *Lionslayer*'s quarterdeck, Kataton rolled his protruding eyes and gave Pinocchio a slow nod. Goliath pumped his fists excitedly in the air. The aleya circled around Wini and her sisters. All eyes were fixed on their presters, awaiting instructions for departure.

"Shall we launch, Your Majesties?" Cinnabar called from the helm.

Pinocchio heaved a sigh. He cast one last glance back to his father and then at the Moonlit Court towering up from the steaming jungles of Abaton.

"All right," Pinocchio said. "To Venice!"

A monstrous cheer rose from the decks as the ships soared off, leaving the lagoon and flying out over the sparkling ocean.

"TO VENICE!"

GLOSSARY

ABATON — An island in the southern Indian Ocean inhabited by species not found elsewhere in the known world. Long ago, **Prester John** united the four **elemental** races under his rule and established the kingdom of Abaton in relative isolation from the outside **humanlands**. Geographically diverse, Abaton features volcanic jungles in the northern realms, with deserts, grasslands, and snowcapped mountains to the south.

ALCHEMY — A branch of human science devoted to engineering and design based on magic introduced into the **humanlands** from Abaton. Examples of alchemy include: the building of mechanical wings for Venice's airmen, war machines, and **automa**. Because human alchemists cannot perform alchemy without **elemental** assistants, many in Abaton consider the practice theft and a corruption of Abatonian magic.

ALEYA — A race of orblike, floating creatures who tend to inhabit the jungles of **Abaton**'s Farrago realm. While often quite shy, some aleya have been known to play tricks on unsuspecting travelers.

ANCIENTMOST PEARL, THE — The mysterious object that is the symbol of authority for **Abaton**'s **presters**. Prester

John kept the workings of the Pearl secret from his subjects. It was generally believed to be the source of his long life and his extraordinary magic.

ARACHNOBAT — A race of Abatonian creatures that are a hybrid of bats and spiders. Their terrifying appearance led many after **Diamancer**'s Rebellion to claim they were "monsters," although there is no evidence of any malicious activity by these creatures.

AUTOMA — Alchemical machines made of wood and gears that resemble humans, act with limited independence, and are used throughout the **Venetian Empire** as servants and guards.

CALDERA KEEP — The ancient city of the **djinn** located in the southwestern reaches of the Caldera Desert. The city is renowned for its obsidian architecture and lava canals.

CELESTIAL BRIGADE, THE — An elite troop of knights who defended **Abaton** for many centuries prior to **Diamancer**'s Rebellion. Soon after, **Prester John** disbanded Abaton's military.

CHAMELEON CLOTH — A fabric developed by **gnomes** that allows whatever it covers to appear nearly invisible. The material assumes the camouflaged appearance of the adjacent surroundings.

CHIMERA — The most populous race of **Abatonians**. Chimera are humanoid with features of a particular species of mammal, bird, amphibian, reptile, or fish.

CRESCENT PORT — A medium-sized merchant town in **Abaton**. With its proximity to the **Moonlit Court** and its large lagoon-harbor, Crescent Port serves as the primary port for Abatonians journeying to the capital on boats.

DEEP ONE, THE — The colossal sea monster that guards the waters of the Indian Ocean around **Abaton** and prevents human sailors from reaching the island. The Deep One is one of the four primordial guardians of Abaton and an **elemental** being of water.

DIAMANCER — An adviser in **the Moonlit Court** who led a rebellion in the twelfth century against his king, **Prester John**. Abatonians today are uncertain what race of creature Diamancer was. Some **gnome** historians speculate that he was the last of a fifth elemental race known as aethers. Diamancer was cast into an enchanted sleep and imprisoned along with his followers after the rebellion.

DJINNI (PL. DJINN) — One of the four races of human-oid **elementals** native to **Abaton**. Djinn are fire elementals and exhibit magical powers over heat and flame.

DRAKE — A race of reptilian, fire-breathing creatures that were considered "monsters" and disappeared from **Abaton** after **Diamancer's** Rebellion.

ELEMENTALS — Magical beings originating in **Abaton** who draw their powers from the elements: air, earth, fire, or water. The four major races are intelligent humanoids: **sylphs** (air), **gnomes** (earth), **djinn** (fire), and **undines** (water). Also four primordial elemental beings—**the Deep One**, the Everwaiting Pyre, **Regolith**, and **the Roc**—serve as guardians over Abaton.

FANTOM — The principal mechanism that allows an **automa** to function. An **alchemy** invention originating in the **Venetian Empire**.

GNOME — One of the four races of humanoid **elementals** of **Abaton**. As earth elementals, gnomes exhibit magical powers over metal, rock, and materials of the earth. Because their flesh has a consistency most similar to clay, gnomes can split apart at will into smaller versions of themselves, as well as fuse back together.

GRIFFIN — A race of Abatonian creatures with the hindquarters of a lion and the front of a raptor, usually an eagle or falcon. Lacking the powers of speech and high thinking, griffins were domesticated in ancient times by **sylphs** and are primarily used for transportation by those in the **Mist Cities** and in the southern plains of **Abaton**.

GROOTSLANG HOLE — The ancient city of the **gnomes** located at the southern edge of the Farrago Jungle where the Plains of Lemuria begin. The city holds the largest number of libraries and historical texts in **Abaton**.

HIGH NOBLES — The leaders of the four **elemental** houses. Within Abatonian society, the elemental races hold a dominant, elite status, particularly those that belong to noble families. The noble elementals select a High Noble to govern their cities and are often called on for governmental affairs at **the Moonlit Court**.

HUMANLANDS — All kingdoms and civilizations around the known world, with the exception of **Abaton**.

KIRIN — A species of single-horned, horselike creatures often called "unicorns" by those from the **humanlands**. Their coats have white or silver fur in the front portions, transitioning to scales of iridescent hues along the hind legs. Known for their swiftness, their gentle natures, and their ability to fly, kirin are wide-ranging across all the realms of **Abaton**.

MANTICORE — A species no longer found in **Abaton**. With the body of a lion, a humanoid face, bat wings, and a tail that projected dangerous spines, manticores were considered "monsters" and disappeared from Abaton after **Diamancer**'s Rebellion.

MEZMERCURIAN THE FIRST — A legendary **chimera** knight who led the **Celestial Brigade** against **Diamancer** and his rebels.

MIST CITIES, THE — Built upon an archipelago of floating rock, the ancient city of the **sylphs** is located at the southernmost tip of **Abaton**.

MOONLIT COURT, THE — The palace of the **presters** of **Abaton**. First built by **Prester John** in ancient times, the palace is a sky-high tower of delicate white stone. The name derives from the way light seeps through the palace's translucent walls.

NAGA — A species no longer found in **Abaton**. Naga have a humanoid torso and arms with a snake tail from the waist down and scales covering their entire bodies. Considered "monsters," they disappeared from Abaton after **Diamancer's** Rebellion.

NAIAD — A race of water-dwelling creatures found throughout **Abaton**. Lacking the powers of speech and higher thinking, naiads are often considered a delicacy to eat, especially among **undines**.

PISCARAY — The ancient underwater city of the **undines** located off the northeastern coast of **Abaton**. Most of the buildings are built from living coral, and several quarters of the city have been sealed to accommodate air-breathing visitors.

PIXIE — A race of minuscule flying creatures found in most realms around **Abaton**. They become luminous by feeding on air. Lacking the powers of speech and higher thinking, pixies are widely used as a light source both in Abaton and more recently in the **humanlands**.

PRESTER — The title given to a ruler of **Abaton**.

PRESTER JOHN — The long-lived magician-king of **Abaton**. Although little is known of Prester John's origins, the source of his near immortality and magical powers was credited to the **Ancientmost Pearl**. He protected Abaton from human interference as well as internal and outside threats until his eventual death in **the Deep One**.

REGOLITH — One of the four primordial guardians of **Abaton** and an **elemental** being of earth. In ancient times, the giant descended beneath the ground under what is today **Grootslang Hole**.

ROC — One of the four primordial guardians of **Abaton** and an **elemental** being of air. An enormous raptor composed of mist and cloud, the Roc's current location is known to few in Abaton.

SLITHERSTEED — Enormous millipedes used for transportation primarily by gnomes and wealthier chimera merchants traveling across the Plains of Lemuria.

SLOSHING SHROUD — An enclosed cloak made from **naiad** scales and filled with water worn by **undines** to allow them to breathe when outside the water.

SUPERFLUOUS WORM — A race of rare Abatonian creatures with the ability to be bifurcated into separate worms who share the same thoughts and speech. **Gnome** nobility have used them for centuries to communicate with others in **Abaton** across vast distances.

SYLPH — One of the four races of humanoid **elementals** of **Abaton**. Sylphs are air elementals and exhibit magical powers over the air. Having no wings, sylphs cannot fly. However, due to their weightlessness and control over wind, many sylphs are able to glide short distances.

UNDINE — One of the four races of humanoid **elementals** of **Abaton**. Undines are water elementals and exhibit magical powers over water. Undines are unable to leave the water and thus are rarely encountered away from bodies of water unless they are wearing **sloshing shrouds**.

VENETIAN EMPIRE, THE — Currently the foremost empire in the **humanlands**, Venice was historically overshadowed by its larger neighbors, including the Byzantine Empire and the pope's Holy Roman Empire. However, after trade began with **Abaton** and Venetian alchemists began designing war machines and **automa** technology using Abatonian **elemental** magic, the empire grew in wealth and military might, soon conquering the entire Italian peninsula and eventually coming to control nearly all the Mediterranean region. Many human kingdoms around the world (most prominently the Sultanate of Zanzibar and the Aztec Confederation) have pledged allegiance to Venice under threat of conquest. The Venetian Empire is ruled by an emperor who is known as the doge.

WYVERN — A reptilian species no longer found in **Abaton**. With long necks, winged forearms, and a powerful tail capable of producing destructive blows, wyverns were considered "monsters" and disappeared from Abaton after **Diamancer**'s Rebellion.

ACKNOWLEDGMENTS

I'd like to extend my gratitude . . .

To my editor, Rotem Moscovich, whose spectacular story sense and thoughtful guidance brought out all the best parts in *Lord of Monsters*. Also to Heather Crowley, Martin Karlow, Maria Elias, Dina Sherman, Jamie Baker, Seale Ballenger, Andrew Sansone, and the rest of my extraordinary team at Disney-Hyperion.

To my agents, Josh and Tracey Adams, for their many talents, enthusiasm, and warmhearted support.

To my first readers and faithful friends in Adverb Fight Club: Jennifer Harrod, J. J. Johnson, and Stephen Messer. Also to the writers, teachers, and friends who lent their creative advice and generosity: Tom Angleberger, the Bat Cave crew, Tom Carr, Andrew S. Chilton, Alan Gratz, Greg Hanson, Lois Pipkin, Amy Kurtz Skelding, Sharon Wheeler, and the wonderful Carolinas' kid lit community.

To my family—Bemises, Butchers, Bauldrees, Byes, and Gorelys—for being my greatest champions.

To Jason Leininger Hugh for his special help inventing marvelously gruesome monsters.

To all the loyal and passionate fans. Every book I write is for you.

Most of all, thank you to my wife, Amy Gorely, and daughter, Rose. I'm the luckiest.